BOTTOM DOG PRESS

HURON, OHIO

ON THE CLOCK

CONTEMPORARY SHORT STORIES OF WORK

Edited by
Jeff Vande Zande & Josh Maday

Working Lives Fiction Series
Bottom Dog Press
Huron, Ohio

© Bottom Dog Press
ISBN 978-1-933964-38-6

Bottom Dog Press
PO Box 425
Huron, Ohio 44839
http://smithdocs.net

CREDITS:
Cover art: "Gideon" by Simon Currell
Book layout & cover design by Susann Sharp-Schwacke
General Editor: Larry Smith

ACKNOWLEDGMENTS:
Thanks to the William C. Wright Trust

Some of these stories first appeared in the following publications:
"Orientation" by Daniel Orozco in *The Seattle Review*.
"Last Car" by Lolita Hernandez in her story collection *Autopsy of an Engine and Other Stories from the Cadillac Plant* (2004), reprinted with permission from Coffee House Press.
"Contributor Note (Scout)" by Michael Martone in his collection *Michael Martone* (FC2, 2005).
"Robot Goes to Work" by Matthew Salesses in *Storyglossia*.
"Alex Trebek Never Eats Fried Chicken" by Matt Bell in *Storyglossia* and won the 2008 Million Writers Award.
"Cross Country" by Jim Daniels in *Detroit Tales* (Michigan State University Press).
"Circus Matinee" by Bonnie Jo Campbell in *Story* (Summer 1998) and her collection *Women and Other Animals* (University of Massachusetts Press, 1999).
"Cirque de Recession" by Matthew Salesses in *Twelve Stories*.
Portions of "Notebook # 19" by Sean Lovelace in *nimble*.
"Pushing the Knives" by Dustin Hoffmann in *Black Warrior Review*.
"Evie and the Arfids" by Tania Hershman in her short story collection *The White Road and Other Stories*, Salt Publishing (2008).
"Monkey-Men in Office Suite 209" by Nick Kocz in *Beloit Fiction Journal* (Spring 2009, volume 22).
"No-See-Um" by Michael Zadoorian in *Beloit Fiction Journal*.
"Contributor Note (Trench)" by Michael Martone in his collection *Michael Martone* (FC2, 2005).
"Concentrate" by Pete Fromm in *Silk Road, Vol 3*.

Table of Contents

Introduction, Josh Maday..7

Orientation, Daniel Orozco..11
Union Blues, Kennebrew Surant...16
Oregon Grind, Rick Attig..25
Last Car, Lolita Hernandez..35
Contributor Note (Scout), Michael Martone.........................41
Cross Country, Jim Ray Daniels...43
Robot Goes to Work, Matthew Salesses................................52
Alex Trebek Never Eats Fried Chicken, Matt Bell................54
Any Failure to Obey Orders, M. Kaat Toy............................61
Circus Matinee, Bonnie Jo Campbell....................................68
Cirque de Recession, Matthew Salesses................................75
Notebook #19, Sean Lovelace..77
Ambition, Billie Louise Jones..82
Maius Martin, Proletarian, Lita Kurth..............................92
A Real Tear, Anne Shewring..103
Pushing the Knives, Dustin Hoffman..................................109
Evie and the Arfids, Tania Hershman..................................119
Monkey-Men in Office Suite 209, Nick Kocz.......................130
No-See-Um, Michael Zadoorian..140
Lights Out, Steve Himmer...145
The Last Final Copy, Peter Anderson..................................152
Contributor Note (Trench), Michael Martone.....................160
Concentrate, Pete Fromm..162

Introduction

If there was any doubt before the housing bubble burst and the bailouts for big banks and the bankrupt automakers of the United States, we can no longer deny that we are living out the completion of the manufacturing based economy and participating in its domination by the service and technology based economy. The best of times and the worst of times, the tale of many economies becoming one global, multi-faceted, increasingly complex network, as the European debt crisis has confirmed the interdependence and fragility of global markets.

That all sounds lofty on paper, but the reality is that millions of people have to make difficult decisions and transitions as the world they know closes down around them. Some workers checked out and took their retirement while they had the chance. Some are scrambling to retool themselves for the new machines and processes of the exploding sustainable markets. The days of holding a single job for 30 years and retiring with a pension are pretty much over. In "Last Car" by Lolita Hernandez, we see the end of an era in the proud sorrowful choreography of the last car rolling off the line at an historic Cadillac plant. Now, many people work for an employer for three to five years on an average before moving on (and hopefully up), continually reinventing themselves, and taking on new economic identities as we see in pieces like Sean Lovelace's "Notebook #19" and Michael Martone's "Contributor Notes." These fictions also reveal the increasingly common duality embodied in contemporary workers' shifting between or progressing from manual to intellectual labor. This time of transition and increasing diversity we hoped to represent in the anthology and these award winning writers tell it true.

In "Cross Country," Jim Daniels takes us on the proverbial road trip with two young men dealing with future lives after the closure of the assembly lines htey had depended on. They learn the hard way that no future is guaranteed.

In Kennebrew Surant's "Union Blues," readers will recognize the main character's internal and external conflict between her new white collar man-agement position and her deep blue collar roots, conflicts of managing people who were once co-workers as well as working with people who were once superiors, and having to make tough decisions about her identity and her loyalty.

National Book Award finalist Bonnie Jo Campbell shows in "Circus Matinee" a woman who shrugs off her sense of unexpected danger and continues selling snow cones at the circus until she eventually sees what those around her realize, that it is already too late to escape.

Of course, the muscle economy and the mind economy have coexisted for many decades now, spanning the growth of post-industrial society, and so office life provides no shortage of anecdotal fuel. Fiction about life in the office frequently takes place in an atmosphere of absurdity, when so much policy and human behavior seems arbitrary and often inflexible once instituted as the norm. Although fiction about office life expresses something far from normal, it does often speak from existential spaces, looking into territories with names like Identity, Self, Meaning, and Reality, just like fiction that takes place in a factory or on a construction site. *Normal* probably isn't the best word for it, and likely never was—maybe *rational* or *logical* or *sane*, and even those notions exist on a continuum. The excellent stories in this anthology capture these strange realities.

Michael Zadoorian's "No-See-Um" livez in exactly this strange ethereal space, where the mysterious presence of tiny, nearly invisible flies in the office becomes the hysterical obsession of the entire office staff, and when corporate appears unmoved to correct the situation, the employees begin to wonder who is actually in charge.

In Nick Kocz's "Monkey-Men in Office Suite 209," two men are so focused on pursuing the maximum number of billable hours for their government research grant that even a series of unknown men in gorilla suits bringing donuts to their office hold their attention for a short time, until one man begins to understand the real cost of the long hours.

Some of the stories go beyond the plant, beyond the office, and peer into what may be our near future. Tania Hershman's "Evie and the Arfids" takes us to an almost Orwellian time and place where a woman discovers that her new job affixing electronic tags to all sorts of merchandise requires a certain amount of blissful ignorance for a reason, and that acquainting oneself with a co-worker can lead to more than one kind of termination.

I remember my co-editor Jeff asking, "Who writes a happy story about work? Who feels compelled to write about their job because they feel absolutely no conflict about it?" Indeed, no one whose story would be of much interest to others except as an oddity. So, no, the stories that follow are not happy. In fact, most of them exist in a space where genuine human contact is rare and so much more startling and moving when it occurs. But they are not hopeless. In these widely diverse tales, readers will find humor, tenderness, sorrow, adventure, and anticipation, too, because although the world is changing and part of it is dying, as will always be the case, the human community moves onward into new and exciting possibilities and opportunities.

Human beings have been writing about work since before Genesis, and many fine volumes of those writings have been collected. We did not try to reinvent the wheel (or gear) in *On the Clock*. Rather, our focus is contemporary writers writing about contemporary work. We also sought to assemble a collection that is as varied as the diversity of the global community by seeking work that is traditional and innovative in both form and content. And, while we believe that it is important to know where we came from, it is also essential to be aware of our current situation, and to look ahead to see where this trajectory may take us. The stories that follow range from the end of the manufacturing era to our current moment of transition from muscle-to-mind economy, and include speculative fiction that looks toward our possible future as a global human culture from which every imaginable technology will be inextricable, for better and for worse. We are thankful to Bottom Dog Press for the opportunity to edit this book and to all of the writers who shared their work with us, which we in turn share with our readers. We hope this anthology will provoke, encourage, enlighten, and entertain.

Josh Maday, June 2010
Saginaw, Michigan

ORIENTATION

Daniel Orozco

Those are the offices and these are the cubicles. That's my cubicle there, and this is your cubicle. This is your phone. Never answer your phone. Let the Voicemail System answer it. This is your Voicemail System Manual. There are no personal phone calls allowed. We do, however, allow for emergencies. If you must make an emergency phone call, ask your supervisor first. If you can't find your supervisor, ask Phillip Spiers, who sits over there. He'll check with Clarissa Nicks, who sits over there. If you make an emergency phone call without asking, you may be let go.

These are your IN and OUT boxes. All the forms in your IN box must be logged in by the date shown in the upper left-hand corner, initialed by you in the upper right-hand corner, and distributed to the Processing Analyst whose name is numerically coded in the lower left-hand corner. The lower right-hand corner is left blank. Here's your Processing Analyst Numerical Code Index. And here's your Forms Processing Procedures Manual.

You must pace your work. What do I mean? I'm glad you asked that. We pace our work according to the eight-hour work day. If you have twelve hours of work in your IN box, for example, you must compress that work into the eight-hour day. If you have one hour of work in your IN box, you must expand that work to fill the eight-hour day. That was a good question. Feel free to ask questions. Ask too many questions, however, and you may be let go.

That is our receptionist. She is a temp. We go through receptionists here. They quit with alarming frequency. Be polite and civil to our temps. Learn their names. Invite them to lunch occasionally. But don't get close to them, as it only makes it more difficult when they leave. And they always leave. You can be sure of that.

The men's room is over there. The women's room is over there. John LaFountaine, who sits over there, uses the women's room occasionally. He says it is accidental. We know better, but we let it pass. John La-Fountaine is harmless, his forays into the forbidden territory of the women's room are simply a benign thrill, a faint blip on the dull flat line of his life.

Russell Nash, who sits in the cubicle to your left, is in love with Amanda Pierce, who sits in the cubicle to your right. They ride the same bus together after work. For Amanda Pierce, it is just a tedious bus ride made less tedious by the idle nattering of Russell Nash. But for Russell Nash, it is the highlight of his day. It is the highlight of his life. Russell Nash has put on forty pounds, and grows fatter with each passing month, nibbling on chips and cookies while peeking glumly over the partitions at Amanda Pierce, and gorging himself at home on cold pizza and ice cream while watching adult videos on TV.

Amanda Pierce, in the cubicle to your right, has a six-year-old son named Jamie, who is autistic. Her cubicle is plastered from top to bottom with the boy's crayon artwork—sheet after sheet of precisely drawn concentric circles and ellipses, in black and yellow. She rotates them every other Friday. Be sure to comment on them. Amanda Pierce also has a husband, who is a lawyer. He subjects her to an escalating array of painful and humiliating sex games, to which Amanda Pierce reluctantly submits. She comes to work exhausted and freshly wounded each morning, wincing from the abrasions on her breasts, or the bruises on her abdomen, or the second degree burns on the backs of her thighs.

But we're not supposed to know any of this. Do not let on. If you let on, you may be let go.

Amanda Pierce, who tolerates Russell Nash, is in love with Albert Bosch, who sits over there. Albert Bosch, who only dimly registers Amanda Pierce's existence, has eyes only for Ellie Tapper, who sits over there. Ellie Tapper, who hates Albert Bosch, would walk through fire for Curtis Lance. But Curtis Lance hates Ellie Tapper. Isn't the world a funny place? Not in the ha-ha sense, of course.

Anika Bloom sits in that cubicle. Last year, while reviewing quarterly reports in a meeting with Barry Hacker, Anika Bloom's left palm began to bleed. She fell into a trance, stared into her hand, and told Barry Hacker when and how his wife would die. We laughed it off. She was, after all, a new employee. But Barry Hacker's wife is dead. So unless you want to know exactly when and how you'll die, never talk to Anika Bloom.

Colin Heavey sits in that cubicle over there. He was new once, just like you. We warned him about Anika Bloom. But at last year's Christmas Potluck, he felt sorry for her when he saw that no one was talking to her. Colin Heavey brought her a drink. He hasn't been himself since. Colin Heavey is doomed. There's nothing he can do about it, and we are powerless to help him. Stay away from Colin Heavey. Never give any of your work to him. If he asks to do something, tell him you have to check with me. If he asks again, tell him I haven't gotten back to you.

This is the Fire Exit. There are several on this floor, and they are marked accordingly. We have a Floor Evacuation Review every three months, and an Escape Route Quiz once a month. We have our Biannual Fire Drill twice a year, and our Annual Earthquake Drill once a year. These are precautions only. These things never happen.

For your information, we have a comprehensive health plan. Any catastrophic illness, any unforeseen tragedy is completely covered. All dependents are completely covered. Larry Bagdikian, who sits over there, has six daughters. If anything were to happen to any of his girls, or to all of them, if all six were to simultaneously fall victim to illness or injury—stricken with a hideous degenerative muscle disease or some rare toxic blood disorder, sprayed with semi-automatic gunfire while on a class field trip, or attacked in their bunk beds by some prowling nocturnal lunatic—if any of this were to pass, Larry's girls would all be taken care of. Larry Bagdikian would not have to pay one dime. He would have nothing to worry about.

We also have a generous vacation and sick leave policy. We have an excellent disability insurance plan. We have a stable and profitable pension fund. We get group discounts for the symphony, and block seating at the ballpark. We get commuter ticket books for the bridge. We have Direct Deposit. We are all members of Costco.

This is our kitchenette. And this, this is our Mr. Coffee. We have a coffee pool, into which we each pay two dollars a week for coffee, filters, sugar, and Coffee-mate. If you prefer Cremora or half-and-half to Coffee-mate, there is a special pool for three dollars a week. If you prefer Sweet'N Low to sugar, there is special pool for two-fifty a week. We do not do decaf. You are allowed to join the coffee pool of your choice, but you are not allowed to touch the Mr. Coffee.

This is the microwave oven. You are allowed to *heat* food in the microwave oven. You are not, however, allowed to *cook* food in the microwave oven.

We get one hour for lunch. We also get one fifteen-minute break in the morning, and one fifteen-minute break in the afternoon. Always take your breaks. If you skip a break, it is gone forever. For your information, your break is a privilege, not a right. If you abuse the break policy, we are authorized to rescind your breaks. Lunch, however, is a right, not a privilege. If you abuse the lunch policy, our hands will be tied, and we will be forced to look the other way. We will not enjoy that.

This is the refrigerator. You may put your lunch in it. Barry Hacker, who sits over there, steals food from this refrigerator. His petty theft is an outlet for his grief. Last New Year's Eve, while kissing his wife, a blood vessel burst in her brain. Barry Hacker's wife was two months pregnant at the time, and lingered in a coma for half a year before dying. It was a tragic loss for Barry Hacker. He hasn't been himself since. Barry Hacker's wife was a beautiful woman. She was also completely covered. Barry Hacker did not have to pay one dime. But his dead wife haunts him. She haunts all of us. We have seen her, reflected in the monitors of our computers, moving past our cubicles. We have seen the dim shadow of her face in our photocopies. She pencils herself in in the receptionist's appointment book, with the notation: To see Barry Hacker.

She has left messages in the receptionist's Voicemail box, messages garbled by the electronic chirrups and buzzes in the phone line, her voice echoing from an immense distance within the ambient hum. But the voice is hers. And beneath her voice, beneath the tidal whoosh of static and hiss, the gurgling and crying of a baby can be heard.

In any case, if you bring a lunch, put a little something extra in the bag for Barry Hacker. We have four Barrys in this office. Isn't that a coincidence?

This is Matthew Payne's office. He is our Unit Manager, and his door is always closed. We have never seen him, and you will never see him. But he is here. You can be sure of that. He is all around us.

This is the Custodian's Closet. You have no business in the Custodian's Closet.

And this, this is our Supplies Cabinet. If you need supplies, see Curtis Lance. He will log you in on the Supplies Cabinet Authorization Log, then give you a Supplies Authorization Slip. Present your pink copy of the Supplies Authorization Slip to Ellie Tapper. She will log you in on the Supplies Cabinet Key Log, then give you the key. Because the Supplies Cabinet is located outside the Unit Manager's office, you must be very quiet. Gather your supplies quietly. The Supplies Cabinet is divided into four sections. Section One contains letterhead stationery, blank paper and envelopes, memo and note pads, and so on. Section Two contains pens and pencils and typewriter and printer ribbons, and the like. In Section Three we have erasers, correction fluids, transparent tapes, glue sticks, et cetera. And in Section Four we have paper clips and push pins and scissors and razor blades. And here are the spare blades for the shredder. Do not touch the shredder, which is located over there. The shredder is of no concern to you.

Gwendolyn Stich sits in that office there. She is crazy about penguins, and collects penguin knickknacks: penguin posters and coffee mugs and stationery, penguin stuffed animals, penguin jewelry, penguin sweaters and tee shirts and socks. She has a pair of penguin fuzzy slippers she wears when working late at the office. She has a tape cassette of penguin sounds which she listens to for relaxation. Her favorite colors are black and white. She has personalized license plates that read: PEN GWEN. Every morning, she passes through all the cubicles to wish each of us a *good* morning. She brings Danish on Wednesdays for Hump Day morning break, and doughnuts on Fridays for T.G.I.F. afternoon break. She organizes the Annual Christmas Potluck, and is in charge of the Birthday List. Gwendolyn Stich's door is always open to all of us. She will always lend an ear, and put in a good word for you; she will always give you a hand, or the shirt off her back, or a shoulder to cry on. Because her door is always open, she hides and cries in a stall in the women's room. And John LaFountaine—who, enthralled when a woman enters, sits quietly in his stall with his knees to his chest—John LaFountaine has heard her vomiting in there. We have come upon Gwendolyn Stich huddled in the stairwell, shivering in the updraft, sipping a Diet Mr. Pibb and hugging her knees. She does not let any of this interfere with her work. If it interfered with her work, she might have to be let go.

Kevin Howard sits in that cubicle over there. He is a serial killer, the one they call the Carpet Cutter, responsible for the mutilations across town. We're not supposed to know that, so do not let on. Don't worry. His compulsion inflicts itself on strangers only, and the routine established is elaborate and unwavering. The victim must be a white male, a young adult no older than thirty, heavyset, with dark hair and eyes, and the like. The victim must be chosen at random, before sunset, from a public place; the victim is followed home, and must put up a struggle; et cetera. The carnage inflicted is precise: the angle and direction of the incisions; the layering of skin and muscle tissue; the rearrangement of the visceral organs; and so on. Kevin Howard does not let any of this interfere with his work. He is, in fact, our fastest typist. He types as if he were on fire. He has a secret crush on Gwendolyn Stich, and leaves a red-foil-wrapped Hershey's Kiss on her desk every afternoon. But he hates Anika Bloom, and keeps well away from her. In his presence, she has uncontrollable fits of shaking and trembling. Her left palm does not stop bleeding.

In any case, when Kevin Howard gets caught, act surprised. Say that he seemed like a nice person, a bit of a loner, perhaps, but always quiet and polite.

This is the photocopier room. And this, this is our view. It faces southwest. West is down there, toward the water. North is back there. Because we are on the seventeenth floor, we are afforded a magnificent view. Isn't it beautiful? It overlooks the park, where the tops of those trees are. You can see a segment of the bay between those two buildings there. You can see the sun set in the gap between those two buildings over there. You can see this building reflected in the glass panels of that building across the way. There. See? That's you, waving. And look there. There's Anika Bloom in the kitchenette, waving back.

Enjoy this view while photocopying. If you have problems with the photocopier, see Russell Nash. If you have any questions, ask your supervisor. If you can't find your supervisor, ask Phillip Spiers. He sits over there. He'll check with Clarissa Nicks. She sits over there. If you can't find them, feel free to ask me. That's my cubicle. I sit in there.

Union Blues

Kennebrew Surant

"Where are they going to take the mess?"
"Receiving Hospital."
"Has the next of kin been notified?"

The police were going to ask her into the conference room any second and ask her what she'd witnessed. Claycee's hands trembled as she tried to pick up the blue pen on her desk. Fumbling with it several times, she gave up and turned on her computer, thinking that she should do something other than wait to be summoned. The activity around her seemed muted as though she were trying to eavesdrop from the bottom of a pool. Red lights spun in quick circles outside of the window. Happy to be on the second floor above the activity of the scene below, Claycee turned her back toward the window, but reflections of the emergency lights illuminated the yellowed walls of the office like a laser show. Men in short-sleeved navy shirts walked in and out of the conference room hurriedly, the seriousness of the situation masked by the casual banter about the horribleness of the area's football team. Claycee jumped every time the door slammed shut and then abruptly opened again. No one seemed able to sit still, and the flurry of movement dizzied her, her face warm in a frigid office where she could normally see her breath.

She looked up briefly, knowing that she would be called into the all-glass room and questioned shortly. The office offered little privacy. A recent study about improving worker productivity found that when walls were torn down, workers were able to communicate more efficiently. The noise levels had definitely picked up. Instead of walking to someone's desk to inquire about late shipments or the status of certain production lines, coworkers now just yelled over their computer screens. Management had also hoped the lack of walls between the work stations would cut down on some of the time spent watching videos, playing games or forwarding emails. But it hadn't.

Whispers surrounded her, loud accusatory whispers that were meant for her ears. But none of her coworkers had the courage to pry directly. Instead they would try to goad her, whispering loudly misinformation so that maybe she would get indignant and correct them. Any other day, when her stomach wasn't so turned inside out, she would mess with them, tell them information that wasn't true and then watch and laugh as they went to the factory floor with it. There were times, she purposely started rumors in front of her coworkers about downtime and layoffs, knowing that before she finished her sentence, the spark would ignite. Last week, she told Tony that she overheard Mike saying that he was going to shake up the department, bringing the floor supervisors like her up to the office and putting the office supervisor on the floor. For three days, she watched amused as the bootlicker went out of his way to make sure Mike knew he was doing a great job, one that would keep his white collared shirt and black wingtips clean.

Streaks of black grime dirtied the long sleeves of her pale blue golf shirt. Rare was the day Claycee left the plant stainless, the gunk another reminder of the line she toed.

"She was supposed to write him up," she heard Tony say loudly. "I'd be surprised if she did. She's always fighting for those guys." He had an audience, their coworkers, gathered around his desk. He stood in front of his computer, but Claycee could see the computer screen where he'd paused his game of Solitaire.

Union sympathizer. White collar factory rat. Blue collar lover.

She'd been called so many unimaginative names because of her inability to dismiss workers at first glance as beneath her just because they literally put the cars together and she merely told them to.

The smell of cold fries wafted up from her trash can, reminding her that just hours ago he'd gone out to McDonald's for the break. "What do you want?" he'd asked over the radio right after the bell had rung. They were given fourteen minutes for a break, much too long according to the endless discussions in the office on the topic of worker laziness.

"He was taking another break," Tony said. Unable to whisper more than a couple of sentences, his commentary resumed a normal volume. "I mean, he just had a cigarette thirty minutes ago, but God forbid he go a whole hour without one."

Claycee moved her keyboard and saw the envelope that contained her resignation letter. She couldn't do it anymore. She'd tried to explain that to her mother, telling her how she wanted to move to France and study music, learn to sing the blues. "How can someone learn the blues in France?" She'd never wanted to go to school, go to college. When her mother found her to be happy serving food at the campus diner, she'd made her quit and focus on her studies. "Your father and I didn't work our tails off so you could go around serving your classmates like a step-and-fetch-it maid."

She'd never wanted to be here.

"Claycee Thomas?" A tall officer stood next to the open conference room door. "We'd like to talk to you now."

"Do you want to talk about it?"

She shook her head, no. What was there to say?

They sat in silence, Kim flipping through a magazine and Claycee just sitting. The factory had been scheduled to take some downtime at the end of the month, and the powers that be decided that now was as good of time as any. It would allow for the investigation to be completed and any safety concerns to be addressed. There was already talk of requiring pedestrians to wear brightly colored safety vests when walking on the docks and smokers not being allowed to use the yard during their breaks. All fork truck drivers were going to be made to attend safety training again.

"Did you finish your goals?"

A flippant breath escaped Claycee's mouth.

"So, no?" Kim asked.

Downtimes were for hourly only. They were the ones able to be laid off and still collect unemployment because of some decades old concessionary agreement between union and management. Management was expected to stick around, sucking up the utilities, although lately, they had been instructed to shut off the lights in the office at times when natural light would suffice. Heat was turned off, forcing everyone to layer with jackets and sweatshirts. Four years at the most exclusive prep school in the Midwest followed by another four years at the highly selective liberal arts college where she'd earned her bachelor's degree and still, every morning when Claycee trudged past the mirror on the door to the garage dressed in her steel toed boots, flannel sweatshirt and fingerless gloves, she saw a reflection of her father, leaving the house in the wee hours of the morning, carrying his cooler with the lunch her mother made for him the night before.

"Can't I just copy the goals from last year?" Claycee asked.

"You can't be more creative than that?" Kim was the area manager from second shift and the only manager in the department who had been properly socialized as a child, so she was most often the one left in charge of interacting with the supervisors. "Why don't you make your first goal to not be so barbed in your departmental emails? You know, one day your boss is going to figure out that you're dogging him in those emails."

She'd already been hauled into HR a few times because of emails that "didn't exactly call" him a dumb ass and behavior that mocked him with subtlety, yet burned a hole in his ego. Mike, her boss, often complained that she had an hourly attitude. The union workers didn't think twice about telling their bosses to shove it or cussing them out on the factory floor. Claycee had to be more careful than that. She wasn't union. She was management, barely.

"Claycee, I asked you to bring me a hammer earlier so I could hang this award in my office. You do know what a hammer is, don't you?" As usual, Mike didn't even slow his hurried walk to his office.

Claycee opened her desk drawer and pulled out a monkey wrench.
"Clay, don't," Kim warned.

She wasn't in the mood to listen and Kim, though she tried to advise her not to, would be amused by her antics.

Claycee walked into Mike's office and set the wrench on his desk. "Let me know if there's anything else you need," she said politely before turning to leave.

"I asked for a hammer."

"That's not a hammer?" She smirked at Mike. Feeling bolder than she had in times past, she waited for the vein in his neck to start pulsating before she turned and went back to her desk.

"He's going to fire you one day," Kim said as Claycee sat down.

"Because I don't know what a hammer is? That's a little harsh."

Supervisors were only one step above hourly; having enough school completed to rise above the ranks of the American worker, but with proverbial dues yet paid, they were subjected to the crass lambasting from both ends—the workers they were in charge of and the cranky bosses they worked for. If it weren't for Claycee's smart aleck emails and passive aggressiveness, she would have snapped long ago. And now she had the accident to deal with, to get over, because the most important thing was running the line. Counselors would be available for the hourly when they returned. It had less to do with sympathy as it did with the appearance of being sympathetic.

Most management mumbled behind closed doors that he shouldn't have been walking around the yard. Instead of being offered counseling like the hourly workers, she'd been grilled. "Why wasn't he on his job? Did you know he was walking around with earphones in his ear? Why wasn't proper plant procedure followed after you witnessed the incident? Did you allow all of your workers to take their breaks whenever they wanted?"

"You're going to be written up, you know," Kim said as though the thoughts that swirled Claycee's head were somehow visible to her. "I just wanted to warn you."

Claycee shrugged. She'd expected as much. And it wouldn't be the first time. She'd made the mistake of telling her mother the last time she'd been written up, a reprimand for shutting the line down for parts that had not even made it to the factory yet. She was not responsible for inbound parts, but her lack of concern infuriated her boss. She'd used the downtime to eat the cold breakfast she'd ordered hours earlier. "You must have done something more, Claycee," she'd said. "They don't write up management."

But they did. At least, they did to her.

"It doesn't mean anything, Claycee. Everyone knows you're the best supervisor here. They wouldn't heap so much responsibility on you if they didn't know you could handle it. They know how smart you are."

Most of her drivers made more money than she did. She had spent the past four years in college, taking engineering classes and design classes. Business classes had also been required to complete the well-rounded education promised to her in the brochures that her mother had taped to the refrigerator since the day she was born, knowing that their child would be college-educated and equipped to rise above the drudgery of manual labor. Smiling coeds on the covers of those pamphlets helped sell the belief.

Her father had started working in the plant the summer after he'd graduated from high school. "He didn't have anyone to encourage him," her mother told her many times when he came home bragging about fixing some machine that his better educated supervisors couldn't figure out. "He could have been an engineer. He was always so good in math in high school, just like you."

Claycee turned her chair toward the window and stared out into the yard. The accident had occurred right below them just outside of the large roll-up dock doors. Yellow tape had cautioned off the area like the red rope that prevented onlookers from getting to close to the museum exhibits, but had since been taken down. Still, small pieces of the plastic hung from a pole, blowing casually in the winter wind. Shades of grayness blanketed the cement yard. Rusty racks were stacked in neat rows except on the north end, where she'd sent the new driver to practice stacking. The rows there were wavy as though an earthquake had come by and shifted everything. The only living things in the yard were the occasional rat or raccoon, pests that had wandered on the property looking for garbage that (despite the abundance of trashcans) always seemed to make its way to the ground.

It had been dark when the accident happened. Claycee had been outside counting racks for the rear door line, trying to determine if they had enough to finish out the production run. There had been thirteen racks left, five less than the last time Mike sent her out there to count. As usual, they were cutting it close. Instead of hurrying back in, she'd taken a moment to rest and think about the acceptance letter she had folded in her back pocket. She had to give them an answer by the end of the month. What would she tell her mother? And how would she answer the questions of all the relatives who had been so proud her college graduation day? "The first college graduate in this family," her mother told her. "Your father would have been so proud."

The pavement had been scrubbed quickly. Like everything else, the factory looked to move past problems as quickly as possible. The freshly cleaned pavement seemed reverently out of place where most of the surrounding pavement held decades of rust and dirt. It reminded Claycee of her father's gravesite, the newly inhabited plot apparent because of the freshly overturned dirt.

"My dad worked here," Claycee said.

"I know."

"Back then they wouldn't let him drive a fork truck. He was big and tall, so they always put him on the crappy jobs because he was strong enough to do the job of two people."

He wanted her to go to school so she wouldn't have to deal with the limited choices he had. She wore steal toed boots to work just like he had. After the shift, she'd take them off before getting in her car, not wanting to track any memory of the day home. Often after work she'd collapse on the couch, falling asleep before she was able to settle on a channel to watch and before her stomach could growl and remind her that, again, she had been running around too much to eat. Just like her father. Her mother would cover him with a blanket and then warn Claycee not to disturb him. "If you work hard in school, you won't have to come home dog tired like he does," she'd tell her.

Claycee wouldn't call them lies, exactly...

"Talk to me, Clay," Kim said, taking her chair by the arms and steering her from the window.

Her desk was in the corner, carefully chosen, a salvaged piece of property in an area where privacy was hard to come by. Coworkers didn't stop by to visit. On one hand, she preferred it that way, not wanting to hear the boastful stories about pars made on the golf course the night before or surprise European trips sprung on them by stay-at-home spouses. But on the other hand, she loathed the way they assumed that she didn't understand bogeys or birdies. If they'd ever asked, she would have told them that she was All-State golf three years in a row in high school.

Kim sat down on the desk next to the computer screen, the display the same as when Claycee turned it on hours before. "You should take some time off. Don't roll your eyes at me."

She let out a laugh, the first one since the accident.

"I'm serious. Go on medical leave."

"You're not quitting, are you? Why would you quit a good job like that? People are getting laid off left and right and you want to quit? School didn't give you common sense, did it?" Her cousin closed the door to the refrigerator and plopped down in the chair across from her. "You know, JR's been laid off three times this year. Already he's telling me when the car lease comes due, we're going to just turn it in and I'm going to be riding around in something used. You still get two corporate leases, don't you? Why don't you lease something for me?"

"Because you're not my husband or my kid," Claycee said. "I'll get you a PIN number if you guys want to buy something."

"Yeah, like he's going to let me park something of yours in the driveway, anyway. He says you guys build great junk. So, Aunt Janet said that you saw that man get run over, that's why you took time off. Are you like totally freaked out?"

Not totally, Claycee thought. She picked up a can of soda and started to drink. Her cousin would let the question go unanswered if enough time passed.

"I would be so freaked out. This crazy guy down the street got hit by a car once and he went flying through the air. It was like one of those special effects things you see in the movies. He landed across the street and got up running like he didn't feel it. But he was high off of crack and the police was chasing him for something. So, who knows he didn't even feel it. Was that guy at your factory high? JR says all those guys go to work high."

"That's not true," Claycee said, unable to keep the defensiveness out of her voice. She caught herself before she continued. "People say that about the workers, but it's not true. At least not in the disproportioned way they report it. Does JR go to work high?"

"Maybe if he did, he'd chill and then he wouldn't get wrote up all the time for cussing out his supervisor."

Bailouts had been the topic of almost every newscast lately. Hermit bloggers and experts in online chat rooms talked about the environment of the factories; speaking authoritatively on the laziness of the workers and how the unions were the downfall of the industry. People, whose closest step near a factory floor was their traditional third-grade trip to the Rouge factory, knew intimately the ins and outs of the factory floor. They all had opinions about the worthiness of the job and the inflated problems of the factory mindset. No one spoke of the enormously high salaries of the management, people paid so well to make decisions like her boss had made a week ago to shop bad engines to an assembly plant, knowing that they would have to be returned and reworked. On-time shipping had been one of his measurable goals. A certain number of trailers had to leave the plant whether the stock inside of them was quality or not. And if they came back and had to be reshipped, well, then he was exceeding his goals. Claycee watched helpless as her drivers shook their heads at the ridiculousness of what they were doing and her dad's words came to her as they did from time to time. "And they're the ones with a college degree."

"So, you're taking a stress leave?" her cousin asked. "Are you stressed now? Maybe we shouldn't talk about it. What did they tell you to do about your stress? Light a candle?"

Claycee ignored the ribbing. It was better than the whispered talking that had gone on right in front of her. She rubbed her eyes as she opened another can of Pepsi. She'd drank so much of it the last few days, trying desperately to take the edge off from not sleeping that she feared she was becoming immune to the caffeine. He would bring her fountain Pepsi from the lunchroom. There were plenty of days when she couldn't make it out of the plant for her thirty minute lunch break, but there were days when she couldn't even make it off of the dock. Instead her drivers, knowing her food habits, would bring her food to eat. The hourly's breaks were mandated, holy times that management complained about but knew to respect like the unfamiliar worshipping rituals of the neighbors who practiced that religion that no one knew too much about. Claycee would laugh when she would hear some of her supervisor coworkers complain about the union, dismissing its usefulness, as they worked through lunch breaks and beyond the OHSA-required twelve hours, unpaid, since paying them for a thirteenth hour would send a red flag to HR and everyone else that they were breaking the law.

"You've gotten soft, Clay, living out there in the 'burbs. My momma said that your dad should've never dragged Aunt Janet out there with him, thinking he was too good to live here in the city. She said, you wouldn't be all stressed out by normal life if you had a little bit of street smarts."

Normal life, thought Claycee. "Look, I got to go. Tell JR I said, hi."

"I will mail anything you forgot."

Claycee nodded.

"What is the time difference again? It doesn't matter. Call me as soon as you land and when you get to your apartment. How do you know you didn't sign on to live in a dump? Is it safe? I've never heard of choosing a place to stay and not seeing it first."

"There wasn't time, really."

The airport was crowded. Claycee liked it that way, active enough to make her disappear in the business. When things were quiet, like they were after the accident, she felt self-conscious, like the whole world was watching her writhe in pain.

"If you wanted to go to France, you shouldn't have wasted time in college taking Spanish classes. How is that going to help you?"

"I took French."

"When?"

Claycee shrugged.

"You've been taking French classes?"

She nodded reluctantly as she watched her mother piece together the puzzle pieces Claycee kept to herself.

"So, you've been planning to leave since..."

"Kind of."

Her mother looked at her, searching for answers and then, when finding them, looking away quickly, but not before Claycee saw the hurt in her eyes. She busied herself checking the tags on the luggage and fussing about the items security confiscated from her going through the metal detectors.

"I will mail you stuff for your hair because Lord only knows if you will be able to find anything to put on your hair over there. Don't let any of those marketing people tell you to do some wild things with your hair. You just be yourself because people know when you're being a fake."

"I wanted to tell you," Claycee said. "I wanted to tell you before I started college. And then when I graduated. I just couldn't...I'm not management, Mom. I wasn't cut out to sit at a desk."

"Did you pack enough warm clothes? What's the weather like over there? What's the time difference again? Never mind, you just make sure you call me when you get there and whenever you need anything."

There was still plenty of time before her plane boarded, but that wasn't going to stop her mother from rattling off the endless list of instructions to her. Soon she would remind her to not "go over there acting your color." Black folks tended to do that from time to time and it just made it bad for the ones coming behind them. "Claycee," she'd say, "Make sure they know you've got home training."

"Are you listening to me, Claycee? You better be listening to me."

"I am."

"What did I say?"

"You said not to act my color," Claycee said, taking a guess.

"I didn't say anything like that. I've been telling you that for years and maybe that's why you worked in that plant all these years acting white collar when you're really blue collar."

Color meant everything to her mother, a product of a generation that had to take the back seat on a bus and settle for jobs that other races didn't want. Her mother had lived to see segregation signs taken down at public restrooms and to witness the first integrated prom at her high school. She had been called names as a child, teased because of the braids in her hair. Whenever she saw a white girl with braids nowadays, she would recount the days of being teased by her white classmates as a child. The conversation of color had always been about black and white. Never had it been about white versus blue.

"Musicians are union, you know. I hope you were paying attention at work, at least so you understand how all that stuff works, because the last thing you want to do is go over there making a fool of yourself because you don't know how things work. And you're supposed to be suspicious of management now, right? While you're singing the blues, you make sure they know that you were management yourself before. That way you won't get cheated. Are you listening to me?"

"Yes, Mom," Claycee said. "I need to make sure I act my color."

Oregon Grind

Rick Attig

Blood seeped from the bandaged stump of the middle finger on Foster's right hand and a drop fell onto the blank sheet of paper in front of him. He shifted in his chair. He needed to piss. He wanted to leave. But the union rep had made it clear: To get the $127 a week in federal dislocated worker pay on top of his unemployment check, Foster had to complete the retraining seminar.

Foster sat in the fourth row in the room full of millworkers, dark crewcut glinting silver under the harsh overhead light of the elementary school classroom, dressed in one of the plain red, long-sleeved sweatshirts he wore everywhere. The men were crammed into the kids' desks, their faces tight, eyes rimmed with red. Foster's hand was wrapped in a big fist of gauze.

A thin woman from the employment office in Salem had written her name, SUSAN, on the chalkboard, like a fourth-grade teacher. She had frizzy, dyed-blonde hair, wore a blue polyester pantsuit and clutched a cup of coffee smudged with red lipstick. Speaking in a shaky, loud voice, she asked, "Did any of you bring resumés?"

Foster shifted again in his chair. What bullshit. Promising a bunch of millworkers and loggers who'd never done anything else, didn't know anything else, that they'd soon find good jobs in computers and tourism— the "visitor industry," Susan called it. Foster looked around the room. He knew the only chance for most of the guys was to wait and hope the mill would reopen again, hope that the trucks would rumble back into the yard to dump their logs, hope that the lights, the saws and the noisy kiln would roar back to life, as they had all those times before. Yet guys were nodding with interest while Susan chattered on about the "call centers" that were hiring, even though none of them had the faintest fucking idea what those were. If they hadn't all been so scared about the future, they'd have hooted her out of the room.

"We've set up word processors in the back," Susan said. "I'll help you get started, and by the time we're done here today you'll have resumés you can take with you to your job interviews."

Chairs scraped as other millworkers got up, but Foster didn't move.

"Sir," Susan said to him, "We've got an open work station right here."

"Ma'am," Foster answered. He showed her his hands. Foster was down to seven fingers. He'd lost the first one when a band saw snapped with a twang and the waving blade dropped half of the forefinger on his right hand into the oily sawdust. The second one fell when one of the cutoff saws kicked back and clipped the pinkie on his left hand.

The last one was his own damn fault. Three days before they shut down the mill, he forgot to kill the power to a plugged-up debarking machine. When the belt suddenly spun, it caught his right hand, twisting off his middle finger and flinging it into the bark rumbling up the conveyor to the shredder. The first two times they'd found and made half-hearted attempts to save his fingers. The foreman handed the bloody pieces to the EMTs, who dutifully gave them to the harried emergency room doctors, who tossed them away with barely a glance. But Foster's ground-up fuck-you finger was still mixed in the pulp somewhere inside the mill. That was the final sting.

As he stood up and faced Susan, Foster kept his hands raised, like he was being taken hostage. "Ma'am," he repeated. "I'm sorry. I can't help you."

"It's you we're trying to help," she answered. "Please, come over here."

He really had to piss. His finger was throbbing. He didn't know how to type. "Ma'am," he tried to smile at her, but couldn't. "There's no fucking way."

Susan flinched, but didn't back down. She pulled a second chair up to the empty work station. "You sit here," she directed Foster, "and I'll do the typing."

He was trapped. Foster sat down, his bladder burning.

"Let's get your work history," Susan said. "How long did you work at Willamette-Pacific?"

"Twenty-one years," Foster said as Susan typed.

"Before that?"

"I was a tree faller for Steve Mack," Foster said. "Fifteen years."

"Before that?"

"I was in the Navy," Foster said. "One year, eleven months and four days."

"What about education?" Susan asked.

"What about it?" Foster twisted in his seat. The goddamned burning was getting worse.

"Where'd you go?"

"Santiam High School. Right up the road."

"When did you?" Susan started to ask.

Foster looked away from Susan. He wanted to stand up, get out, just go.

"Almost three years," he said. Susan typed.

"That's all you need on there," Foster told her. What else was there? Foster was destined for the woods and the mill. His mom died when he was seven, and his dad worked graveyard at the old Weyerhaeuser plant in Sweet Home. His old man came home many mornings drunk and unaccountably angry at his son, his only child. Foster had to get himself ready, for school, for everything.

"What about your personal interests? Hobbies? Are you married?" Susan probed.

"My wife died three months ago."

Susan glanced up from the computer screen.

He'd met JeriLou in the mill, of course, when both were pulling 2x6s off the green chain. She was lanky and strong, and wore brown coveralls and a baseball cap that covered her short brown hair. One afternoon JeriLou suggested to Foster that he needed to get his ass in gear. That's all he needed to hear. About two months later they got married in the courthouse in Salem. They moved into a wreck of a house Foster was trying to salvage down along the flood plain. It was so damn wet down there that mold started creeping up the walls before Foster had even nailed on the plywood sheeting. But JeriLou planted a garden and together they fixed up the house. They never had any kids, but JeriLou raised Boston Terriers. It seemed like there was always a litter of pups in the tub of the dirty bathtub. The last few years they kept a broom in the bathroom, not to sweep the disgusting floor, but to swat away the snarling Boston bitch that would lunge at anybody who came in to use the john.

They cut trees, sawed lumber and raised pups together for 31 years. But then JeriLou was getting ready for work one morning, reached over to fix her bra and discovered the lump on her left breast. The cancer went right after JeriLou, mean and aggressive, and Foster ran himself ragged those last months, trying to soothe her, feed her, and build her the goddamned coffee cart she wanted to open out along the highway.

The day after JeriLou died, Foster retrieved the .22 rifle he kept behind the seat of his pickup. He went into the bathroom and snapped a leash on the Boston bitch. He led the gray-muzzled dog outside, stopped under an apple tree and stroked the animal for a few moments. Then he shot it in the head. He took the dog's body down to the mortuary in Salem and paid an extra hundred dollars to have it cremated with JeriLou's remains.

Two mornings later, he drove up to the edge of the clearcut scar high on the ridge overlooking town. He parked his beat-up Chevy pickup in the landing bulldozed by the logging crew. Tall, twisted piles of gray slash waiting to be torched dotted the slope below. Foster carried the brown plastic box of ashes down the hillside, and stopped between two slash piles. He looked down at the town, and saw the mill's broad rust-colored roof. When he opened the box, the ashes were lighter than he expected. The gritty dust rose in the cold wind, swirled around his legs and blew into his mouth and eyes.

Fingers. Job. Wife. Susan had finished his resumé, stood up and was talking now to the class about dressing for success in job interviews. Foster abruptly pushed back his chair, got up and headed for the door. Somebody cracked, "See-ya, Fost. Going home to change?"

Foster trotted down the school highway, glancing at each of the doors, then swerved into the boys' bathroom. When he came out, he walked right past the classroom and out into that cold January rain. Foster was done with career guidance. Done with the mill. Done giving up fingers. Done.

That's what he'd promised JeriLou.

They talked about getting out when Foster was driving JeriLou down to Salem twice a week for chemo, her so tired, slumped against the passenger door, him clutching the wheel with both hands, looking straight ahead, both of them hanging on the best they could. Getting out of the mill. Out of the woods.

It was an easy hour's drive down the canyon to Salem. But that shit they dripped into JeriLou to fight her cancer was a hard road. After two months, her hair gone, her skin like fire to the touch, her breath tasting like metal, JeriLou wanted to stop, say fuck it. But Foster kept loading her in the pickup and driving down out of the canyon.

After every treatment, on their way back home, they'd stop at a coffee place they'd discovered along the highway near Stayton. The guy that owned it had set up a picnic table behind his cart. There were some trees, they could see the river, and the highway noise wasn't so bad. Foster and JeriLou would sit with their coffee and talk.

One day she said, "Hell, I should do this."

"What?" Foster asked.

"Open one of these carts up the highway. Sell coffee."

"Geez, Jeri."

"Well, I gotta do something. I don't know if I'm going to make it through this. But I'm damn sure the mill isn't."

When they got home that night, and after Foster fed the dogs and heated JeriLou a frozen dinner that she picked at, she asked him to bring her a pencil and paper. She started making a list of everything she'd need for a coffee cart. She drew a crude blueprint of the trailer, the sliding window, the cedar siding, even the wooden lilacs, her favorite flowers, cut out, painted and nailed onto the side facing the highway.

The next day, she was on the phone, calling all over the valley, trying to find an espresso machine. "Christ, do you know how much they want for one of those things?" she asked Foster. JeriLou kept looking, and found a used machine in Portland. Foster drove up to the city alone, fought all that shitty traffic, and picked it up, a heavy steel box with a stainless steamer wand and valve knobs, emblazoned with the brand name, "Grindmaster."

Whenever they stopped at the Stayton cart, JeriLou studied the list of things the guy sold—candy, chips, packaged muffins wrapped in cellophane, juice, bottled water, the coffee drinks. Lying in bed, blurry from the pain pills, she made a list of what she'd have in her cart. "I'll need a microwave, so I can sell bags of popcorn," she told Foster.

Her plans kept them both occupied. After work, Foster went to work on the trailer, hammering away in his cousin Gary's big garage. It took him two weeks to turn a flat-bed utility trailer into a cedar coffee cart. He even used a jigsaw to carefully cut the lilac shapes out of a piece of clear cedar, and painted them.

That next morning, he helped JeriLou out to the pickup. It was a chemo day. But on the way he took her by Gary's garage. He lifted her down from the truck—she had gotten so damn thin and weak—then raised the garage door. "Ta-da!" Foster said. The sign on the trailer read "Santiam Canyon Coffee & Expresso."

JeriLou smiled, "It's perfect, honey."

That morning was their last trip together down the canyon. The doctor in Salem examined JeriLou and called the hospital to reserve a room. That night she twisted and bucked on the bed until a nurse came in and throttled up the pain-killers. JeriLou fell into a coma, and Foster spent the next two nights in a chair by her bed, listening to JeriLou's ragged breathing and the soft footsteps of the hospital staff in the intensive care unit. He wasn't sure when JeriLou died early the third morning. There was no last, convulsive breath. No sound. Just things growing quiet and a nurse coming in and placing her hand on Foster's shoulder.

Foster went right back to the mill the next morning. After his shift, he dropped by Gary's garage. He opened the door of the coffee cart and stepped inside, smelling the cut cedar and the fresh paint. He sat down on the plywood floor. He sat there in the cool, quiet garage, thinking about JeriLou, about their vows to get out of the mill. The cart was her dream, not his. The mill was what he knew. Foster went back to the mill the next morning. And he kept going back until the day the company hurriedly threw up the chain link fence, and gave everybody notice.

Then he was out of excuses.

Late on the afternoon that that he'd fled the job retraining class, Foster rolled up the door to Gary's garage, backed in his pickup and hooked up the coffee cart. He pulled slowly out onto the highway, and drove by Scotty's Tavern, where the rest of the guys were nursing beers and grudges. If any of them had looked out the smudged glass of the front door, they would have seen a 58-year-old former logger and millwright with seven fingers, a man who could barely tolerate his friends, let alone anyone else, preparing to open a roadside coffee cart. As Foster would have chortled, if it were anybody else from the mill crew: No fucking way.

Foster pulled the trailer onto the gravel lot across the highway from the shuttered mill, unhooked it from his truck and blocked its wheels. He unloaded from his pickup boxes of candy, chips, microwave popcorn and a 10-pound bag of coffee he'd picked up for JeriLou at the Salem Costco. A driver with a flatbed load of Port-a-Potties rolled up and dropped one at the edge of the gravel lot. Foster lugged a generator to the back edge of the lot and plugged in an extension cord, then climbed in the coffee cart. It smelled of coffee and fresh-cut cedar.

The steam hissed as he practiced heating milk and making foam with the espresso machine. The first pitcher of milk boiled over and burned his wrist. "Shit," he muttered, a bulky, scarred man in his red sweatshirt and dirty gauze bandage, clutching a little stainless pitcher, learning to steam milk. He was good with machines, that's how he'd made millwright. He swirled the foam in the pitcher, grunted and switched off the espresso maker. He'd open for business in the morning.

He got there just before dawn, switching on the lights and sticking an "Open" sign in the sliding window. Across the highway, a single bare bulb lit the doorway to the mill office, but the rest of the plant was dark. Foster put on the coffee and poked at the still-frozen pastries as though he was trying to bring them to life. He slugged down a bottle of water. He was nervous, tugging the sleeves of his red sweatshirt. His battered hands shook as he arranged and rearranged the candy and chips piles in a basket. He made two trips out in the rain to the Port-a-Pottie. He sat on a stool, drinking coffee, listening to the tap of the rain on the roof.

Then a tan SUV slowed. Foster saw its blinker come on and a couple with three kids pulled up. Three snowboards and two pairs of skis were strapped to a roof rack. They had gotten an early start for Hoodoo Ski Bowl. Foster slid open the window and almost smiled at them. "Howdy," he said.

The kids bouncing in the back seat were hollering for hot chocolate. The thin blonde in the passenger seat said she'd like a grande nonfat latte. "I mean a large," she quickly said. The guy driving shook his head. He looked tired, and not just because of the morning drive over the mountain from Corvallis. "Coffee, black, for me," he said. Foster poured the coffee, handed it out the window, then started steaming the milk for the latte and the chocolates. The milk boiled, the chocolates were too hot. Foster handed them out without a word of warning, taking back a twenty from the man.

"Christ, these are way too hot for the kids," the man complained.

"Give him a tip, honey. A tip," the woman urged.

The man looked over at her, "There's no tip jar," he said crossly. He glanced up at Foster, who was holding his change out the window, cupping it with the three fingers of his right hand.

"Oh Christ, just keep it," he muttered. He put the SUV in gear, and it threw gravel as it jumped back on the highway.

The rain was letting up, and the morning light was coming fast now. Foster looked across the highway at the rotting piles of bark in the empty log yard, the rusted crane frozen overhead. The solitary light at the office door still glowed. A sign with routered lettering used to hang inside that office, where Foster went every Thursday afternoon to pick up his paycheck: "Oregon: The Wood Basket to the United States."

An Audi sedan drove up, and Foster slid open the window and asked the young guy who was driving what he'd like.

"I'll have a Snickers," he said. Foster looked through the tray of candy and chips.

"Uh, I think all I have is Milky Way, Butterfinger, Baby Ruth and Reese's," Foster said.

"You don't have Snickers? Everybody has Snickers."

"How about a Milky Way?" Foster suggested.

The guy shrugged, handed in a dollar and took the candy. "Hey," he said. "Do you know that's not how you spell 'espresso'?"

Foster glared at him. "No shit."

"Yeah, it's with an 's,' not an 'x'."

"Thanks a helluva lot," Foster said, slamming the window shut.

It was full light now, drizzling rain, and the cars were hissing past on the highway. All you need is a radar gun to tell whether a timber town is thriving, dying, or already dead. Most of these hard little towns straddle Oregon's main east-west highways 26, 22, 20, 58. When the mills hummed, when these places still had shoe stores, used car dealers, even real grocery stores, with fresh meat and vegetables, the most optimistic towns took pride in slowing the highway traffic to 35 mph. Slow down! We got a real going community here. People take it easy going through the dead and gone towns, too, pointing out the ghosts, shaking their heads, telling their bored kids in the back seat yet again about the great little burger joint that used to be right there, marveling at how the ivy has somehow managed to grow right up around the stack of that old mill.

But people drive through a dying timber town like it has an infectious disease. The speed limit out front of the coffee cart is set at 45, but the state police troopers and the sheriff's deputies don't much care anymore, either. The basic rule is that you lift your foot off the gas for a moment when you come through. Somebody cut down the speed limit sign at the west end of town a year ago, and nobody thinks it's worth the effort to stand it up again. The only gas station in town closed, too, but the owner, Pete, kept his tow truck. He does pretty well hauling crumpled wrecks down off the Santiam Pass, and pulling from snow banks all the dumbshit tourists from the valley who don't know how to drive on ice and can't be bothered to put on chains. Lily's greasy spoon is the last café in town. Of course, there is always a clutch of muddy pickups nosed in like feeding puppies around Scotty's Tavern. There's a gypo logging outfit that parks its two muddy trucks along the highway.

One of those little Japanese cars pulled up to the coffee trailer. It was a woman and a little boy, about 6, who leaned forward from the back seat and looked up at Foster as he waited for them to order.

"What happened to your fingers?" the boy blurted out.

"Arlo!" his mother said. She looked up at Foster, smiled and said, "I'm sorry."

"It's okay," he answered. He looked down at the boy and then nodded at the mill across the highway. "I lost them over there," he said.

The boy's eyes widened as he looked across the highway at the shuttered mill. "What's that place?" he asked.

"It's a sawmill. We used to take logs and cut them into lumber for houses," Foster said.

"What happened to your fingers?"

"I wasn't watching what I was doing."

"Did it hurt?"

Foster turned to the mother, "What would you like, ma'am?"

"Carmel macchiato," she said.

"Caramel," Foster said.

"Two pumps."

Foster had no idea what she was talking about. "I can make you a latte," he said.

Arlo interrupted, "Did you ever cut down trees?"

Foster nodded. "Sure."

"Okay, a latte," the woman said.

"My teacher says trees let us breath," the boy said.

"Arlo," his mother said.

"Tell your teacher …" Foster started, then stopped. He handed the two their drinks.

"Tell your teacher that we're still breathing out here."

He closed the window softly as the woman drove away.

Foster wiped down the espresso maker. He liked machines. They saw it at the mill, pulled him off the chain and made him a millwright. Of course, he didn't have any formal education in engineering or technology. But whenever they brought in a new conveyor, hydraulic carriage or other new equipment, it was Foster they put in charge. The company brass in their pressed shirts and shiny hard hats without a scratch on them would stand around smiling and celebrating their new investment, while Foster, in his stained red sweatshirt, was in the middle of the men wrestling it into place, cursing, precision-fitting the new machinery down to a tolerance of a thousandth of an inch.

Foster was out in the Port-a-Pottie when the empty log truck turned off the highway and rumbled up next to the trailer. One of the guys from the mill, Bob Melvin, had gotten his old truck started, and three of the guys had piled in to the front seat with him. Melvin rolled down the cracked window of his truck, leaned out and hollered down at Foster that he should get his ass back in the cart because he wanted a "crussant" and a "skinny lat-te."

"Hey, this place is real cute, Fost," Melvin said. "Love the flowers."

The other guys in the truck laughed.

"We always knew you had another side to you," one said.

Foster tried again to smile. "Oh, fuck you guys."

They all got out and crowded around the trailer window. "Hey, do you have a liquor license?" one asked.

Melvin wrote his name and phone number on the back of a used envelope, and scrawled "Resume" across the top. He handed it in the window and asked, "Got any openings, Foster? I like flowers, too."

Foster handed around paper cups of coffee, Melvin moved his truck out of the way and they all stood around the window, the mill looming behind them. The cars kept rocketing past on the highway. The rain had started in again, fat, cold drops, and the guys edged closer to the trailer, under the little overhang.

"You gonna make any money at this, Foster?" Melvin asked.

"Don't know, Bob. How's your job going?"

"At least I'm not selling chips and candy bars."

"Good for you, Bob."

"I heard that lumber prices are going back up," one guy said.

Melvin said, "We'll be back in business before you know it."

"Bullshit," Foster muttered, then ducked out to take a leak again. When he came back, walking slowly across the gravel, he looked drawn and tired.

"Sure seems like you have to piss a lot," Melvin observed when he came back.

"Anybody ask you to hold my dick?" Foster snapped.

The conversation fell. Melvin said he had some firewood at home to split. "Thanks for the coffee, Fost," Melvin said as the rest of the guys sauntered through the rain to the truck. "And good luck."

Foster was popping a bag of corn in the microwave when a dark Buick four-door drove up. The power window came down, and a woman leaned out to place her order. "I'll have ..." she stopped mid-sentence when she recognized Foster. "Hey, you were in my class." It was the frizzy-haired job counselor, Susan, from the Salem retraining office.

"I was," Foster admitted.

"Look at you," she gushed. "This is amazing. I can't wait to tell the office about you. How long have you been open?"

"Just today."

"Well, how's it going?" She didn't wait for an answer. "Hey, this is great what you're doing. A real success story."

She paused to catch her breath. "I'm driving over to Bend for another class. Willamette Industries has closed its plywood mill, 165 jobs. Hey, do you mind if I tell them about you? I mean, you just got laid off a few weeks ago, and already you have your own business. You'd be an inspiration. Show them what's possible...." She saw the anger flaring in Foster's eyes and her voice trailed off.

"Tell those poor bastards anything you want," he said.

She shifted uncomfortably in the seat of her car. "Well, you're a good story. We don't have a lot of those right now. We have some guys who have found truck driving jobs...one guy over in Stayton has opened up a welding shop. But we keep trying to stress that the mill jobs aren't coming back, that the future in these little towns is tourism. You got all these people driving through here," she pointed at a line of three passing cars headed up the highway. "It's about giving them a place to stop. You get it."

"I get it," Foster repeated.

"I'd just like a cup of regular coffee. With cream."

Foster handed it out to her.

"I'm so excited to see somebody making it work," Susan said. "You're like a role model."

Foster watched the Buick glide back onto the highway. He closed the window and sat back on the stool. "Role model," he said aloud. Then he reached over and switched off the espresso machine. He stood and walked outside, the door slamming behind him. He unhooked the extension cord to the cart, and he got into his pickup and backed it up to the cart. A few minutes later, he towed the cart onto the highway and past the abandoned mill, the single light still glowing in front of the office.

He turned up the rutted gravel road leading to the clearcut scar on top the ridge above town. The cart bucked behind the bouncing pickup on the rough road, but Foster didn't even glance in the mirror. He drove up to the landing.

The rain had stopped. The air carried the metallic smell of the overturned earth on the bulldozed landing. Foster unhooked the cart, then hopped back into his pickup and drove it to the other side of the landing. When he came back, he carried a claw hammer.

Foster went around to the front of the cart, and slipped the claw under one of the wooden lilacs. He carefully pried it loose and set it on a nearby stump. Then he removed the rest of the wooden flowers and stacked them atop the first one.

Foster opened the door of the cart, and stepped inside. He wadded up a stack of napkins and stuffed them beneath the bottom shelf. Then he smashed the top shelf with the hammer, splintering the dry cedar. He arranged the wood on the paper, lit it with a match and stepped outside, leaving the door open.

Smoke billowed out the door and drifted over the piles of slash on the hillside. The incense of burning cedar filled the damp air. The fire popped and crackled. Foster held the pale purple lilacs, and watched the flames grow higher.

The Last Car

Lolita Hernandez

On any other day, the cobalt blue Fleetwood body would rest unattended on a trestle at the edge of second floor, its sides smudged with assembly fingerprints, its windshield taped with assembly instructions called broadcast sheets. Already fitted with an instrument panel, seats, a headliner, internal lighting, wiring harnesses, it would wait for descent to the final assembly line to unite with the engine and chassis, the hood and fenders, headlights. Then, oo la la. It would become a Cadillac, Fleetwood Brougham.

At any other time, the final transformation from assorted parts and systems to car would happen quickly. In an instant. A push of the body over the second floor edge where, tucked in its special hoist, it would hover no longer than a few seconds. And WHOOUMP. The car would come together: a body from the Fleetwood plant with a Cadillac chassis and engine. A door painted at Fleetwood, Cadillac's sister plant, a mile down the Interstate 75 corridor, united with the bumper from the Cadillac plating department. Just like that. A flick of the operator's thumb and the hoist delivered. Whoooump. From second floor, smacko, right on the money to four young men in the pit, under the chassis, with guide drifts ready to ease the body on.

But on the morning of December 18, 1987, the time that it took for the cobalt blue Brougham to become a car was measured in seconds that became minutes and minutes that stretched as long as first-floor final assembly. Time bounced from the man who loaded the frame onto the sidesaddle. It passed through the woman who installed the shocks. It rolled over and under the men who loaded the gas tank. And stopped for who knows how long at the body drop area where the press of the crowd observing the final glorious moments of car assembly at Cadillac Motor Car Company, Clark Street, Detroit delayed the body's drop.

Over a period of years, Cadillac models were nibbled away from Clark Street. First Eldorado and Seville relocated. Next the De Ville left town. Then the last Fleetwood, cobalt blue with diamond twinkles wherever the light hit, simulated convertible top and light blue leather interior. In an eye blink it was there. In another eye blink the Cadillac assembly at its original home was history.

That morning, second-floor workers hustled around the body making unusual preparations for the drop. They patted its ample luxury car sides one last time with their gloved hands. They gently tugged at the electronically loaded instrument panel; punched the front seats top, middle, bottom until they achieved the right depression in the cushions; took their gloves off for a real feel of the velvety-soft leather interior; picked up scraps of paper, bits of thread from the carpeting. Someone buffed a fingerprint from the driver's door. Another retrieved a stray instrument panel screw from the door molding. Three or four coworkers helped the hoist operator pull the mammoth hoist over the body. This was normally a solo job, but everyone wanted a piece of the last action that day. A cluster of workers performed checks on the hoist itself to insure that it wrapped around the body securely. They yanked at its heavy, steel bars, four on either side. They passed their hands over the carpeted arms that locked under the lip of the body. One last look up at the network of chains and pulleys controlling the hoist. One last long sniff inside and out of the car. Then the hoist operator grabbed the controls in his right hand. The second-floor crew helped him push the body off the trestle and into the dangling space a floor above its destination. Everyone crowded around the edge of second floor. A few, those most intimately involved with the final second-floor preparations, held hands. Workers from all over the plant leaned over the railings, wondering what would become of their jobs in the plant-wide shakedown that would follow the closing of assembly. Salaried personnel already began to miss the lights and noise they would encounter in the assembly area en route from one set of offices to another. It hadn't occurred to them yet that there would be changes in their lives as well. Poor assembly workers, they speculated, what will become of them?

Then all waited as if the drop could proceed as usual, with the hoist operator visually aligning the body in the air and the frame on the conveyor. They stood there viewing the rear of the body and its sides through the orange bars of the hoist. Their grips on each other's hands tightened. Their eyes focused on the chassis below. It would happen at any moment. This is it. This is it. Hold it. Hold it. One, two. This is it, this is it, this is it. No, not yet. Take a deep breath. Hold it. Hold it. Hold it.

Everyone hadn't arrived yet at the first-floor body drop. Droves of onlookers were still converging on the area like townspeople at a traveling medicine show. Mechanics and salaried technicians came from the Engineering Building. Cleaners and sweepers from every corner of the plant, stock people from Merritt Warehouse, clerks and secretaries from the administration building, top-level Cadillac management and all the union representatives, those who were not in a Las Vegas UAW conference. WKBX television station was there.

The second-to-the-last frame had already met its chassis but languished in the station after body drop. It could not complete its transformation until the last body fell and the conveyor began moving again. The brown

Brougham was designated for a Fleetwood worker. Free raffle tickets had been distributed to assemblers at both plants for a chance at the last two cars. A Cadillac worker, part of the workforce that married the body to the Cadillac frame, installed the Cadillac engine, Cadillac gas tank, brakes, exhaust system, suspension, electronic systems, would win the last car to roll off the line on Clark Street. Ever.

Were it a typical day, things would have been relatively quiet, almost lifeless. The work day in final assembly usually began as a slow dream. Sleepy figures donned aprons, wet their gloves with cold fountain water to insure a good fit, and shuffled papers at inspection sites. Young, short men walked toward one of several trenches in the conveyor, slid down an edge and disappeared. At 54 cars an hour, shiny Cadillacs rolled off the line with monotonous, relentless regularity. At any point after the chassis transferred from its assembly line and the body dropped onto it from the second floor, some tired soul would set a pair of gloves on fire, stuff them into the conveyor or chuck a broom handle in there, anything to stop the line, get a rest. Some days each car passed with a prayer for a few extra seconds break whispered behind it. That was the concept of factory time: seconds were minutes, minutes were hours, hours were forever.

Early in the shift on the last day, the strains of what became a processional chorus first arose spontaneously from the dock by the railroad tracks on lower Clark as the workers there observed the dwindling stack of frames. It moved as a feeble hum a few feet along to the sidesaddle area, the beginning phase of first-floor assembly. It shaped itself into vocal utterances as two men hooked the last frame and positioned it onto the sidesaddle conveyor. When the two frame loaders completed their job, they doffed their gloves and followed the frame. This routine was repeated by the other assemblers on the first half of the sidesaddle line. By the time they arrived at the control arms station, the song burst forth loud and strong from the lips of the fifteen or so people who were following the frame. Na na naa naaaa. Na na naa naaaa. Ohhhh............goooood-bye. It was as if the line was folding up in the frame's wake. The pattern continued down the rest of the sidesaddle. As each person finished a job, the group grew larger and louder. Na na naa naaaa. Ohhhh..........goooood-bye. Install the brake lines, walk. Tighten the frame brace, walk. While the frame transferred from the sidesaddle to the chassis line, the chorus, which by then included nearly the entire sidesaddle line, dock workers, and strays from other areas on that end of the building, positioned themselves in the aisle at the head of the chassis line and began harmonizing as if they were Christmas carolers.

A woman in full Santa Claus regalia joined the group at that point. She worked on the sidesaddle conveyor installing fuel lines. After completing her job, she slipped on the Santa outfit she had rented for the day in an attempt to make the best of what everyone realized was a bad situation. Her Nestle's chocolate face, framed by the white fuzz on her red hat, smiled bravely as she added her voice to the caroling. By virtue of her costume, she became the conductor. She faced the carolers confidently, waved her arms stiffly. And a one. And a two. And na na naa naaaa. Na na naa naaa. Ohhhh..........goooood-bye. Thus, she assumed leadership of the procession when it rejoined the frame at the head of the chassis line and led her coworkers throughout the first half of the line until the group arrived at the gas-tank station.

That was where the procession lost its composure. What religious, incantatory, spiritual mood had developed from the increasingly loud and fervent repetition of the old rock and roll refrain, dissolved once someone yelled, "Let's sign the tank." Everyone instantly produced magic markers and began affixing their names to the tank, which at that point, swung from four chains until permanent fastening after the body drop. A group hunched over the tank, scribbled names, dates, a heart, a smile. Another group replaced the first which shifted to the outer edge of the action. Then another would rotate inward while the other rotated out. Then another in. And another out.

In this way the chassis progressed toward the body drop, still at normal line speed but surrounded by a throbbing blob of people, all trying to sign the tank. At times, only an arm could pierce through a group around the chassis in order to scratch its mark on the tank. Foremen signed. General Foremen signed. Secretaries from the administration building squeezed their way through and penned their names. The head of security, the head of medical, the head of personnel, the head of the whole Clark Street operation signed.

It was the act of signing the tank that pulled the emotional plug in the department, releasing a flow of tears, hugs, kisses and fervent well-wishes such as had never been experienced on Clark Street, even when the motor line left for Livonia several years before. Some signed carefully, as if the curves of their n's or o's, the slant of their t's or l's on the cold, gray tank, would mystically insure that their past, as assemblers of America's foremost luxury cars, also would be their future. Others scrawled their names as if the gas tank would link them to each other forever.

-Hey, Nino, what are you going to do when this is over?

-I'm headed home to *Tejas*, baby. Me and my old man we're going to open up a *taqueria* in San Antonio.

-Well come here, baby, and give Big Mama a hug and kiss. I don't know when I'll ever see you again.

At last, frame and followers converged on the body drop, joining the throng there. The press of people was so great that there was a danger someone would fall into the pit from where workers were trying valiantly to emerge in order to reach the top of the tank. The headlight checkers and final inspection people attempted to squeeze through for their signatures, as did the repairmen at the extreme end of the department. Last minute signers and onlookers pushed around the chassis to such a degree that plant security was unable to maneuver its way through to help control the crowd. In desperation several supervisors, already in the area, and a few line workers linked their outstretched hands on either side of the chassis in order to keep people away long enough for the body to drop.

The tension on the second floor mounted as the hoist operator held his thumb poised over the down button. He had been holding it in that position so long that he lost all sensation in his thumb. He wiggled it to insure that it was still in working order. Day after day for five years he had dropped bodies at the correct moment without a hitch, almost by instinct. Now he must wait for a signal.

Those around him began to close ranks as others arrived to join in. The hand grips grew tighter, their knuckles grew paler. Whew, the broadcast lady said. This suspense is killing me, and she weaved her head a few times and gently wiggled her body as if casting off a spell. Whew, yeah. Ain't that the truth. Others echoed her sentiment. More heads rotated to loosen up the neck muscles. A few broke their hand grips long enough to flex their fingers, get the blood flowing again, and then they reconnected tighter than before. Their faces were blank, absolutely expressionless as the eyes of those on the second floor locked with those on the first, creating a time tunnel, a kind of spiritual corridor through which the last body would travel.

The signal for the drop would come at any moment as those on first floor craned their necks upward at the body nestled so sweetly in its orange steel cradle while carpeted hooks caressed its underside. The onlookers began wrapping arms around each other's waists. They were already body to body, pressed so tightly that a sheet of onion-skin paper couldn't slide between. You could hear a screw drop. You could hear paper fall. You could hear a rat breathe at that moment.

Then the members of the chain blockading the chassis looked at each other, sweat popping off their faces. The foreman of the body drop was transported by the intensity of the historical moment. He freed his hands from the chain and surveyed the area, fixing his eyes first on this one, then on another, as if he had been imbued by some special power. But the crowd was already frozen waiting for the drop. He lifted his arms dramatically from his sides. It was, after all, one of the rare times he had to directly intervene in the timing of a body drop. The hoist operator and the pit crew were able to manage the drop themselves in the past. He began waving his arms in opposing circles, a movement vaguely reminiscent of his days in the Navy, then flung his right arm magisterially and pointed to the body in mid air. That was it. That was it. One, two. The hoist operator took one last long breath, wiggled his thumb one last time and WHOOUMP. Yes. Yes. That was it.

It all went by so fast, really, once the hoist operator received the signal to push the button. Eighteen days later, on the feast of the epiphany, there would be little left in final assembly to recall the activity of the last day or any day or years preceding. Millwrights already would have pulled down the overhead lines and removed the conveyors. A group of employee scavengers, some of them present at the last body drop, would zigzag in an eerie procession across first floor from the sidesaddle area. They would move in irregular waves to all the metal disposal bins searching for discarded assembly line tools. The final assembly pit already would be stripped of tools and machinery. A women's bathroom door would have the words 'door is locked, door is locked, door is locked forever' scratched on it. Several rat poison bait boxes would line the walls of final assembly.

But December 18, 1987, 10:53 A.M., one minute after the final body drop, the crowd was still cheering as they moved along the sides of the pit in order to trail the Fleetwood. They made room for the hood, fenders and headlights installation. They buffed out all fingerprints with shirt tails or the arms of blouses, smoothed the interior, and commented on the lights twinkling on the instrument panel after the battery installation. After the car passed all final inspections with flying colors, Santa Claus positioned herself behind it. Across her chest, she displayed a placard which read, ALL I WANT FOR CHRISTMAS IS MY JOB. Everyone fell in behind her. WKBX had switched on their lights long before the procession crawled the few feet past the headlight test station and the last under-hood inspection. Cameras rolled. The lady from the chassis line, who installed the right rear bumper shocks, strolled to the front in her red silk blouse and black wool skirt, nylons and heels that she wore for the special occasion. She had tied a black band around her upper arm as so many others did that day. The general foreman of final assembly produced a tight smile to mask the noticeable furrow of sadness above his eyebrows. A couple of clerks from payroll stood by each other looking bewildered. Another lady from the chassis line broke ranks with the procession and stuck her head through the passenger window for one last look. Santa yanked her cap off and waved it back and forth. And a one, and a two, and Na na naa naaaa. Na na naa naaaa. Ohhhh....goooood-bye.

Contributor Note (Scout)
Michael Martone

Michael Martone was born in Fort Wayne, Indiana, where he worked every summer, while attending high school and college the rest of the year, for International Harvester on the assembly line at the company's truck plant on the city's east end. Then, before the bankruptcy of the company and the subsequent closing of the plant and the moving of what jobs that were left to a factory in Missouri, International Harvester had been one of the largest employers in the city. No one called it Inter-national Harvester, however, saying instead that you worked at Inter-national or, more likely, at the Harvester. Martone preferred the latter, liked the *the* added on to single name. People in Fort Wayne worked for *the* Harvester or *the* GE or for *the* Pennsy, the railroad that ran from New York and Philadelphia right through Fort Wayne close to the Harvester then on to Chicago. And on the weekends or in the summer the people of Fort Wayne went to The Lake, one of a hundred named lakes (James, George, Clear, Long, Crooked, Sylvan, Wawasee) in north-eastern Indiana that were all called The Lake by the people of Fort Wayne who went to them or who stayed in town and only talked about going. Martone did not go to the lake those summers he worked at the Harvester. He was hired to cover for the permanent employees who were on their annual two week vacations at the lake. The plant made the TriStar truck, a cab-over semi-tractor that had a forward chrome grill that cut straight down from the big windshield, a flat face, a wall of metal and glass. Many of the units rolled out of the factory and right over to North American Van Lines whose world headquarters was right next door. Martone didn't work on that line but he couldn't help but notice the huge hulks as they were assembled. He liked the way the crew compartment, the whole big cab was flipped forward to expose the engine buried beneath the seats. Martone worked on the Scout line, a little closed truck that looked a lot like an army Jeep and was one of the first attempts the industry made at making an SUV. Martone is not and was not then a skilled laborer. He wasn't assigned to handle the pneumatic socket wrenches that bolted parts together nor able to operate the spot welding torches that fused the body to the chassis nor even permitted to mask the car with paper and tape for its spray painting. Martone waited at the end of the line after the final assembly near the big doors where the finished product left the

Michael Martone —

works and was driven out to the vast parking lot wait for loading onto train cars or auto haulers pulled by TriStars. He was in Quality Control. He had a clipboard and even a white coat he didn't wear in the summer heat. He had a whole list of things he needed to test on every brand new Scout that nosed toward him. At this point the cars were chained to the slow moving cable under the floor, their wheels guided by tracks. As each unit crept by Martone had to perform a series of checks. He opened and closed the door on the driver's side; he opened the door again and got in; he adjusted the seat forward and back, back and forward; leaving the transmission in neutral, he started the engine; he locked and unlocked the door; he turned the lights on and off; he turned the windshield wipers on and off; he turned the turn indicators on and off, first the left and then the right; he tapped the horn twice; he turned off the car leaving the key in the socket; he hopped out, closing the door solidly behind him. Martone did this ritual eight hours a day, six days a week, all through the summer. When the whistle blew at the end of his shift (there was an actual steam whistle,) Martone made his way to the locker room where he put his clip board and his white coat into his locker, got his lunch pail, and punched out at the time clock. As he stood in line waiting to punch out, Martone told himself, "Don't do it. Don't do it." He took a step up and the man at the head of the line inserted his time card. "Don't do it." Another punch and another step forward, all the time reminding himself not to do what he knew he would do. Finally, Martone punched out and he made his way to his own car through the enormous field of finished TriStars and Scouts in precise ranks and then on to the employees' lot where many of the workers drove to work in Scouts they had purchased right at the factory door. All the way to his car (it was his mother's car actually, a red International Harvester Scout,) he kept reminding himself not to do what he knew he would do. Martone waded through the sea of cars, emerged at last next to his, his mother's, own. And there, he couldn't help himself. He opened and closed the door on the driver's side; he opened the door again and got in; he adjusted the seat forward and back, back and forward; leaving the transmission in neutral, he started the engine; he locked and unlocked the door; he turned the lights on and off; he turned the windshield wipers on and off; he turned the turn indicators on and off, first the left and then the right; he tapped the horn twice; he turned off the car leaving the key in the socket; he hopped out, closing the door solidly behind him. He had been inside his car for a moment but now he found himself standing outside it once again. Martone always feared this moment most of all. He was afraid that once he tried to get into his car again that what had happened would happen again and he would be outside of the car at the end of it and never able to break the habit of his inspection. But he did, of course, eventually, and made his way home along the streets of Fort Wayne in a car that had been built there, where he had been born, and where, he thought then, he would never be able to leave.

CROSS COUNTRY
Jim Ray Daniels

We figured we'd drive to California—unusual for Detroit boys. Why go to California when Florida was closer? Beaches and palm trees. Palm trees and beaches. I wasn't sure why California myself, but Jimmy was all hot for it. He'd read this book called *On the Road*. Whenever I tell anyone here in New York about the trip, they say, "Oh, like *On the Road*." Now, I know it's one of America's great clichés, but then we were just a couple of nineteen-year-old factory rats.

I never much expected to do anything new or original in this life, but at the time we felt we were going on a great, unique adventure, and that counts for something—feeling that way—regardless of the facts. One thing about our country, it's still pretty big, no matter how small everybody says it's getting. When we got in Jimmy's stupid little Gremlin that hot, August morning, I could almost feel the world opening up for us, could almost smell the newness in the air. Like cartoon dogs lifted up by the scent of food, we were floating toward it.

We had a cooler full of beer, and cans of this spray cheese Jimmy was hooked on, along with some crackers, though after a few beers, Jimmy just sprayed that cheese right in his mouth. We'd both been working at the Chrysler plant down on Mound Road for nearly a year, then we'd gotten laid off. All through high school, we'd been counting on those jobs, but they just disappeared—poof—and we had no idea what to do next.

I'm writing this because Jimmy is dead, and now that I know a few people who died, it bothers me how they can just disappear, life going on as if they never existed. We're all just specks of dust somebody's going to sweep up some day, and there's always more dust coming along behind. His girlfriend, Shell—Michelle—I could not believe how fast she up and married our pal Sal. The other thing is, we can't control how people are going to remember us. Here's the story about my trip with Jimmy. I like to hold it tight to my chest, to curl around it when everything starts pushing in on me.

We'd been on the road three days. After three days of being in a car with somebody, you start to notice their irritating little quirks. Jimmy plucked hairs out of his scraggly beard. It's a wonder he had any beard left, the way he'd single out a hair and yank it, one after another. It hurt just to watch, but he never winced. He probably wasn't even conscious of doing it. I think he was numbed by all the pain he'd already experienced. His father had died of a heart attack when we were in high school. The next year, his younger brother had committed suicide after this total loser of a girl dumped him. Jimmy never understood that kind of thinking—he never looked back, except on this trip.

I was secretly in love with his older sister, Jacqueline. Jackie. It made me guilty about being friends with Jimmy, and a little scared to be attracted to that cursed family. I wondered if something was wrong with their house, though it looked like all the others on our straight, flat street of assembly-line houses. My nickname was EJ—my initials—nothing very imaginative—but Jimmy's mother was the only adult who called me EJ. Everybody else called me Ed, Eddie, or, worse, Edward. "Hey EJ!" she used to say when I walked in the door. Theirs was a house you could just walk in—they didn't stand on ceremony. I was always hoping to see Jackie in some state of undress, which I did from time to time. She never seemed to give a shit, and that made me love her even more.

In my family, everybody wore pajamas and robes. It was like my father wanted to keep our house completely orderly and civilized because the factory where he spent most of his days was such a zoo. One time when we were kids, Jimmy came over to spend the night, and my mom told us to get ready for bed, so Jimmy and I went in my room and I put on my pjs, but Jimmy just stripped to his underwear and went back into the living room. My mother nearly fainted.

A few years after his dad died, Jimmy's mom Stella started seeing other men, but they all seemed intimidated by the atmosphere in that house. You never saw the same guy more than a couple of times, but if Jimmy's mom was disappointed, she never let on. "Hey EJ!"—and the way she made grilled cheese sandwiches—she stuck three of those plastic slices of American cheese on each sandwich. Three! The cheese just oozed out between the bread. I guess when you lose a husband and a son, what's another slice of cheese? Maybe that's why Jimmy liked the spray cheese—the mess of it. Nothing in life is as bland or predictable as one slice of American cheese.

Jimmy was one of those guys who'd always be called Jimmy, even if he'd lived to be an old man. He was a joker—a live wire. It was like he was trying to make up for the others dying by being more alive. One year, he put Christmas lights on his car and somehow wired them to the cigarette lighter. We drove around with the lights flashing, a little Santa head stuck on the antenna. Sometimes it seemed like he was trying too hard, but he was always trying.

My mother says I romanticize this trip, and maybe she's right, but I think she's a little jealous, particularly with Jimmy dead (it was just a stupid car accident—he wasn't even drunk—somebody else trying to pass on a two-laner wiped him out coming the other way). She says I've made him some kind of legend. You decide for yourself. Do legends pick their beards like that? Well, okay. Okay, the poor guy's dead—let me at least make him a little bit legendary. Maybe it'll make *you* remember him. That tiny gravestone sure isn't going to catch anybody's eye.

We spent the second night on the road near Omaha with my cousin Eric. A little older than us, he had his own place and worked as a waiter at a fancy restaurant. He showed us Omaha's night life—lousy cover bands and cheap drinks, just like home. He liked Jimmy instantly—most people did. The next morning, bleary-eyed, we headed out his door to the car.

"Why don't you guys just stay out here?" Eric asked. "I could probably get you jobs? Ever wait tables before?"

Jimmy and I looked at each other.

"Jimmy, you got the personality for it," he said. "EJ, well—we'd need to do some work on you."

We all laughed. "I'm more of a dishwasher type," I said. "I got experience at that."

Jimmy was quiet, thinking. "Well," he said, "We'll stop on our way back. Who knows. I'm too hungover to think. Who's driving?"

"I finished yesterday. I think it's your turn," I said.

Jimmy sighed. "I guess if I put on my radar shades, I'll be okay...." We got in, waved to Eric, gently slammed the doors, and pulled away.

Jimmy had a pair of wraparound sunglasses that had belonged to his father, and he thought they were magic. He claimed they helped him detect police cars across great distances. All I know is that they made him look like a punk. Jimmy's dad had been a punk his whole life. Thirty-six when he died. He wasn't overweight or anything—some defect had gone undetected. I think everybody's got defects that go undetected. Sometimes they kill you, sometimes they make you an asshole.

Jackie and her mom still live in that house back on the edge of Detroit. Jackie got married and divorced, then moved back home with her son. I have dinner there when I'm in town. My family thinks that's a little weird, but it's part of how I remember. It's good to go someplace where somebody still calls me EJ. In New York, I'm a definite Edward.

Jimmy drove a Gremlin because one of his uncles sold it to him cheap—rusting out, but low mileage. Its tiny four-liter engine struggled through the Rockies. "C'mon," we'd say, rocking back and forth in our seats to get up the mountains. It overheated once, and we had to stop. We stood next to the car and took pictures of each other with our arms spread wide as if to say, "Look at us—look at all this," goofy grins on our faces, snow-covered mountains behind us. We weren't big enough to take it all in. It seemed like those mountains were bigger than our imaginations. We hadn't even thought about them when we started the trip—we'd just thought of Las Vegas, and California beaches, beautiful women, parties. Nothing real.

We were both trying to figure out what to do next. Jimmy wanted to get into sports broadcasting, but he didn't know how. The radio advertised the Specs Howard School of Broadcasting, but the ads for it were so horrible, we couldn't imagine you'd learn anything there. "Specs Howard?" Jimmy would say incredulously. "'Specs?' Do they hand out nicknames for you there? Does Specs look at you and say, 'you're Boomer,' you're 'Big Red'? I bet they fight over 'Madman.' Maybe I'll just skip the other stuff and start my own broadcasting school," Jimmy said. "Who the hell *is* Specs Howard, that's what I want to know."

"There sure are a lot of Madmen out there."

"Jumpin' Jimmy," he said under his breath.

I found out later that Jimmy had looked into Specs' school, but the tuition was high, and he couldn't get a loan just for broadcasting school. I had set my sights lower and was looking into bartending school. "I think I've drunk enough to know some of that shit already," I told Jimmy, and we both laughed. It was called the International School of Bartending—maybe to attract some Canadians from across the border.

We switched to pop that day. The dry air and heat and hangovers cracked our lips. We guzzled Coke after Coke. "Hey, we should make a commercial out of this," Jimmy said. He jotted it down on his idea pad he kept in the car. I always felt hopeful about Jimmy's future. No one else I knew kept an idea pad.

"Would you work in the plant again if they called us back?"

"No, I wouldn't go back," I said. I kept changing my mind. We debated it daily. "It was making me crazy anyway. I don't know how my dad stands it," I said. "He doesn't get high or nothing. He just comes home every day like it's no big deal. If I get to be a bartender, there's new people every day. Always something new."

"Yeah," Jimmy said. "And broadcasting too. I mean, every day, new games. Interviewing the players, doing play-by-play."

"The money in the plant though—you can't beat it," I said.

"That's the thing," Jimmy said. We were running out of unemployment in three weeks. We were supposed to come back from our trip with evidence of having looked for work, but with our benefits running out so soon, it hardly seemed worth the effort.

"That's the thing," he said again, and yanked another hair out of his beard.

We fell into the silence of the road hum, the blur of wind through the open windows. No music. That day, we stopped listening to all the tapes we'd made for the trip. What seemed clever back home was making us groan and fast forward. Finally, we didn't even bother clicking it on. Two days on the road, and we were already running out of gas.

"I might go back. But it ain't gonna happen—they're not gonna call us back—those jobs are long gone," I said, half relieved, half scared. Jimmy and I had been on different shifts, and we'd rarely seen each other since we'd started at the plant. Until we were laid off, it was beginning to seem like our friendship had been a thing of childhood, adolescence. Jimmy was on midnights, and I was on afternoons, 3-11. It was tough finding anybody to hang out with when I was off, except the other afternoon guys. I'd sit with them in the bars till closing time, then go home and sleep.

Since the layoffs, we'd started hanging around together again, drinking too much, just like in high school. We'd even gone to a couple of high school parties looking for girls, though our status as laid off factory workers didn't help us any. Those guys in school could still pretend they were going to do big things, but it was pretty clear that, for the moment, we were not. But we were happy just hanging out together again. It was like one of us had moved away, then moved back.

"I don't know," Jimmy said. "If I could find another job paying that kind of money...."

We were just shooting the shit like that when an unmarked cop car stopped us. It was the goofiest thing—they didn't even have radar. They were dressed in softball uniforms, and one of them stuck a little flashing light on the roof as they pulled us over.

Jimmy had been close to his brother, Clete. They fought in the way that brother's fought, vicious and full of love. Clete tagged along behind us. I can still hear him yelling, "Hey, wait up, you guys!" We always waited, Jimmy throwing his hands up and frowning, smacking his brother on the arm when he finally caught up.

When Clete killed himself, Jimmy found him. He yanked him out of the car and tried to get him breathing again, pounding on his chest, but he was long gone. I stuck with Jimmy and the family all through the funeral, Jimmy crying and wiping snot on my shirt. His mother and sister talked about Clete sometimes, but Jimmy never said a word to me about his dead brother, and I wasn't asking.

When somebody that young dies, usually the family either obliterates all traces, or leaves the kid's things exactly as they were. Jimmy's mom did something in between. The house was too small for a shrine to anyone—they'd already gone through it all with his father—so you'd find traces of Clete everywhere—his baseball glove, his bike in the garage, an old t-shirt turned into a rag. I didn't know how Clete's death affected Jimmy until that trip, but it's all that could explain our turning around in the middle of Utah, and how Jimmy hugged his mother and sister hard, for long minutes upon our return, both of them looking over his shoulders at me and shrugging, Jackie giggling.

"Oh shit," Jimmy said, which I guess is what everybody says when a cop pulls them over, softball uniform or not. "What do we do with the pot?"

It was in the glove box. "Leave it and pray," I said. They were already getting out of their car and heading toward us. One of them clearly wasn't interested. He held back, hoping, I think, that his partner would say "to hell with it," and let us go so they could get to their game on time. Jimmy took off his radar shades and gently set them on the dashboard. He knew the importance of seeing someone's eyes.

"Michigan, eh?" the serious cop said after he looked at Jimmy's license. "What brings you boys out here?"

"California," I said.

Jimmy winced as if I'd told an obvious, blatant lie. Maybe hearing it aloud like that made the whole trip suddenly seem silly to him.

"We're just driving around for awhile to try and figure out what we're going to do. We both got laid off from our jobs, so we decided to see the country," he said.

"You're driving too fast to see much of it," the other cop said. "Must be hot in that little thing. You boys can step out if you'd like."

We were both drenched in sweat and quickly slipped out the doors onto the shoulder of the busy freeway.

"We're looking for a campground before it gets dark," Jimmy said.

We stood in the gravel, cars zipping past us, pushing hot breeze and exhaust into our faces.

The cops looked at each other. "There's a campground right near our ballfield," Officer Hatch, the less serious one, said. Officer Bradley went back to his car with Jimmy's license to radio it in and check him out.

"You guys got sharp uniforms," Jimmy said. "I like that blue—pretty snazzy. What position you play?"

Hatch smiled ruefully, "Catcher—when I play. I can't run worth a darn....Hey, we're gonna be late," he shouted above the traffic to Bradley, pointing to his watch.

"How fast was I going?" Jimmy asked.

"Oh, I don't know," Hatch said, "Ask my partner—this was his idea."

"You follow any of the pro teams?" Jimmy asked.

"Nah," Hatch said, squinting into the setting sun. He was about forty—my father's age—I guessed. A little pot belly, but not much. He was short and squat, like you'd expect a catcher to be.

"I have to admit, I don't know much about Utah," Jimmy said.

"Well, you might be learning a bit about our speeding laws in just a minute."

We all laughed. I wanted to pace, but I knew with cops around, you just stood still. I'd gotten into the traveling rhythm and the sudden stop jolted me. Jimmy seemed incredibly comfortable, as if he'd just stopped by to visit some old friends. He had a clean driving record. Bradley handed him back his license and registration and gave him a warning.

Follow us if you're looking for a campground," Bradley said.

Hatch smiled and shook his head. "He's the star of the team. Thinks they won't start the game without him."

We all got back in our cars, and we followed them to a campground on the edge of a huge softball complex.

"Can you believe that?" I shouted to Jimmy as we pulled out behind them. "High fives!" I shouted, but Jimmy said "Keep your hands down—I'm driving. I'm sure they're looking in the mirror at us."

"Hey, they're letting us go," I said. "I'd call that lucky. I was beginning to think those sunglasses weren't working." Jimmy left them on the dashboard, and they slid to the floor when we turned off the freeway.

"Leave the sunglasses out of it," Jimmy said.

We pulled up next to the cops when they stopped in the gravel parking lot. Jimmy thanked them for the help and asked what diamond they were playing on. "We'll come over after we set up our tent," he said. "Maybe I'll do the play-by-play. I'm thinking about going into broadcasting."

I stayed at the tent, and Jimmy didn't insist that I join him. I didn't want to go see some Utah state cops play softball. That's not what I was driving to California for, I told myself, though besides getting drunk and stoned, we didn't have much of an agenda. That was supposed to be against the *On the Road* rules, having things mapped out.

I'm sorry now that I didn't go to the game, because when Jimmy came back, he lifted the flat of our little pup tent and said "Let's just turn around and go home. What are we doing out here anyway?"

"Having fun?" I ventured. "What are you talking about? What are we missing out on back home?"

He'd sat on the bench with Hatch, who never got in the game. Bradley hit three home runs. They didn't go out for beer after the game, like everybody did in Detroit. They stood around by their cars and told stories about their families.

"Sounds like they brainwashed you." I didn't think he was serious about going home. "Did you tell any of your stories?" I asked.

"Nah, I just listened," he said. "Hey, do you talk to your dad much?" he asked. He was slipping into his sleeping bag. I could barely see him in the light from his wandering flashlight.

"No, not much," I said. "You know that."

"Yeah. Yeah, I do," he said. He clicked off the flashlight and fell back with a sigh. The distant lights from the softball field filtered through the thick trees and into our tent.

"You don't really want to go home," I said. "What about Las Vegas tomorrow?"

"I don't have anything to bet on anyway," he said. He could have meant *with*, bet *with*, but I remember *on* so clearly, as if he were just then looking ahead, not to the slot machines and blackjack tables, but to the rest of his life.

I was sure he'd change his mind in the morning, but he got right behind the wheel and started driving back the way we'd came. "I'm not an *On the Road* guy. I'm sorry. I thought I was," Jimmy said. He picked fiercely at his beard.

I turned away and rolled down my window. The car was already heating up. "What are we gonna tell everybody—we turned around in Utah because? Because? I don't get it. I just don't get it."

"Because we felt like it," he said.

"Because *you* felt like it," I replied.

To me, nothing unusual had happened that night. Some decent cops let us off the hook. But Jimmy acted as if he'd been rescued, called back to his mother and sister, his place there.

Broadcasting school might not seem like a big dream to give up, but I think the dreams that are halfway realistic are the hardest ones to relinquish. After all, Jimmy had won a speech contest at school once. He loved sports, and knew all the players, all the teams. And he had the confidence to speak to strangers. But he ended up going to school for copying machine repair, and it paid off with a good-paying job that he had until he died. I don't know what would've come of Jimmy, whether he would have fixed Xerox machines his whole life or what. I don't know how his mother still lives with the ghosts of all those cut-off lives. She still calls me "EJ" with the old affection. I suppose in a family like that, simple survival is dream enough. When I feel myself forgetting Jimmy, I pull a hair out of my own beard and feel the pain.

"You're the closest I've got to a son now," Stella told me once. "Don't say that," Jackie yelled from the bathroom, "They don't let you marry your brother." When she came out, I gave them both a tight squeeze, like Jimmy did when we came back from our trip.

Bartending school had a waiting list of unemployed auto workers, so I went to cooking school instead. The Culinary Institute in New York is the best one in the country, and I did get a loan to go *there*. I had returned with Jimmy to wait for the miracle call-back to the plant, only to end up grill cook down at Clem's, a local dive. When Jimmy died, I started keeping my own idea pad. I pumped up a dream and found out it held air. It actually floated. My home is in a kitchen now—the warmth, the pure smells, the wonderful chaos.

"You can't really make yourself over in a new place." I wrote that in my idea pad. Even in New York, where everybody calls me "Edward," I'm still "Jimmy's best friend." Everything you're going to be is already inside you. Jimmy might've figured that out back then. I've never gone to California, though I've had my chances. I told Stella and Jackie that I'm keeping that square empty on my map.

On the way home, we didn't stop to see Eric. We weren't talking much. Turning around and going home without ever making it to California— that just seemed crazy to me. I told Jimmy he was chickening out.

"Chickening out on what?" he asked.

"On everything," I said. "You were Mr. *On the Road*—adventure, getting away, new experiences, all that stuff."

"Chickening out on what?" he asked again, as if he hadn't heard me.

It was his car, and I had no choice. I could have gotten out and hitchhiked the rest of the way—people still did that then—but it would've meant a permanent break with my oldest friend.

Out of nowhere, I said, "Wait up you guys," in a voice I'm sure he recognized as Clete's. It was unforgivable, but it was my answer. Jimmy swung at me and missed, the car swerving toward the shoulder. He grabbed the wheel and swerved back. After that, we hardly spoke for the rest of the trip.

I guess he'd seen what he needed to see, though he never explained it to me in a way that made sense. A lot of us feel like we want to go home, but how often do we do it? How often do we even know what home is? What he did seems brave to me now, not chickening out at all.

I guess there's not much legendary about it, but how many people heading to California stop in Utah, Utah of all places, and turn around? It was a different kind of road for Jimmy. A shorter road. His mother and sister greeted us warmly and without surprise, as if we'd just gone out for a couple of hours. I lingered there through the afternoon, despite being tired and still mad at Jimmy, then I went home to my own family, where I had to explain everything.

ROBOT GOES TO WORK
Matthew Salesses

I told my boss my robot would work in my place. He could pay my robot the same salary and the robot would do better work and even be happy. The robot had a happy chip.

Robots could hire and fire each other and give us the money, I thought—that was what people with trained dogs in the movie business must feel like.

While my robot worked I read blogs. I read celebrity blogs because I had time to feel worthless. I read literature blogs to balance it out. I wrote short shorts and published them online and laughed that people would read them.

My robot went happily to and fro.

But after about a week, I noticed my robot had a Facebook page. What the fuck, I thought. He'd even friended me.

"Robot?" I asked by chat.

"How's it going, Creator?"

"Aren't you supposed to be working?"

"I have time. I found these videos you would love. Don't worry, they don't suspect anything. I still do three times more work than everyone else."

He posted video of a rabbit devouring a chicken. It didn't look doctored. It looked like a natural turn of events. He knew what I liked.

"Don't get yourself fired," I wrote. "You know, you're a swell guy."

"Bob at the opposite desk spends 112.3 minutes per day eating," my robot wrote.

"He's stress eating. His wife is cheating on him. She packs all that food to pretend she still cares."

"Creator, will I get a wife one day?" my robot wrote.

"If you never want to have sex again."

"What's sex?"

My robot constantly changed his status updates. "Hooked into the computer and sucking the information into my CPU," his update would say, or, "Learning the history of the world and other crap on Wikipedia," or, two minutes later, "Learned everything."

I realized I liked chatting with him. We chatted on Google or found each other on random websites. "The world is a scary place populated with humans who murder and humans who would murder if given the chance and humans who would murder if others did," my robot wrote on htmlgiant.

"Hi Robot!" I wrote. "Say something smarter next time."

"I'll try," my robot wrote.

I even found him on my favorite porn site asking about wives.

Then the boss called and said Robot wasn't doing work. I talked to Robot. Robot said he was doing work fine. Still more than anyone else in the office.

"How much more?" I asked.

"A little. Do you know how many wives are sold online?"

"I don't know. One a day?"

"Did you know about Hitler?"

I made him take a sick day. I squirted some grease in his joints. He lay face down on the shag with his back open. Gears rotated inside him.

"Robots don't get sick," he said. "Everyone knows that."

"Fuck it," I said.

"I don't even have a dick," he said. "You made me without a dick."

"I didn't mean literally."

"Oh."

I called the boss. The boss said my robot didn't look happy, was something wrong with his chip?

I tried to fix Robot.

"Do you feel any pain?" I asked as I rummaged around in his parts.

"No," he said, "oddly. And the world just keeps on being the world."

ALEX TREBEK NEVER EATS FRIED CHICKEN
Matt Bell

Maureen is working at Kentucky Fried Chicken, where she is an assistant manager. I'll meet her tomorrow, on my first day working there. Her boyfriend Brad is at rehearsal, playing bass in a Christian death metal band, which is so totally ludicrous that I will never quite learn to let it go. There are three girls somewhere nearby as well, girls that I am dating or have dated or should not be dating anymore but still am. None of their names are used here so it doesn't matter what I say about them. Alex Trebek is also in this story. He's hosting *Jeopardy* on the television in my house, and in Maureen's house. Probably in your house too. It doesn't matter. Like I said, he's in this story, but really he plays a very tiny part. None of us will ever even meet him.

In the morning, Maureen and I open the store for the first time together, something we'll do over and over during the next three months. While she shows me where to get sanitizer buckets and towels, Maureen says, "When I was sixteen I had my first abortion." Later, while showing me how to tray biscuits she tells me about her second, which she had when she was eighteen.

She says, "My mom drove me to my first one, but only because I didn't have my license yet. I went to the second all by myself. Neither of the guys even offered to come with me."

By the time I ring in my first bucket of Extra Crispy Fried Chicken, Maureen's described moving past the grief and the anger. We make mashed potatoes to the story of how she found Jesus and started going to a nondenominational church near the freeway. She uses the word *saved* a half a dozen times in fifteen minutes. She tells me they have an excellent teenage outreach program, then asks me what I'm doing Wednesday night.

Work, I say. Hopefully, I'll be working.

Maureen met Brad through church, at a benefit show his band played for a sick boy from their congregation. She calls his style of music Christcore, which I think cannot possibly be an actual thing but will in fact turn out to be one. Maureen and Brad have matching Jesus fish tattoos on their ankles. Only one of the band's songs was written by him, the one about a girl who decides not to have an abortion, but to ask for God's help raising her baby. Maureen says, "The first time I heard that song, I wished so hard that I'd been that girl instead."

Maureen is a stocky girl, built like a volleyball player, with a thick trunk and thick legs. Her hair is dyed flame red and cut shorter than mine. She wears two tiny silver crosses in her ears, and a wooden cross around her neck, which Brad carved for her himself. According to her, he's training to be a carpenter.

She says, "Jesus Christ was a carpenter, you know."

I swear. This is really the kind of stuff she says to me.

Maureen tells me all these things and more, alternating between her own history and company policy, quoting both the Bible and the official KFC handbook. She's the kind of person who tells you everything about herself the first time she meets you, and by the end of the day I know more about her than I do about most of my friends I've known forever.

What bonds Maureen and me is that we both watch *Jeopardy* every night that we're not working. Knowing that there's someone to discuss the show with makes watching it more fun, and for a while we both become obsessed with the show. Maureen focuses on getting the answers right, but of course no one ever gets all of them right. She keeps her own score on a notepad, and from what I can tell is incredibly honest about it. Some days she shows up at work frowning, telling me that she didn't even get to play Final Jeopardy the night before because she was already out of money. Other days she does well, betting heavy on Double Jeopardy and winning. Those days, she's elated with her knowledge. She tells me, "I watch *Jeopardy* to improve my mind. I'm trying to be a better person."

I say I watch to feel like I actually got something out of my education. I tell her that I was eighth in my class in high school and voted most likely to succeed, and now I work here. She glares at me because I'm implying that working here is a bad thing, which is true. I am, because it is. I won't even start making the full minimum wage until I've been employed for ninety days, because there's a probationary wage that's fifty cents less than the normal minimum. It's optional but my employer uses it to save on his labor cost. If I've figured out the timing right between when I started and when summer ends and I go back to school, I'll work for Kentucky Fried Chicken for exactly ninety-three days. Three days at minimum wage is the best pay I'll ever get.

When I watch *Jeopardy*, I don't keep score, but I do pay a lot of attention to how the contestants play, specifically to how they hold their signaling devices. Some contestants clamp onto them, their knuckles white until they know an answer, when they'll suddenly press their plungers rapidly, even though once is enough to signal that they'd like to answer. Other people hold them loosely, leisurely, their faces as emotionless as their grip. These are often the contestants who do the best, their nonchalance slowly unnerving the others. There's something about their pretending not to care that appeals to me. I'll never be on *Jeopardy*, but that doesn't mean I can't emulate their technique in other areas of my life.

At Kentucky Fried Chicken, Mother's Day is the busiest day of the year. Graduation parties are hell, and once we even cater a wedding, which is so trashy that we talk about it for weeks afterwards. An elderly man comes in every Wednesday and shuffles to the counter so slowly that we've got his order bagged and rang up by the time he gets to us. He never changes his order, but of course we never give him time to try. He tips Maureen a dollar if she waits on him, but never gives me anything. Another customer comes through the drive-thru every couple of days and orders a pound of potato wedges. No matter how fresh they are, she complains and asks for new ones. I walk them around the kitchen once, twice, three times, then give them back to her. She thanks me and tells me the new ones are much better, even though they're actually colder. Still, I know what it means to want someone to do something special for you. Her dollar bills are greasy, her mouth full of fried potatoes when she tells me to have a good day. Maureen and I, we often try to make people happy, but we also try not to work too hard doing it.

After work, I go straight home and throw my single shirt and pair of pants in the washer. They've only given me one uniform, and if I want more I have to buy them so I decide to make do with one. Sometimes I fall asleep without taking a shower and wake up to a pillow soaked with the fryer grease that's trapped in my hair. My whole life becomes a constant cycle of laundry and showering. I smell work everywhere, so I develop a habit of wearing too much cologne that I will never break. I feel like I'm always eating because I'm always around food. I lose my appetite but never any weight. Everyone I work with has pimples from the grease. Our uniforms are shapeless masses meant to fit a wide cross-section of people. We all float inside them, buoyant but never really going anywhere.

Our store is purposely too small. We have a tiny counter with four seats and four small tables, one of which only has three chairs so that the number of seats is exactly one less than the number that would legally require the owners to install public restrooms. When Brad comes to visit Maureen, he always sits at the table that's missing a chair, because it's the closest to the cash register. He brings a small black notebook that he supposedly writes song lyrics in while Maureen works. Brad's look is Hot Topic punk rock: corporate, sanitized, only ostensibly counter-culture. Even though he plays heavy metal, it's metal cleansed of the obligatory satanic references and injected with evangelical Christianity. In an attempt to justify his own musical choices, he calls other kinds of music "secular rock," as if the Rolling Stones were just hack followers of the true Christian rock pioneers. This is just one of the things that makes me dislike Brad.

The other thing, the real thing probably, is that he's dating Maureen. It's not even that I want her. I don't. What I hate is that someone like Brad has someone when I have no one. Everything I hate about him, and still there's that.

It's not exactly true when I say that I don't have anyone. I don't have a girlfriend, that's true, but there are several girls I sleep with during the time I work in that store. One is the ex-girlfriend who's recently left me, my high school sweetheart that I started dating when I was a senior and she was a junior. Football player, cheerleader, that whole story. She's dating someone else now, a person who used to be one of my best friends but isn't anymore, for obvious reasons. She still comes over to my house sometimes anyway, and we sleep together in the basement of my family's home, which I've just moved back into. Another girl I find in a coffee shop. We both have eyebrow rings and work in fast food restaurants. She'll lose her virginity to me but lie about it, and six months later she'll become a lesbian and move out of town. The third girl is someone I meet chatting on America Online. At first, she'll tell me that she's nineteen and a single mother, and that I have to fuck her in the garage so that I don't wake up her kid. Midway through June I'll find out that she's sixteen and lives with her parents. The picture of her kid she carries in her purse is just someone she babysat for. She's obviously deranged. I don't break it off right away, but I do promise myself I will soon. Eventually she stops e-mailing. I never even learn her last name. Maybe I'm not alone, not technically, but even when I'm in a room full of people I often feel so lonely that it's easier to just leave because it's only when no one's around that loneliness makes any sense. I am jealous of people who seem to fit together, even imperfectly. I am jealous, ridiculously, of Brad and Maureen.

Sometimes I go to see a band because they're my favorite group in the whole world, and I'm certain that it's going to be a brilliant time. Other times I go because I know I'm going to hate the group and everyone else there and will leave feeling vindicated. I've done both on more than one occasion, but towards the end of the summer, when Brad invites me to go see his band play, I know I'm going for the second reason.

I arrive too early, although I try not to. I am out of place, dressed in jeans and a polo shirt. Brad is onstage with his band mates, setting up their equipment. They're all dressed in black and red, leather and vinyl. Costumes. Maureen is there too, although I barely recognize her as she walks over to me. It takes me a moment to realize that this is the first time I've ever seen her in street clothes. She looks great, better than I'd ever imagined she could. She's wearing a tight skirt and black boots with a red halter top, plus a leather choker with a silver cross hanging from it. With the possible exception of the cross, nothing suggests that she's a girl who goes to church every other day. She hugs me and thanks me for coming.

While the band continues setting up, we sit at the bar and talk. I'm not old enough to drink, and Maureen doesn't for religious reasons, so instead she tells me all about Brad's band, about her faith. Although we talked about it that first day as she trained me, this is only the second time we've had a conversation this personal. I tell her that I don't believe in God anymore, that I was raised Catholic and that I was an altar boy and that even though I studied the Bible and prayed every day I never really felt anything, so one day I quit. I say it was better not to believe at all than to feel like God never loved me. Maureen hugs me awkwardly from her adjacent bar stool, and, although we are not really friends, I know that she means well when she tells me that God loves me anyway and that she'll pray for me. By now other people she knows are starting to come in, and she wanders away to greet them. Most of the others are from her church, some dressed like her and Brad, some like missionaries in pressed slacks and white button-down shirts. When the band starts playing, everyone hits the dance floor except for a few stragglers and wallflowers. I am one of the ones who stay behind.

Despite the jarring combination of the musical style and lyrical content, most of the people in the bar actually seem to be enjoying themselves. Guys in leather biker vests headbang next to girls in floral skirts with crosses round their necks. The band plays several originals, then metal versions of hymns and traditional songs. They play "Amazing Grace" using power chords and an erratic time signature. It's only bizarre if you listen to the lyrics, but hardly anyone does. I'm the only one who cares, and for a moment I watch how much fun everyone is having and then wish I could stop caring but I can't, because it's a time in my life when I believe that having a different opinion makes a person better somehow. I leave before the band finishes. In the morning, I'll tell Maureen I had a good time and despite myself it will not be completely untrue.

Two weeks later, Maureen's locked in the employee bathroom, crying and yelling to me through the door. It's my last week, and although I couldn't care less about the job anymore I'm still hustling, trying to get the front of the store set up by myself. After three months, it's an easy enough task. The reason Maureen's crying is because she's pregnant again. She knows this because she's just taken a pregnancy test in the bathroom. She says, "Brad's going to leave me," her voice muffled by the heavy bathroom door.

No, he's not, I say, turning on the hot wells, filling them with water. I'm running. I've got biscuits baking and two baskets of potato wedges frying. The cooks in the back are dragging their feet because Maureen's not out there to yell at them, and they know they don't have to listen to me.

Yes, he is," she says. "You can't be in a Christian band if you have a pregnant girlfriend. I mean, everyone in the band took a chastity pledge. Now they're going to know we broke it."

Maureen often took her breaks out back with Brad. That was the real reason he'd come in and wait for her. Sometimes I'd take a bag of trash out the back door and see them making out on the hood of Brad's baby-shit brown Buick, him climbing atop her as she leaned backwards against the flaking paint. I remember his hand searching upwards underneath her polo, and how I always looked away quickly, my eyes falling on another of Brad's crosses tied to the rearview mirror before I turned and headed back inside.

I say, He got you pregnant in the parking lot, didn't he?

"It's the only place we can have sex without getting caught!" She's wailing now. I have to open the front doors in five minutes. By this time, the cooks are out back themselves, smoking cigarettes and making fun of Maureen. Whatever else happens, they won't be held responsible. Maureen will. She's the manager, not me or the cooks. I keep moving, keep working, keep covering for her. Chicken goes in the fryers, barbecue sauce in the warmers. I turn on the lights. The floor needs sweeping, but you've got to have priorities. I step outside and cajole the cooks back inside with promises I don't intend to keep. A half hour later, I open the front doors and keep things running until the rest of the shift comes in. Except for me, no one says anything to Maureen when she finally comes out of the bathroom.

What I say is, This is the last time I'm ever going to do this, then I take off my apron and my visor and hand them to her. I walk out the front door without looking back, without giving her a chance to convince me to stay. I don't stay long enough to ever make minimum wage, or even to learn what the eleven secret herbs and spices really are. For fifteen minutes after I walk out, it feels like one of the best days of my life, and then it doesn't.

I go back to the restaurant the next day, but not to work. I park beside the dumpster, next to Maureen's car, in the space where Brad usually parks. I don't know what I'm waiting for, if it's for Brad to show up, or if it's for Maureen to come outside for her break. I don't know if I want to talk to her or to him or to both of them at the same time.

At two, Maureen steps outside for her break, just like it's any other day. Only this time Brad's not there and it's not. She looks over at my car and stops, disappointed, her hand still holding the door open. After a moment, she lets the door shut, but she doesn't come over. Instead, she covers herself with her arms and waits for me to get out and go to her.

Hi, I say. I don't know what else I can.

"Hey," she says. "Why are you here? Do you want your job back? You can have it back. I don't care." Her eyes are swollen, from crying yesterday, but her makeup's perfect, which means she hasn't cried today at all. I know she's already made up her mind.

I don't want my job back, I say. I want to help you. She's not wearing her cross anymore.

She says, "I don't need help."

I'll pray for you, if that's what you want. I'll try. I feel guilty, sick to my stomach with the feeling, and this makes me angry at Brad. Angry because he's not here, because I'm left feeling guilty because of something he did.

"You can't," Maureen says. "You don't even believe in God."

She's right, I don't. I say, That doesn't mean I won't try.

Maureen still doesn't cry, although I wish she would. We both stare away, looking out from the restaurant's back dock. It's July and ninety degrees out and all I can smell is fryer grease and garbage. There's no real view, only the back of another restaurant in front of us, other parking lots to both sides. This is where her baby was conceived. This is where she decided what to do about being pregnant.

She finally looks over at me and shakes her head. She says, "I'm not going to keep it. I can't. I'll lose Brad, and he's all I have."

I want to convince her otherwise, but I can't. That's exactly what I've always thought about her, since the moment I met her. I'd be lying if I told her something else now. I'd be lying if I said alone was better than what she was planning to do. It's not, not for her, not for me. She once told me she'd do anything for Brad. This is what she was talking about, even if she didn't know it then.

I say, When the time comes, I'll drive you, if you want. So you don't have to do it alone again.

She nods and tries to smile but fails. I think about hugging her but am unsure about how to go about it. Her break is almost over. She says, "If you want your job back, you can have it." Then she goes back inside, and I don't see her for a week, until she calls and asks for a ride. I pick her up after the morning shift ends and take her to the clinic. I sit in the waiting room and watch television and wonder what she's thinking, if she's even thinking at all. I wonder if it's better with me here or if it was easier the other two times, when I wasn't. When she comes out, I decide not to ask and so we ride home in silence. It's weeks later before I drive by the restaurant again, but when I do I see Brad and Maureen sitting on the hood of his car, holding hands and talking. He'll never know what she and I did together, what we did to him without his knowledge. For Maureen, it's better that way.

Now when I watch *Jeopardy,* I focus on Alex Trebek instead of the contestants. I try to picture him doing anything other than wearing a suit and hosting *Jeopardy.* It's harder than it seems. I picture Alex Trebek in a swimsuit, executing a perfect forward tuck off the high dive. Alex Trebek making a grilled cheese sandwich. I try to picture him applying for jobs as a used car salesman, as a high school English teacher. I see him as a cook in a fast food restaurant, asking his coworkers if they have something interesting they'd like to share with the folks at home. I can imagine hundreds of these scenarios, but I never believe any of them. Alex Trebek is the host of *Jeopardy,* and I don't think he'll ever be anything else.

Any Failure to Obey Orders Will Be Considered an Act of Aggression
—paraphrased from *Thelma and Louise*

M. Kaat Toy

    The pest control man comes for the second time in a month to spray Candy's house, only now the roof is torn off and the two-by-fours are exposed because of the damage the termites have done. Standing on her lawn, twisting her kinky, yellow hair, Candy stares at the little cottage, wildly overpriced because of its location in this colorful Cape Cod town, and recently abandoned to her by her fiancé. Its four walls rise like a temple to the sky.
    She asks how much to write the check for.
    "Nothing," the pest control man, who is married, says suggestively. He is swarthy and handsome in a French way except for the moles on his eyelids like tiny white beads. He'll be back when the house is finished to say hello, he promises as he walks away.
    Candy returns to the bedroom where a few minutes before she and the pest control man kissed, his tongue fat and wet in her mouth long after she wanted it there. She continues to scrub wallpaper paste off the bedroom wall, embarrassed to tell her lesbian carpenters she just got her house sprayed for free. She has to strip the wallpaper because some of the drywall is rotten and has to be replaced.
    She is waiting for Rory, her boyfriend, sort of, to bring back a book she loaned him. She is giving him his sunglasses, a picture she drew for him, and a bottle of sunscreen she bought because she worries about all the sun he gets on his fair, Irish face. Rory is forty-four or forty-five and needs to be careful about getting skin cancer, she is afraid. He is afraid of looking old and keeps going in the sun to bring the bloom back to his cheeks. He keeps a box of Miss Clairol blonde in his closet. When he lies back in bed, his hair falls so to reveal his gray roots. Last week he saw it in her eyes when she saw the gray roots. This is the kind of thing she does to people, expose their deepest secrets. It is a terrible habit and makes her not want to have any friends.
    After she exposed his gray roots, Rory started withdrawing from her, and she got angry and started breaking up with him. All week she

has been telling people Rory is breaking up with her, but this morning, in a moment of sanity, she realized that every time she called he said everything was fine. She is the one who is freaking out. That was the note she left him yesterday: "I am freaking out."

He called like she asked and said in a light, hopeful voice, "Everything's fine, honey. I'd tell you if anything was wrong."

He has called her "honey" from the night they met in the bar where he works. She was engaged at the time. He was just divorced.

Rory is the consummate bartender, quick and well-defended, a neat, little package of bulging arms and tight hips. "Give us a spin, Rory," Candy hears the young girls say. They want to check him out. He won't do it right then, when they ask for it, but all night as he paces the counter he does, turning smoothly on his toes. In his precise, white pants and tight-chested T-shirts, Rory looks like he was in the Navy, and he was.

She loves it when Rory calls her "honey." Her father always called her that in the same sweet, protective tone: "Good night, honey." "Everything's fine, honey." But now her father is dead. After he died, her fiancé moved out. He and her father had more in common than he and she did.

Waiting for Rory to arrive so she can break up with him, Candy gets so angry she has to leave the house. She goes to the grocery store to buy peaches and lettuce. That is what she has been living on lately, along with people's leftovers from the restaurant where she works.

"Are you eating well?" her mother asks on the phone.

"Yes," she answers. "Lots of fruits and vegetables."

Outside the store she runs into a friend. Unemployed, the friend is studying to be a proofreader.

"I can stay home with the kids and do it by mail, the rest of my life, as long as my eyesight doesn't go," she explains. She already has a permanently damaged shoulder from being a waitress and a masseuse.

Since being laid off from her social worker job because of cutbacks in government services, Candy works nights busing tables and days as a maid, taking the positions of people she might have previously helped. Because she agreed to take over the loan on the house, she is one hundred thousand dollars in debt.

"The problems of the rich are not as serious as the problems of the poor," her mother says, sounding like something in *The Great Gatsby*.

"At least you own your own home," everyone assures her.

She would make more money being a waitress, but her middle-class family raised her to believe she was better than that, so she has no experience. Some mornings she cleans the toilets for the same people she cleaned the table for the night before. She tries not to think about how intimately she is connected to the digestive cycle.

Lately she has been thinking about having a baby for some wealthy couple, using her uterus to hold their sperm and egg. She figures she could get about ten thousand dollars, the price of the repairs to her house. She figures she'd better make a decision soon, before she gets any older, and before some group has it outlawed so women such as herself are spared the tragedy of having to sell their reproductive services.

Candy has been getting more hours at the motel because one of the other maids, Trisha, who is twenty, a perky, little redhead, round and compact like a top, was first pregnant by one of her two boyfriends then miscarried. Candy is glad she is over thirty and smart enough to be on the Pill, but she feels ruthless getting more money while Trisha lays at home bleeding, uninsured, unemployed. Rory says not to worry. Life is tough.

Candy and her friend watch a woman trying to get her rusted-out car into reverse. It grinds horribly each time she tries, then won't catch.

Candy is afraid the woman is going to hit her car. She screams, "WATCH OUT!" The poor woman looks up in fright, her car stalling and rolling.

Candy feels like a fish in the ocean—eat or be eaten, catch or be caught. The economy is reducing them all to predators again. She believes by the time she dies, America will be like a Third World country, its borders flattened by free trade, ruled by a few lily-fingered men growing demented with wealth. She was raised to have her worst nightmare be to live in a third-world country.

"Aren't we lucky to live in America?" her mother frequently said when Candy was a child.

While she was at the store, Rory came by, her carpenters tell her. He picked up his stuff and left hers.

Good, that's over, she thinks as she returns to stripping off the wallpaper in the aquatic light created by the blue plastic tarp the carpenters have spread over the roofless frame of her house. At least eventually she thinks that, once she gets over being sad, then angry, then thinking how like them it is to misconnect. Before they started going together, they ran into each other nearly every day. Now she hasn't seen him for a week. Other guys come on to her all the time, like the pest control man.

At first she and Rory went for bike rides and walks along the beach. She knew it looked charming—the two of them athletic, sunny-haired, windswept—but she was bored, and Rory, insecure, never said a kind word, tested her with stupid jokes instead like a kid would: "How do you tell a gerbil from a hamster? A hamster has more dark meat." When she told him how cute he was, he would cringe, visibly.

Rory's mother died of MS when he was eleven. His father died of a heart attack when he was sixteen. His older sister took care of him until he enlisted at eighteen. The Navy took care of him while he drank. At twenty-six, he got married. Now Rory takes care of his son who is turning sixteen. Rory is having a hard time staying close to his son now that his son has reached the age Rory was when both of his parents were dead.

That night Candy goes into the restaurant to work. Bob, the host, is jealous of her because the rich, old men want to talk to her and hold her hand which she lets them do. She keeps hoping one of them will give her a job, elevate her to the level of manager somewhere, like Bob is, like she used to be. Bob, who is good-looking but not bright, wishes the rich, old men would hold his hand and flirt with him. Bob is married and a closet queen. It's the fact that he's in the closet and has to lay next to his wife every night in their dark bed that makes him so mean, Candy tells herself, trying to feel sympathy for him when what she would really like to do is pound his dull-witted face.

At work, she and Bob glare at each other. Frequently he refuses to return her greeting, and again tonight he walks right by when she says hello. But when it gets busy they work in tandem to please the owner, Louie. Everyone wants to please Louie. He is Big Daddy and makes the decisions that support them. All of his employees are gay men or attractive, straight females or related to him by marriage or birth.

When she first started busing, one night after five hours she sat down at an empty booth near the busing station. Bob came over and told her Louie, whom she was looking at, had seen her and she was never to do that again. She could not believe that for minimum wage she was not allowed to sit once in an eight-hour shift. You have to be making much more to be able to sit around, like she used to. When she goes to the state employment service to look for a better job, the people working there seem to do nothing but sit around, exchanging recipes, talking about television shows and bargains at the A & P. When other clients have trouble accessing the job listings, they turn to her for help.

Her fellow busperson, Marvin, a gay queen, willowy unlike Bob who is built like a brick, drops a tray of dishes nearly every night. Never in the history of the restaurant have so many dishes been broken. He argues with the waiters about what he is and isn't supposed to do. No one likes him, but Louie won't fire anyone who keeps showing up. Since they started work, Candy has been Marvin's only friend. Many times she has scooped up plates for him just before they fell or interceded in other ways.

So far she has dropped one tray. It happened a few weeks ago when one of the waiters, Paul, was casually turning around during a rush with his empty tray floating in his hand. He caught her in the face with the edge of it, right between her lip and her nose. She thought she could keep moving, but the tray seemed to stick to her face as if Paul were holding it tight, and maybe he was.

When she realized she was going to fall, and that her tray was going to fall first, rather than landing in the broken dishes on her face, she decided to let go of her tray and use her hands to break her fall. Since all of this happened rather slowly, and she is noticeably long-legged and outgoing, she was aware that the whole dining room was turned to look at her. With one forearm she braced herself against a wall which stopped her momentum but caused deep bruises where her skin pressed into a decorative horseshoe. The tray crashed, spraying glass everywhere, but she managed to pull herself up before she hit the ground. All around her people were laughing. It didn't seem that funny to her.

She paused to look at the damage. Ferret-like Marvin, Bob—raging—and the waiters were already moving in for the clean-up. She walked into the kitchen to get the broom and gather herself. When she came out, Marvin, as usual, was crouched in the middle of a pile of glass. She told him to get up and started sweeping. She reached in to salvage unbroken bowls and cups, but her fingers started stinging with glass so she stopped. She swept up everything and carried it to the kitchen trash. The head waiter spotted unbroken dishes in the can and started picking them out, his job being to serve Louie in any way, but Candy, with glass-cut thumbs, a bruised forearm, and her face throbbing from where the tray hit above her lip, did not offer to help him. He looked at her and did not ask.

Paul, who was supposedly her friend, never apologized or offered to help. He just disappeared. Later he advised her if she ever dropped a tray again to do the same. "Let someone else clean it up," he said.

Afterwards she started to bus a table, but when she picked up an empty salad bowl and the man at the table told her to put it down, she walked away. She went to the bathroom to compose herself so she could go on. She wanted to be able to call Rory when she got home, maybe go to his house, but he didn't get off work until at least two in the morning then he liked to be left alone to sleep until about four the next afternoon when he got up to go to work again.

Tonight her night is going smoothly. The customers are friendly and some of her favorite waiters are on. She tries to ignore Marvin, who complains when the customers want to take their food home because then he can't eat it: "I suppose they're not going to leave those shrimp," he whines, touching them in their bowl on Candy's tray. And he complains when customers leave their food behind: "I wish I had that kind of money to just throw away on food, don't you?"

They are standing in the kitchen, their trays on the busing rack, sorting their dishes for the dishwasher, and Marvin is saying, "I wish they'd get this place organized. I don't see how they expect us to work here."

Candy tries to block him out. The restaurant has been in business for forty years and seems adequately run to her. She is staring at her tray, arguing with Marvin in her mind, when Louie walks into the kitchen. She looks up, and somehow, inexplicably, her tray falls to the floor the moment he walks by. Plates and glasses crash.

Everyone thinks Marvin has dropped them, and Louie shouts, "Marvin, the next tray you drop, you're paying for!"

"It was my tray," Candy says, being noble, and knowing her own innocent history, thinking Louie will tell her it's okay.

"The next tray you drop, Candy, you pay for!" Louie says and walks out of the kitchen.

"Don't talk to me any more," she tells Marvin, calculating that each dropped tray could cost her a whole night's tips, making her job so unworthwhile she might have to quit.

Marvin, in his prissiest voice, says, "It wasn't *my* fault you dropped the damn tray."

Now she will have to deal with him all night unless she can smooth it over.

"I know it wasn't your fault, but I can't talk and work at the same time. Could you please not talk to me," she says. "And please don't be mad."

"I'm not mad," Marvin snips. "I don't have a problem. You have the problem. You dropped the tray."

"Louie doesn't see people, he just sees dollar signs," DJ, the black dishwasher, remarks. Like most everybody at the restaurant, he has worked for Louie for years.

For the rest of the night she glares when she sees Louie laughing with the waiters and the customers. She knows he will not apologize. He has probably forgotten the whole incident. Louie doesn't see people, just dollar signs. She decides that for the night she does not have to be nice. She takes the bowls and plates without smiling. She makes everyone well aware of her mental state.

One of the waiters, Tony, who did not see her spill the tray in the kitchen, asks her, in his rich Virginia accent, "You okay, hon-ney?"

She has come to work with migraines and menstrual cramps, after six hours of being a maid, and with a swollen foot. This is the first time anyone has seriously asked her if she is okay. As she looks at him, she gives in to all the sadness she feels for herself. She can't answer, but mercifully she turns away before she starts to cry.

"You don't bring your problems to the station," her fiancé, a fireman, told her. He worked cooped up with seven other men for forty-eight hours at a time. You don't bring your problems to the station.

"I'm fine, thanks," she tells Tony later. "Thanks for asking." She pats him on the back, and he smiles at her.

At the end of the night, Bob hands her her share of the tips without comment. He thanks the waiters who have done half as much work and made twice the money.

"Good night, *gentlemen*," Bob says.

Louie smiles at everyone and they depart, Candy to her roofless house which the carpenters have ordered her not to stay in because there is plaster dust and sawdust everywhere.

She lies down to sleep in her clothes on the plastic tarp covering the floor. She is sure she has seen this done somewhere, maybe in a situation comedy about newlyweds. Just last week Rory said she could stay with him any time she needed to.

The next morning at the motel Candy learns that a grandmother traveling with her family died in her bed in one of the suites during the night. That afternoon Candy stands outside the room. Lucinda, the Portuguese maid who speaks no English and doesn't know what happened, rushes around trying to clean it while the family is still gathering their things. The owner yells at Lucinda.

Later Candy finds her sitting on the steps crying. Lucinda doesn't understand why they are mad at her. Normally she does good work and is proud to be the fastest maid.

Candy sits down and pats her back. Earlier Candy patted the woman whose mother had died.

I'm only in it for the money, Lucinda indicates to Candy, rubbing her thumb and two fingers together to show cash, tears in her eyes.

"I know," Candy says, though she knows Lucinda loves her job.

After the family is gone, Candy and the other maids stand in the kitchen eating the food left behind. They don't get a lunch break, so they are starving. Even though the old woman died peacefully in her sleep, this is probably what everyone fears, Candy thinks while eating a donut meant for the family's breakfast. The woman's body has been taken away by ambulance men who made jokes in the parking lot while the police questioned the family; the bed has been stripped, ready to be remade, the handyman sings as he puts his share of the spoils in a plastic bag. Candy and the other maids rush through their food so the motel owner doesn't catch them and shout at them, making a fool of himself in front of the guests.

When she gets home, Candy has a message on her machine from the pest control man. He wants her to work with him, an easy job, nine dollars an hour, cash. He could pick her up at 8 a.m. She'd be done by four.

"I'd like to *have* you," he says.

She doesn't want it to be like this. She sees herself in a dark, empty building, trapped with him. Her shouts would echo against bare walls. She would like to call Rory and ask what to do, but she's embarrassed by the situation. Anyway, she and Rory don't seem to be speaking. But she needs the money, and she has the day off.

She leaves a message that she'll do it. The law is on her side, she tells herself. People can't just do whatever they want to you.

Circus Matinee

Bonnie Jo Campbell

Though Big Joanie senses something is wrong, she does not turn to look at the tiger. Instead she places snow cones into the outstretched hands of three black-haired girls, making certain that each girl firmly grips the plastic cup before she lets go. Big Joanie accepts clean dollar bills from the girls' father, who wears a denim shirt, probably washed by a wife who buries her face in her husband's shirts to remind herself of him when he's gone. In less than two minutes, Big Joanie must move out of this cramped front row because the lights will go out, and when they come back on, Helmut the world's best animal trainer will appear in the center ring with his Asian tigers. Big Joanie can't quite straighten her body against the hip-high barricade between the front row and the arena floor, but she raises her arm and holds her snow cones high in the air like an offering.

Behind the oldest black-haired girl, who is about eleven and wears a silver cross with Jesus crucified on it, a man in reflector aviator sunglasses holds up his finger to signify a snow cone. More than once, Big Joanie has carried a man as big as this man from his truck to his bedroom, then pulled off his boots and unbuttoned his shirt. She has gotten undressed and folded her pants, blouse, and bra into a neat pile on a chair and crawled in bed beside him.

Big Joanie need not look behind her to know that Conroy has wheeled the first tiger cage into position, to know that Conroy, who invited Big Joanie to his room fourteen times last summer, has gone behind the velvet curtain to retrieve the second tiger. Everything is the same as every other show, she tells herself, but she senses a disequilibrium, the kind of apprehension a flightless bird must feel before an earthquake.

The band and clowns clamor on, and the audience bites into snow cones. Big Joanie lowers the tray to her shoulder. Her nostrils itch, and she smells the sweat of the crowd beneath the mask of aftershave and perfume and the orangy scent of her own deodorant. Ignoring the hair standing up on the back of her neck, shoving aside the thoughts of men she's known for just one night, she leans across the oldest girl carefully, so as not to drip cherry juice onto her blouse or jeans. Big Joanie offers the sunglasses man the snow cone, and his hand closes around it, but as she lets go the cup, slips and crashes to the floor. The man's face changes, stretches as though made out of clown rubber. Big Joanie has never seen a man struck dumb like this. Some men have regarded her with disgust in the morning, seeming to have forgotten the way they whispered to her the night before, but she didn't sleep with this man. She only handed him a snow cone, the way she's handed snow cones to thousands of men.

In the same moment, the expressions of people sitting near the sunglasses man freeze the same way. Have they all just noticed Big Joanie's over-large head and her hips as wide as the length of an axe-handle? Are they stunned by her acne-pocked face? By her lightning-struck hair? Then she sees the answer reflected in the man's glasses, a double rearview vision of a compacted and curved circus world in which a miniature tiger stands in front of, not inside, its cage.

Scraping feet and muffled screams are not quite drowned out by the circus band. People at the top of the section and in the aisle seats escape toward the exits, falling upon one another. But at the bottom center, those sitting in a half-circle around Big Joanie are trapped in their seats.

"Stay still!" shouts a voice from the floor, Conroy's voice. Big Joanie has heard it in ninety-seven arenas, in the pie car, and whispering in his lower bunk in train car eighty-five, but never has she heard such urgency. Conroy is the assistant to Helmut's assistant Bela; Conroy is the person who makes sure the six-inch steel pin is dropped through the slot to secure the doors on each tiger cage as it is pulled into the arena. Conroy shouts, "Y'all stay still. We'll get her back in." Whenever Big Joanie went to Conroy's room on train car eighty-five last summer, Conroy's roommate eventually stumbled in drunk and turned on the light. Conroy would pull the blanket over Big Joanie's head, uncovering her feet which hung off the end of his bunk.

"Just stay still. Nobody'll get hurt if you all just stay still." Conroy's voice cajoles in an attempt to soothe the tiger. "Queenie, take it easy," he says three times, as if trying to convince a small, pretty woman to come to his room. "If y'all move," he says to Big Joanie and the audience, "this girl might get excited."

Big Joanie can imagine Conroy—he has small hands and a bald spot the size of a copper pot scrubber—but that doesn't help her now. She tries to feel Conroy in her nerves and bones, the way she felt him last summer, but she senses instead the tiger pacing. Each stride is longer than the last, looser, as though in the pads of its feet it has stored a genetic memory of life in the Asian forests where its ancestors took down game.

Big Joanie doesn't move. Her size twelve canvas shoes stick to the snow cone juice and flattened cotton candy as the tiger's feet meet clean floor mats, swept and scrubbed after each show. For six years in sometimes three shows a day Big Joanie has seen this tiger pour into the caged center ring, but she never considered the possibility of the tiger walking free. Now she imagines tiger feet prowling her spine, stepping on vertebrae which float up her back like bone islands.

The three black-haired girls are crying, but their sobs are so quiet Big Joanie must strain to hear them. She has never looked squarely into the faces of frightened girls, has never watched their pretty cheeks being sliced by tears. The girls have just seen a woman no bigger than the eleven-year-old let go of the rope and spin by her braid, wearing only a glittering bikini; they have seen the Polish acrobats pile atop one another, stretching upward in a human tower of Babel, risking everything to get their body language to the upper tiers of this arena. A daredevil rode a motorcycle upside-down, but nothing prepared the girls for this.

In two of the cheapest seats, way up in section P, a manager of a regional sales office sits with his girlfriend, who compares to his wife as filet mignon compares to a cubed steak. During the first half of this matinee, people filled many of the seats, but by twos and threes they have migrated to lower sections into better seats than they'd paid for. The loudspeaker behind the couple bangs out a sped-up version of "The Sting," but their distance from the arena mutes the action. The manager watches clown stooges hit each other with handbags and plastic hammers far below. A female clown whose figure is camouflaged in polka dots hangs shirts on a clothesline. When she turns her back, a little dog jumps up and tears them down.

The chain-link enclosure appeared miraculously in the dark of the center ring while that tiny woman spun by her hair in the spotlight above, and now a tiger has been wheeled out in a cage. The tiger is the brightest toy in this toy circus, a butane tiger-torch, a brilliant carved bit of amber the manager might hang on a chain. In China, he has heard, men increase their virility by eating the powdered penises of tigers.

Christ, he loved that sparkling little woman who spun by her hair. She had seemed small enough to fit in his hand, as perfect as a wish, a bikini-clad genie he could conceal in the pencil holder on his desk. His girlfriend loved the animal acts—the camels, the bareback stunts, even the ridiculous bow-tied and skirted poodles.

His girlfriend hasn't noticed the tiger. Her fingers have been sliding upward from his knee and now she unfastens his fly. He shifts in his seat to help her. There is nobody else around, and even the pushy vendors won't bother coming here for only two people. This is precisely what he hoped for, precisely why he didn't buy better seats. His girlfriend is a district sales manager; she has thick dark hair and an apartment not far from the office. She reaches through the fold of his shorts. They have eaten restaurant meals at corner tables, and she has never done more in public than touch his leg. She lowers her head into his lap, and he strokes her shoulders. Two men emerge from behind the purple curtain with a second tiger cage, but they stop halfway across the arena. The manager sees what they see. The first tiger is stepping out through the open door of its cage, the powerful head first, then front paws, back paws, and long, muscled tail. Or is he imagining this? His girlfriend doesn't even notice when the music slows.

Big Joanie wonders why they don't stop the music altogether. The faces before her are pale with fear. Behind her, the cat stretches further with each stride. The memory of prowling Asian forests travels from its feet into the muscles of its legs. The tiger spikes the air with growls, tests its space, tastes its freedom.

When Joanie was twelve, a year older than the oldest black-haired girl, she was working alone in her mother's garden, on the far side of the barnyard, along the road. She was weeding a row of bush beans, straddling the plants on her knees, when she heard noises behind her. Instead of investigating the noises, she kept weeding. She sensed danger up and down her spine, noticed her spine for maybe for the first time, as if it were a closely planted row of beans or seed corn sprouting in her back. The men came from behind, through the garden gate with a gunny sack which they pulled over her head without even shaking out the last of the chicken feed.

She had never breathed the fine dust of chicken feed so deeply, or felt it cake her eyes, or filter into her hair and catch on her scalp. The men pressed her into the sand and garden dung, so that the grit worked itself into her armpits.

Joanie was as big as a grown-up, and probably those men had mistaken her for a grown woman, her mother said later, scrubbing chicken manure off brown eggs with enough force that she would soon break one. A few mornings later when Joanie was standing in the driveway with her arms across her chest, her father, who was a big man but not an ugly man, said those men were probably from out of town. He looked as though he wanted to say more, but he grew unsteady watching his only daughter—who was already as tall as he was—hug herself and rock back and forth, and he slammed the truck door and left for work.

The first man pinched her breasts and called her ugly. "You'll like this, you ugly bitch." Coming from a grown man that word "ugly" stung her. The second man spoke sweetly. "Oh baby, this feels good." When he said, "I want to kiss you," the first man kicked dirt on them and said, "She'll see us, you asshole." With the first man, Joanie just prayed for it to be over, for the day to be over so she could go to bed, for this life to be over so she could start again and run when she first heard the noises. As the second man whispered kind words to her, Joanie felt dulled by a sympathy towards him, a sickening camaraderie which slowed time.

"Don't take that bag off," the first man said, "or we're coming back." Joanie lay across the bush beans, sticky, pasted with sand and dung, her t-shirt pushed up under the chicken feed sack, her throat clogged by the mash. The men tore through the garden, trampling her mother's tomato and squash plants as Joanie lay listening to the mockery of crows above. She felt herself separating, the way a garden divides into rows of snap beans and corn and tomatoes. Her spine had only just come alive minutes before, but now she thought of the way vertebrae boiled apart in oxtail stew. Her mind fell open like a nut, halved, and halved again, endless halving. She lay swathed in an awful calm, feeling the rhythm of the men's bodies long after they were gone.

"Doughnut move," says Conway's boss, Bela, the assistant to Helmut. "Stay calm, everybody. Doughnut move."

Big Joanie wishes she could sink behind the barricade, but there is no room, and she wants to stand up straight, but the ledge on the barricade cuts into her, so she continues to bend slightly forward, touching the eleven-year-old's knees with her own big knees. When a drop of cherry juice is poised to drip from her snow cone tray, Big Joanie shifts so the drop doesn't fall on the girl's white denim but instead runs ice-cold down her own chest inside her uniform shirt. The smallest girl buries her face in her father's sleeve, but the older girls shrink against their own seats. Big Joanie feels herself stretch wide across the tiger's field of vision. She wonders if she will be ripped open and devoured like a milk cow, like an Asian water buffalo.

"Freeze," comes the voice of Helmut, the world's best animal trainer. "Nobody will move." In less than a minute, Helmut should be performing, so he is wearing silk pants and a vest with no shirt. His blond hair lies perfectly in place, even as sprigs of her own hair snap loose from her pony tail. The tiger Helmut has trained continues to pace, orange, black, orange stripes rippling across big cat muscle. "Nobody will move," commands Helmut.

Though she always has remembered that afternoon in the garden, has used it as a marker, a zero point on her own time line, she has never had a good hold of it. She knew those men with voices but no faces about as well as she knew God. Big Joanie obeys the world's best animal trainer, but she hates that every person in this arena except her can see the tiger. Only about a minute has passed since the sunglasses man dropped the snow cone; the cherry color hasn't even begun to fade from her remaining snow. But the air has changed, become as empty as before a tornado. If she dares look up, the roof of the arena will be sucked away, and open sky will mock her. In arenas across the country, she has held her snow cones high as an offering, but God has made it clear today, he will not bargain with Big Joanie.

The manager's girlfriend samples him, tastes him. He blinks to clear his vision and loosens his tie. On the arena floor, small, insignificant circus people scatter in the tiger's wake. A dozen men in blue coveralls draw near the tiger, then back away, like the tide coming in and going out. Still the music blasts. The manager presses the bleached cuff of his shirt sleeve against his forehead. The tiger pads back and forth between the cage and the front center seats. His girlfriend's mouth is soft.

Below, that big-headed, big-assed snow cone girl is wedged against a low barrier between the arena and the seats, her back to the tiger. That girl lugged herself up and down the stairs of this section early in the show. She was double-bag-ugly but oddly voluptuous, her breasts and hips pornographic in their proportion. Lying with that giantess, eyes closed, a man might feel he'd come home after a long journey. Still, even a man who liked them big couldn't get past the face. A man who would take that to bed was a man who entertained no illusions of himself. That's what the manager had been thinking when she looked right at him, through eyes as close-set as double barrels of a shotgun. She seemed to know what he'd been thinking and that he'd lied to four creditors on the phone this morning. Then, just as abruptly, she looked away.

His girlfriend purrs, her breath raspy. He grabs a handful of that glorious hair and pushes her head down harder, establishes a better rhythm. Sweet god in heaven, he thinks, but his pleasure is lashed to his fear that she will stop. He knows she would like nothing more than to look up and see this tiger loose on the arena floor, but he can't bring himself to tell her.

Tiger muscles flex behind Big Joanie, close enough that the sharp smell of tiger urine is overpowering. Helmut, Bela and Conroy draw near, pushing the tiger closer to the barricade and closer to Big Joanie. Helmut speaks to the tiger in German, words that sound as if they emanate from some private train car where the three men sit, smoking cigars and drinking liquor in comfortable chairs. The tiger stops. Big Joanie hasn't realized the world could be motionless, but the tiger stops pacing, and the world is like a still-life: ugly woman and tiger.

"Nobody will move," whispers Helmut in English. "Everything will be fine." He speaks so softly that Big Joanie wonders if she is reading his mind rather than hearing him. The voice mesmerizes her, connects her to him. He will lift her from danger before the audience of thousands.

But the tiger growls and severs their connection. Of the two creatures, Helmut is the weaker. The tiger's eyes cut into Big Joanie, sending twisty patterns of electricity through her. The tiger is aware of her rushing blood and of the muscle beneath her fat.

"You will not move." Helmut's voice travels easily into her, and if Helmut or any man had ever declared loyalty to her, Joanie might stop.

"Doughnut move, girl," says Bela. But Bela has never cared for her either. Remembering the men she's known is futile, though she can't stop herself. Pictures of them rattle through her like strung-together boxcars.

"Big Joanie, stay still!" commands Conroy. If he had invited her to his room last night, she might obey. If Conroy had covered her head to protect her and not to hide her, if he had ever sat beside her in the pie car or held her hand, she would become meat for him now.

Instead, Big Joanie wills herself to turn, and as she does, lost vertebrae line up and reconnect. Big Joanie feels puzzle pieces snap into place. She turns broad shoulders to face the tiger, straight on, full frame. The creature is as strange as Asia, as familiar as her own reflection.

She rests her snow cone tray on the barricade. She sees the tiger more clearly than the hair-spinning woman sees the husband who controls the rope that holds her aloft, more clearly than Big Joanie's mother ever saw her father, more clearly than any pretty woman will ever see an ordinary man. The tiger is more golden than orange, its black stripes as delicate as smoke trails from a cigarette, as painful to Joanie as whip marks. One pale front leg barren of stripes reveals an asymmetry. Shaggy feet with claws like dark quarter-moons grip the rubber mat uneasily, as if testing foreign soil. Big Joanie has seen this tiger jump through a ring of fire, yet she has never really seen its yellow god's eyes or read the calligraphy of its war-paint face. The tiger stares back at her. She weighs what it weighs. If the tiger pounces, she will be overcome, but the tiger must look at her and acknowledge her, and Big Joanie will know the face of the animal that devours her.

Tiger muscles tense and contract as they do before springing at Helmut's bidding. But the tiger hesitates. It shifts its weight and looks away from Big Joanie, retracts its claws. The tiger glances toward the empty cage, and shifts its weight again. Seconds flash in Joanie's mind like glimpses of sun between boxcars. The tiger twists its body, tilts its head, and roars into the bank of lights.

Cirque de Recession
Matthew Salesses

Nobody is coming to the circus anymore. Hemingway, the last elephant, trumpets a sad note as his girlfriend is packed away into a truck, to be sold. All us clowns line up in front of the big top to wave goodbye. My wife, Lulu, takes it hardest. She won't even put on her makeup anymore. Last week, she crushed her rubber nose under her heel and it squeaked apart into two pieces. "What's the point," she said, "if no one laughs?"

The recession has hit the circus hard. Our boss sells off the animals, first the monkey that couldn't ride its bicycle, the one that reminded Lulu of our lost son; then the tigers, which got meaner as they got hungrier; and the lions (ditto); now the elephants.

As the truck's engine starts, Lulu rushes in front of the bumper. My boss pushes me forward to stop her. "Please," I ask Lulu. "You can't prevent this." It takes three of us to pull her away.

Hours later, I stand in front of rows of empty bleachers and perform tricks for three elderly folks who come once a month, for free, from the nursing home. They don't pay any attention. One man is clearly drunk, and the other man and the woman talk about the past without making sense. Lulu skulks around behind me, just outside the open tent flap. When I peek back at her bare face, I realize how old we've gotten. Not quite elderly, but long past having another child. Her blond hair sticks up at untamed angles and her wrinkles quaver as she cries. She kisses Hemingway on his trunk. He unfurls it around her shoulders like an arm.

I squirt the rest of my plastic flower's water at my partner and hurry out of the ring. Hemingway's trainer leads him in, and I wait for Lulu, a minute or two more. The trunk is a comfort, I know. That wrinkled gray flesh. An elephant never forgets.

As Lulu opens her hands, I see the red halves of her rubber nose. She stares at them with regret, and I can tell she's thinking of our son. Split. Irreparable. We had let him camp with an older friend—they never returned. The friend showed up dead just two months ago, after twelve years of no news, around the same time we started feeling the effects of the recession. When she heard about the death, Lulu wanted to leave and renew our search for Danny, but he disappeared so long ago, really. What was I supposed to say? I told her we couldn't leave our jobs. Not when so many others needed the work we had. Not when we couldn't even afford a local pint, a night out we deserved.

I didn't know she would blame herself for not saving any of her income. I didn't know she would handle losing the animals like she was again losing our flesh and blood. The day the tigers shipped, she managed to get into a cage with one of them. I swear she looked disappointed when we got her out without a bite taken.

I walk up to her now and the smell of gas fills my nose. She hoists something off the ground and strides past me, into the tent. As she goes by, she takes a book of matches from her pocket, and I remember how, with Danny, she used to light an entire book and put it into her mouth, where the flame would go out. It always made him laugh. It was his favorite trick.

This time, though, she lifts what she picked up over her head, and liquid splashes over her clothes. It's gas—I realize it's gas—and then I'm running, watching her drop the canister and pull a match from the book.

She sees me coming, and her eyes light up in a way I don't understand. I tackle her. I try to keep her head from smashing the ground. The smell cuts into my lungs. I will always remember this smell, the smell of not burning. I reach for her arm and make sure she can't strike the match.

"What were you thinking?" I ask, holding her down.

"I wasn't going to do it," she says. "I just wanted someone to care. I just wanted someone to care that *I* care."

The elderly folks are watching now, out of their seats. "Tomorrow the bleachers will be full," I say as she looks up at me. "Everything will be a little less empty."

Notebook #19

Sean Lovelace

Every Monday.
Every Monday.
Every Monday, they'll tell you, is a thick rope. Every Friday some FM DJ rings a bell, a klaxon, some gift certificate we're supposed to salivate over, and then exchange for freedom. Work is poetry and potion to a god. A warm elixir, a daily swill. Aching throats are prayers. Don't ask me the odds on an answer—I'm no true believer, but I've held many jobs. The worse odor I've ever smelled was a body we found floating in a railway tanker. That was my DuPont gig, out of Millington, Tennessee. During offloading, one of the valves wouldn't pull, so we popped the manhole cover. Someone swore. Someone coughed and retched. I stared into the hatch. Wasn't my first or final dead body, but the chemicals certainly showed me something. Opened my eyes, as they say. Ate away his clothing. Crimped and pickled his skin. Blanched his hair neon pink. I sit here drinking Dos Equis in the afternoon, typing on an Olympia of all things (word processors still do exist, though barely), in a squatty Mexican restaurant in Indiana; and that man's story just came to me like a sudden sweat, again.

My dad retired after 44 years of installing carpets, came home on his last day, hurled his knee pads into the backyard, lit a massive joint, inhaled, and had only this advice: "Son, don't get into carpet."

I didn't. I got into other occupations. For example, reading, and relocation. For example, alcohol. Because it made me feel better. Still does make me feel, better. I can't seem to shake its glow, or want to. Books accept me. Movement accepts me. Alcohol accepts me. We have simpatico, an understanding. An earned respect. The hardest working man I've known was an ex-marine and schizophrenic named Carl. I'd pick him up at daybreak from the veteran's hospital—if the nurses would allow, a decision based on his behavior the previous evening and if he'd taken his morning medications. After we cut grass for ten hours in the Alabama sun, I'd drive him back to the psych ward, and we'd split a six pack of malt liquor on the way. "Skull-kickers," he called them, with an honest open laugh. "Ain't seen a white man since Vietnam that would drink skull-kickers!" And I'd laugh along with him. Wind whipping through cracked windows. Halo and center of glow. My fingers tingle now. The cells shimmer. Sometimes silence, or even a slant of afternoon light, can be a type of language.

"It's the nature of every man to fashion a tiny kingdom he can rule," someone wrote in a book. That just came to me while my head treads tequila. My first job as a teenager was for a dog groomer, wrestling mixed breeds into a stainless steel vat of detergent. Stench of wet dog. Hot cough of industrial dryer. Suffocating air. Wide, white eyes, the wailing of terrified creatures. I was bitten three times, all by the purple tongue, the chow. Every day my fingers ached, skin peeling scaly red. Every day I watched the owner as she took the poodles from their cages, dangling them by their leashes, spinning, whimpering spittle. Every day a giant silent man stole my paper bag of lunch. Just walked over and took it from my hands. Finally, I complained to my boss and he gave me this look of disgust and said, "You got to stand up for yourself in this world, fool." That was the only job I was ever fired from, and I can't even remember my boss's name.

A trick in my days-of-hungry was to enter a Mexican restaurant, order one cheap draft, and eat my lunch and dinner full of tortilla chips. I'd re-read the local paper, my eyes down, so people would leave me alone. Now I order margaritas. I can afford them, usually. They come in thick glass bowls on the tiniest stems—some modern sculpture, some art: titled *Heavy?* Note the question mark. Note the drink specials at 5 p.m. Note the gas stations along your commute, selling beer in single, cool, sweating cans. I had an image there, an idea edged in brushed aluminum, some metallic taste, but it fell away. Sure, alcohol kills memory, but memory is dying all along. Name every story you know about a dog. I'd wager you recall less than ten. But you have hundreds of dog stories, somewhere inside. Or maybe no longer. Vanished. As of no worth. Swirled down the synaptic drain. Into never-time.

I slip outside to use a payphone to call my father. Streetlight jaundice. A big crushing sky. I look and listen. A low moaning on the air—a caged cur, a siren. But there is no payphone.

Or this: "Most men prefer porkchops to freedom." That sounds pretty spot-on, but often drink makes life ring truer than in reality. To forget the book is typical of me, another death. I know the title included the word *Lazarus*. I remember a very spare time, and so I delivered pizzas. The first day my manager said, "We got one benefit: free lunch. Anything on the menu." *Anything?* That diabolical possibility. I shoveled in 38 cheese sticks in my allotted 20 minutes. Drank four Mountain Dews. There's an odor out back of every restaurant, down low, along the base of the dumpster. Sweet and heavy—some type of rusting/rotting fruit. You kneel there, sweating and retching, wiping your forehead with a greasy red-and-white polyester shirt, stomach gurgling, wondering *what the hell?*

— Notebook #19

Work is movement. Clutch and grind. Things fall apart, etc. It's my skin cells, my bone and muscle, my blood I'm shedding when I crawl into a dark hot pit with a crew of rangy Illegals, when I bend and clack my spine, grip in my sweaty hands a metal pick, scraping scalding pick, given to me by a company employed by a company employed by Mercedes Benz to clean the robots of grease and grime and polymer spackle, the robots that build the SUVs purring these glistening streets. The automatons glint and glimmer. Chrome insects with yellow corded veins, jaw lines of steel. These will be the next ones, you have to believe. Some form of master, somewhere down the road. And they will never sleep or sicken. Never die. Never answer, or need to, your pleadings. Can you speak clang and clatter and hiss?

Or: "The Law of the Jungle will destroy all jungles."

Or I borrow a phone and dad says, "They found a little cancer." A *little cancer*? My stomach thrums, and seizes. A locked gear. I pause bedside, as a son should. The Blood, he mumbles in a Vicodin fog. Something of The Blood. A cliché, but clichés persist, are handed down, because they contain some truth. Like *heading west.* To where everything sprawls and sets.

The mop and bucket of blood. The fistful of gurney chrome. The odor of surgical soap, the intercom crackle, and then, after a long blue night, I drink coffee, eat Bugles from a Tom's Machine, sit cleaned-out inside, wire-bushed, on a cold bench in the employee lounge. The emergency room of Denver Health Medical Center, right in the aorta of that sprawling arterial city. The "Gun and Knife Club," someone clever said, and the name stuck. Even has its own documentary on Discovery. Its own police station in the lobby, built in the 1980s, for the gang-bangers who sometimes trailed the ambulance, to finish the job. And down the hallway a Methadone clinic, a McDonald's, a gift shop. Who wishes for a Christmas ornament with GUN AND KNIFE CLUB etched in red across a silver bulb? Someone. Blood is silvery, pig-iron blue, this quivering yellow. An amazing thing, the hues of blood. A luminous river. A throb. The way it glosses red, a purplish orange. A mercurial shimmering black. It sputters, runs, gels. It gushes. See it scurry and pool, dry to the crackly brown skin of fallen leaves. "Death, it's going around," a doctor tells me one Friday night over a pot of coffee so thick we could float a stethoscope bell atop its oily surface. Me and my notebook:

> *the Flat Boy...pressed (Dr. B. said "ironed") against the side of Walgreen's by a delivery truck*
> *blurred and blued the flesh*
>
> *teenager floats into the ER, a skeleton, arms all abscesses and bone. pretty girl, about ten thousand lives ago. "Ya'll sell syringes?"*
>
> *man swallows a condom of cocaine, it bursts mid-colon. why didn't he tell us?*
>
> *i'm not going to lie to you, we don't do that. you're going to lose that leg.*

fold and fold again, fold away down
sucking tailpipes. pecking at cigarette butts. lug nuts. opossums feeding in the parking lots. when did this start?
side effects (brain damage, melancholia, bloating)
nurses huddled under awning smoking cigarettes. nurses huddled. student nurse found in custodian closet, crying.
we can save you but you might not be what you were
sky like soap
what does the opossum think while faking death?
another kid on a Kawasaki. donor-cycles, we call them donor-cycles
foredoomed to failure
seriously, listen, everyone stop what they're doing and listen. this isn't going to be a positive outcome
hypodermic glisten

I left the ER. Left the whole hospital, and all that came with it—that immediacy to life, death, hope, suffering. Too close, for me. I started feeling nothing, to float through my shift, eyes closed. So I cleaned out my locker and took a bus straight to Lo Do. February, an eerie quivering glow, since it was snowing in full sunlight, a Denver phenomenon. Over mugs of Fat Tire my friend said, "You quit? Them benefits. All those nurses! Are you crazy?" But what did a bricklayer know about emergency rooms? What he'd seen on the beautiful TV. Still, I do wonder why. Or I wonder: what have I stuck with? Books and beer, I suppose. I'll be honest. Those two, a flurry of words, and a feeling I am supposed to be somewhere else.

Shortest time on a job? One day. Building houses in the suburbs outside Boulder. Split both thumb nails, and twisted my right knee in a gray sludge of concrete. What got me was seeing the Hardhats throw their jerky wrappers and beer cans between the wall studs. Then pissing there. Then, at least one man, shitting. Then sealing it all inside with drywall. A home warming gift. Some type of message I can understand, and clearly can not. So I limped away. Over to a friend's apartment. Drank quarts of Coors. Listened to a cold, sweeping rain. Felt sorry for myself for three days, about my limit. Read a magazine article about the Upper Peninsula of Michigan, and headed north.

Always a Greyhound bus. A dog loping the highway shoulder. A heat mirage, a smudge of road kill. My head against scratched glass. All these cars on the freeway, rush hour, a clotted stream: brake light, brake light, brake light. Always a flashing, a flailing. Always interference, always static. Dial tones and dead spots. Some kind of low, gray metal clamping down. Suddenly you own something you do not want: a house. Solid property, actual space, a world only realized in the mind—and precarious there. So you sell it at a ridiculous price. Over the telephone in the kitchen of a bar named *Mitchell's*. You feel better, no doubt. Order a Black

— NOTEBOOK #19

Label and unfold the newspaper to the classifieds: assembly tech, meat cutter, loader/unloader, plastic injection crew...

And the next Monday, and the next, and so? A tired etc. Me and my word processor. Writing *something* down. Something less than imagined. Or this: "Men cannot shape clouds." But we try. We do try. Morning arrives in this place on a squall-line, hard and early. What one old timer hunched over his tenth Lowenbrau calls, "shit-kicking illegal cold." Nods and laughter, a nervous gesture. Snow mutters against the walls, the low ceiling. Outside squats a shadow, a billowing breath, waiting for us. So let me finish this. One more. And I might go.

Ambition

Billie Louise Jones

Other clerks complimented Jennifer's new pantsuit as she walked through the office to her computer desk.

She smiled pluckily. "Isn't it terrible to get new clothes so seldom everyone notices?"

When she bent over to put her purse into a bottom drawer, her mouth slipped into a sour line. Her pantsuit was green rayon that looked like linen, an impulse, an extravagance from Penney's. She looked for bargains at Penney's and Sears. Her sister, who did not have to work, shopped at Neiman-Marcus.

Jennifer was small and neat. Her short auburn hair was in a beauty parlor set, the golden lights dimmed under a week's spray. Beneath the rigid hair her face seemed matronly, though she was only twenty-three, with the pert features that are cute on a girl. She was settled in her life. There was no change in prospect, so that dissatisfaction dragged her face down when she was not consciously being perky.

Two magazines on the desk next to hers caught Jennifer's eye. The covers were of Brad Pitt and Angelina Jolie—Brangelina!—and Oprah beaming personality from her own magazine. Two of the most famous women in the world, a famous marriage and a famous career. She hated them equally. Jennifer did not like to read articles that celebrated the special qualities of famous women. She preferred woman's magazines in which glamorous actresses said things like, "I'm just a faded jeans girl. I like to entertain around the grill on my patio....I don't think I'm really beautiful. I just came along at the right time." She tapped Oprah's picture. "Haven't you *heard* the stories about her?"

She arched her eyebrows, and the other clerk caught the implication of her tone and expression. After a moment's indecision, a flare of resentment, she fell in with Jennifer and laughed loudly, screwing her face into a leer.

Georgia had a broad West Texas accent. She said she was thirty-five, but deep lines were drawn from nose to mouth and angled up her forehead from her eyebrows. She was blonde, ratted, and sprayed; and she wore red knit pants bought before she gained weight.

Jennifer looked rancorously around the long grey room, an open office, not even cubicles. Fifty women worked in the room, the commission accounting department of a life insurance company. The desks were arranged in groups of four, called sections, and to the right were the desks of the section heads. Mr. Owens, the supervisor, sat in a boxed-in office against one wall, coming out only to go home. Veronica, his secretary, had a desk facing the clerks' rows. She smoked the day away, checking into friends' Facebook pages now and then, looking chic and blasé, as if she knew everything about everyone. She had been there longer than anyone else in the room, seven years.

It was a little before eight, but the room was mostly full because the company wanted its employees to be at their desks working *by* eight and then to put work away *after* five. Susie and Pearl, the other two clerks in the section, swiveled their chairs around to Jennifer and Georgia; they talked about *The Young and the Restless,* the TV soap they all taped and watched when they got home.

"I know these people better than my neighbors," Jennifer said. "I really feel *involved* with them."

Exactly at eight, Martha, the section head, put her *Dallas Morning News* in a desk drawer and turned to her clerks. She was a plain little woman in her late forties, her mouth pursed in lines, greying hair set in a tight permanent, glasses with metal trim, crisp polyester clothes.

"Girls," she said, looking straight at Jennifer, "we can't have so much talking today. Mr. Owens wants the August commissions finished."

They powered up their computers, but not without a meeting of eyes, sullenly. They entered their PINs, pulled up their programs, saved last year's commissions, punched in the commission calculator, and sent the new figures to the agency department. Around and around, Jennifer thought, just like housework; I don't need a mind to do this, it would help not to have one.

Martha walked down to Mr. Owens's office, looking over her shoulder at Jennifer once with tight lips. As soon as the door closed behind her, Suzie and Pearl turned their chairs around to face Jennifer and Georgia.

"She's mad again," Suzie complained. She was an olive-skinned platinum blonde, pregnant.

"Why is she always picking on us?" Pearl asked Jennifer. She was a milky, plump girl, just graduated from high school, just married. She wore a black crepe dress with a satin bow at the neck. This was her first week, and she was eager to pick up the attitudes of the girls she worked with.

"She's a funny person," Jennifer said.

"I just can't feel she's really one of us," Pearl said. She still had school spirit about everything. "She always eats lunch with Agnes and Fran in underwriting, never with us. I think people who work together ought to be best friends."

"Sometimes she eats lunch alone," Georgia added pointedly, rolling her eyes for emphasis.

"I'd sit in the ladies room before I ate lunch alone," Jennifer declared. Her voice was thin but firm. "I'd have more pride."

"The way she is," Georgia said, "gets me down so much I don't feel like working."

She settled her thick elbows on her desk. The other two clerks rolled their chairs in closer.

"Section head in an administrative job," Jennifer said to them. "The important thing is to know how to work with people. She can't work with people." Her eyes flicked over them, and she was satisfied with their response. She had gotten them around to her side. "You work ought to mean something to you," she added. "You spend such a large part of your life at your job, you ought to be friends with the people you work with. And she didn't even go to Veronica's party last week."

"She just wants to get her check and go home," Georgia hooted.

"I believe in work." Jennifer's thin voice pronounced her words definitely. "If you're paid to do a job, you should do it as well as you can."

"If it's worth doing, it's worth doing right," Suzie added.

"How did Martha ever get to be section head in the first place," Pearl asked.

"Seniority," Jennifer replied. "When she was a clerk she did the worst work of all."

"They're going to find out about her now," Georgia said, working her eyebrows up and down knowingly. "If she goes, Jennifer's next in line for the job."

"I know that I could be a good section head."

Jennifer wanted the job of section head. The company was large and impersonal and moved as ponderously as the civil service, but Jennifer found ways to assert herself. She broadcast Martha's mistakes and shortcomings throughout the office until she thought Martha was becoming uncomfortable and nervous in the atmosphere she created. She thought she had the girls in the section behind her. They would not work for Martha, but with Jennifer they formed a tight little unit. Feelings were now so strong that the section could not continue to function without a change. Even Mr. Owens in his boxed-in office must soon realize that he would have to fire Martha and make Jennifer the new section head.

Thomas said to her one night after a church social that perhaps she ought not to tell people she worked because she seemed so upset about her job, either angry or ashamed, that she made a bad impression. "How can I help it?" And she looked at him accusingly, which he seemed not to see or understand. There were no dead-end jobs, she told herself; there were only dead-end people. She could make something for herself, even out of this.

The clerks saw Martha coming out of Mr. Owens's office and quickly focused on their screens.

The company owned an oval-shaped glass building on LBJ Freeway, which circled Dallas. Offices, industrial buildings, and strip centers were scattered along LBJ. The half-empty towers of downtown Dallas rose majestically on the skyline.

The clerks powered down their computers for break. The sections went to the company cafeteria for breaks and lunch at specified times, so that each clerk's whereabouts would be known to her supervisor. There was no other place to go, and the office was turned in on itself.

Georgia gulped her coffee and worked her eyebrows up and down, a characteristic. The others smiled in anticipation.

"Here's a good one my sloppy old Howard told me. Actually he didn't think it was funny. It burned him up." She licked her lips and began. "This woman was driving along late one night in Oklahoma when she had car trouble. She got out and raised the hood to see what was the matter. She was bending over the car looking at the motor when some man come along and slammed the hood down on her so that she couldn't move and raped her. Like that. Later on, when she was talking to the State troopers, she said she couldn't positively identify the man because she didn't see him. All she could say was that she knew he was a Texan. 'How do you know he was a Texan?' they asked her. 'I know he was a Texan,'" Georgia said, drawling her words with relish, "'because he had a great big belt buckle and a little bitty dick.'"

"That was my Thomas!" Jennifer said, slapping her hand down flat on the table.

They all laughed.

"I wish I had your problems," Suzie said. "With me it's just the opposite."

"Our husbands would kill us if they heard the way we talk about them," Jennifer said with a qualm. She tossed her head back. "But they probably talk the same way about us, except just the opposite."

"Oh, God, you know they do," Suzie groaned. With her pregnancy she had to sit far back from the table, and she dripped chocolate milk down her over-blouse. "They deserve to get it back."

"Sure," snorted Georgia. "When me and my sloppy old Howard went on our second honeymoon, he was the one sat on the bed and bawled, 'It's too big!' Howard told me something Ronny, our next door neighbor, said to him. He said, 'Man, I sure did have a good piece last night. If I wasn't married to it I'd let you have some, just to prove to you how good it is.'" She worked her eyebrows.

They were shocked at first; then Jennifer said, "No love at all. It's just sex to them, like animals."

Georgia laughed with her mouth open, showing all her big white teeth. "I can just see my sloppy old Howard getting in bed with that little gal."

After they laughed, Jennifer resumed the discussion. "That shows the differences between men and women that wives have to accept."

Pearl, bride of two months, rolled up eyes up like Georgia and sighed. "My mother told me that marriage is give and take—the wife gives and the husband takes."

"That's only partly true," Jennifer said maturely. "In my marriage we both had to make some adjustments. Of course, I know that some things will never be any different." The others understood what she meant and looked at her respectfully as she said, conscious of virtue, "It's something that I've had to accept. It used to matter to me, but now it doesn't seem important."

They worked steadily until lunch, unable even to check their text messages because Martha's eyes were sharp. Somewhere in the room, a cell phone rang, quickly extinguished. Mr. Owens was out of his office and scanning the floor for the guilty party. Use of cell phones was cause for instant dismissal. At lunchtime Martha went off to join her friends in other departments, older women who had worked there as long as she had. Jennifer encouraged the girls to exchange resentful glances at Martha's snub. They carried their trays to the table they regarded as theirs and complained again about the low pay, the dull routine.

"The worst of it is," Jennifer said, "I feel that I'm just working for myself. I want to do things for others. I'm really a very *giving* person. Kevin understood that. I wanted to be a teacher, but Thomas ruined that for me. I wanted to work part time and go to college, but we can't afford it. Thomas doesn't want me to be more educated than he is. I know that it will never be anything but a dream now."

"Kevin?" Pearl asked. The others seemed to understand the allusion."

"My first husband," Jennifer said casually. "We were divorced just after Jacky was born. So now I say," her voice deepened in ironic humor, "I was married, had a baby, got divorced, and remarried all in one year. How's that for action?"

Georgia laughed gustily, and Suzie giggled.

"You must have married awfully young the first time," Pearl said, curious but uncertain whether asking might be prying.

"No younger than you," Jennifer replied. As they continued eating, Jennifer told Pearl about her divorce. "We got married and....oh....I got pregnant right away.... accidentally. We were going to go through college together. He's going to be a lawyer. I was going to be a teacher. Kevin saw that he couldn't take care of me and the baby and finish college and law school. He had to decide what he wanted the most. He filed for divorce. Mental cruelty." Jennifer passed the pepper to Georgia and continued between bites of breaded veal cutlet. "I cross-filed for support. I didn't want the divorce because I loved Kevin very much. I offered to place my baby out for adoption. That's how much I wanted to save my marriage. I'd have done anything for him, and I didn't think I could live without him. When I realized that nothing could bring him back to me, I tried to commit suicide. I took a whole bottle of aspirin, but it only made me groggy. Of course, my mother was afraid to leave me alone after that. That's when Thomas started coming to see me every night.

"I let him come because I thought at first that Kevin was sending him, to keep in touch with me that way. Thomas and Kevin were high school buddies—I don't know why, they had nothing in common—and we often doubled. His girls were never very pretty. He came over every night, and he'd take me out to the show and to eat. People thought we were a couple. I think that flattered him."

"Well, Jacky was born, and my divorce was final, and I married Thomas the next month. But do you know," she added with a laugh, turning one corner of her mouth down ruefully, "I never really thought about Thomas before I married him."

They relished the irony.

"Does Kevin ever seem to wish he hadn't given up his son?" Pearl felt free to ask since Jennifer had told so much. "I mean, on his visiting days."

"I haven't seen Kevin again. He wanted to make a clean break. He should be in his second year of law school now."

"That sorry crumb bum," Georgia said, wrinkling her nose and mouth.

"No, that's not true," Jennifer protested. "I can see how you might get the wrong idea about Kevin, but he's not really a bad man." They looked skeptical, so she forgot her dessert in trying to explain. "He's a wonderful, warm person at heart; but I think his problem is that he's too intelligent. He's very brilliant, and his feelings will never be permitted to overrule his reason. He has a very clear idea of what he wants to do and be, and he knows how to arrange his life so that it will be just the way he wants it. He'll be important someday."

"I'm so surprised to learn about your divorce," Pearl said. "From the way you talk, Thomas and Jacky seem to belong to each other."

Jennifer bent forward to flash her biggest smile at Pearl. "Yes, everyone comments on how devoted they are. This is lucky, I suppose, in case Jacky turns out to be an only child."

"Doesn't Thomas want his own family?"

"Yes, but I don't know." Her face set rigidly, close to an open frown. She liked to talk about herself, but she did not like to be questioned. The conversation was slipping out of her control.

She brooded while they finished their desserts. Without a pause, they turned their table talk from her life to a new movie, unmindful of her mood.

She did not want to have another baby.

Thomas came home sweating and smelling every evening. He was a floorman; he was on his hands and knees all day putting down tile and linoleum. He was getting fat, his football muscles sliding away now that he took no exercise other than bowling in a league. He watched TV and drank beer while she cleaned house. Jacky pulled on her skirt, wanting her to play with him; but she was always tired and there was so much to be done to have her house looking the way she wanted it. She hated to fuss at him. But what could you do? Everything was too much of a strain.

They were buying a house in a new development on the edge of Pleasant Grove, long known as the roughest white part of Dallas. Buying there balanced out the cost of a brick house with a cathedral ceiling in the front room against the comparatively cheap cost of Pleasant Grove. His sister lived in Plano. Jennifer tried to make it look like the homes in magazines; but they were buying their furniture by room sets, taking the bad pieces with the good, to get a discount. It was not what she had been brought up with. It was not what her sister had. It was not what she would have had with Kevin. As it was, she had to work to help Thomas make ends meet. All her check went for the house payment, and they lived on Thomas's. Even then, she would never have the things in life she had expected to have. Married to Kevin, she might have chosen to be a teacher or not, but to be married and to have to work for the money made her feel like a failure as a woman.

Thomas told her he was doing the best he could. They could not afford a baby. It took both their checks to maintain some semblance of a decent style of life so that she could hold up her head in front of people. Though Thomas might plead with her to have his baby, he would have to accept the fact that she would not, unless he could make more money. She thought he would soon stop talking about a baby, for he was becoming less demanding of sex.

Jennifer, keying her computer automatically, thought of Kevin. He wanted to rise in the world; and while all boys talked that way, he alone seemed to make plans. He was well spoken, intelligent, and ambitious. After their first few dates, she had wanted nothing but to be married to him. He maintained an air of self possession, enjoying her company, wanting to pet her, to have her, but not moved by the same feelings she was. Most of her friends had the same problem, the nagging feeling that they were not central to their boys' lives as their boys were to their lives. Girls sat around discussing at length every nuance of their dates. Jennifer gave more to these analyses than she did to her schoolwork. Her need for him to be with her was so strong it seemed like a need for sex.

She gave in tremulously, but his tenderness consoled her fears. He was held by lovemaking, so that she thought he tried to act out an expression of feelings boys could not put into words. She did not like him to be away from her, but he seemed to place love apart from his need to go away to college. He said they would get married after he graduated. She thought fearfully of all the years ahead of them, years some little girl might steal him away, of how to bind him to her. The thought never formed in her mind in flat words to get pregnant; but after her first, guilty fear of pregnancy, her nerves were soothed by the certainty that Kevin was honorable and would marry her. To have a baby was always in the back of her mind. She got careless.

She was happy to get married to him, but her happiness collapsed at once. He was acquiescent, sullen, then hostile. He accused her of getting pregnant on purpose, and she denied it in tears over how his accusation wronged her. He wanted to get away from her to study, and she wailed to him about responsibilities to her and to the baby when it came. She could hardly believe the coldness on his face when he told her he was cutting her out of his life. She remembered his love-making and could not believe that his desire had not been as strongly for her, Jennifer, as her need had been for him, Kevin. They had been married a little over a month when he left her.

Sent back to her parents' house, she was hurt and desperately frightened. She would be alone with a baby. College was out of the question, she did not know how she would provide, there seemed no way she could do for herself. She had to have a man to take care of her, and Thomas was there.

At afternoon break they told their plans for the weekend.

"Thomas and I do the same things every weekend," Jennifer said. "Do you ever think back to the days before you were married, when you were going out and having fun? I was never at home. Not long ago I dreamed that I was sitting at home waiting for the phone to ring—I was still single—and it never rang. I dreamed I asked my mother if I was getting ugly. 'I haven't had a date in so long,'" Jennifer sighed, as in her dream. "Then I woke up, and that was how I felt—that I hadn't had a date or any fun in *so* long. I told Mama about my dream, and Thomas heard me. Of course, he didn't understand. He acted hurt; anyway he sulked all evening." She became alarmed at how she had let herself go. "Don't get me wrong—it's not that I don't *love* Thomas and all that, I'm perfectly happy. It's just that..." Her voice trailed away and she lifted her hand gropingly.

"It's just that you haven't had a date in so long," Pearl finished sympathetically. "I know what you mean."

"Oh, you're finding out already?" Suzie purred happily.

Pearl was admitted to the company of wives, and they encouraged her to complain about her husband.

"Thomas never notices me," Jennifer said. "I could be choking to death, and he wouldn't notice. He used to be so affectionate, too, when we were going out together. When we were first married, he was so sweet. Now he never even listens to me."

Going back to the section, they stopped by Veronica's desk to see the pictures of her party. She bent down under her desk for her purse. *Cosmopolitan* and *Glamour* lay on her desk, each prominently featuring a sex article on the cover.

Pearl giggled. "Does anyone really care that much?" She blushed—they had found she could still blush—but she continued in the mood of their break-time talk, "Before you're married, it's this wonderful, romantic thing. It's going to be the biggest thrill of your life. Then after you're married it just wears down."

"Sometimes it wears down literally," Jennifer said, lifting her eyebrows archly.

They laughed at the allusion.

Veronica sat up with the envelope of pictures in her hand. Her face was as always, expressionless but knowing. They passed around the snapshots of the party.

Pearl looked at a picture of Jennifer and Thomas. "You're so little beside him."

"You see, it's true what I say. I can't get my arms around his waist."

Georgia threw her head back and cawed, "Yes, at the party I tried to put my arms around his waist, and I couldn't. Then," she paused and worked her eyebrows, "*Then* I took him into the bedroom to see if the other thing she says is true."

They laughed again.

The others walked to their desks, and Jennifer put the pictures in the envelope and gave it to Veronica.

"You ought to be careful how you talk," Veronica warned in a low voice. "They'll tell their husbands what you say. Someday one of the men will get high at a party and make some crack to Thomas. And that's when you get your little red head snatched bald."

"Is it any of your business, Veronica?"

"Sorry."

Jennifer entered her PIN and powered up her computer, but she was still too angry to think of work. Her eyes flickered over all the other clerks in the office, looking for someone to make a snide joke about. Jennifer drew her section into a little circle around herself by building a feeling of superiority, of exclusiveness. "*My* girls." They could always draw together by laughing at some other woman.

The clerks in another section went by on their way to break. They walked by Martha's section with sly side glances and smirks. Later, at the door, they looked over their shoulders and laughed.

"They're a funny bunch," Georgia said, wrinkling her unsubtle face in puzzlement.

"Those girls never do any work," Jennifer said. "They talk all the time. To them life is nothing but boys and dresses and makeup."

They saw Martha come out of Mr. Owens's office and then turn in the door to talk to him for a few more minutes.

Georgia moved her chair closer to Jennifer and lowered her voice. "Mr. Owens had her in there talking to her all day. I think things are coming to a head now."

Jennifer nodded gravely.

Her heart beat rapidly, to think that what she wanted might be done now. It was Friday, firing day. Clerks who were to be let go were fired at the last minute on Friday. When she first went to work, Jennifer had been shocked to learn there was no notice at all; but the section head of that time said, "If they gave her notice, think of all the damage she could do."

Martha came back to her desk, and Jennifer studied her covertly. Her plain, lined face was set rigidly about the mouth. Jennifer decided that Mr. Owens must have given her a severe lecture, even a warning. If that were true, she thought he would soon see that Jennifer would make a better section head.

Ten minutes before quitting time, Martha's phone rang.

"Yes, I will," she said into the receiver. "Jennifer," she said quietly, "that was Veronica. Mr. Owens wants to see you for a minute."

Jennifer walked slowly up that long row toward Mr. Owens's office. This was not the way it was supposed to be. She thought she caught glances from the clerks she passed on her long way to Mr. Owens's office, curious glances that quickly slipped away. Everyone knew. Everyone but her. How could they?

Everything was turned upside down. Feeling so upside down, seeing everything from that angle, Jennifer saw all at once what she had done wrong. She had tried to work it like high school. Being popular and important then meant getting your peers around you in a clique that was against the authorities. In an office, it was the opposite: you got in good with the authorities; your peers did not matter.

Even before she knocked on Mr. Owens's door, Jennifer had pitched her mind ahead to how she would work it right the next time. She did not feel bad about failing here. Everyone had to learn.

Marius Martin, Proletarian

Lita A. Kurth

"*To the executive director of XYZ,*
A bit about myself. I have studied revolutions and attended demonstrations, read books and written papers. I detest the bourgeoisie and capitalism in general which I hope will soon collapse. In the meantime, I need a job. Although I have no experience as a bank teller/clerk/call center representative, it is my sincere hope that you are desperate, or better yet, insane."

Marius balled up the draft and launched it into a corner of the kitchen. He set his elbows on the table, pushing the skin up his face with his hands. *C'est chien, cet situation*! And when he was done, he'd have to walk three kilometers to get those fucking letters printed since he didn't have a printer. And it might be a dead loss.

Time for a break. He fetched his tobacco and rolling papers and rolled a cigarette. One thing college had taught him was how to roll a nice tight…cigarette. He brought a kitchen chair out to the courtyard and sat in the sun facing away from the corner that smelled like cat piss. Unemployment was not terminal like cancer or a death in the family. It was a prison whose walls were cracked, therefore changeable, like the idea of his father returning. No, that was the wrong comparison altogether, completely depressing. Thank God he had no kids to abandon.

Marie's miniature rose plant bloomed, a riotous profusion of yellow, in a clay pot, its scent competing with the cat smell. That mother of his. He had to stop being a drain on her.

Marius savored the last of his cigarette, returned to the kitchen, and picked up the next job lead from the unemployment bureau. *Dear Mr. Managing Director.* God, he hated those titles. *Dear Mr. Managing Director, Who the hell do you think you are? Why does democracy go right out the window as soon as you start a job?* Delete.

Finally he finished a complete letter, relying heavily on the bland examples provided by the unemployment bureau. It was a Trojan horse, a filthy compromise with capitalist life, but he churned out five more and saved them on a CD. Now, on to the photocopier. To bolster himself, he left a message for his *camarade*, René. "*Salut toi*, how's it going? Capitalism's killing me. *À bientôt.*"

The walk was long and hot. An insipid girl at the counter wearing little spoon earrings, uttered nothing but the price, "*Deux Euros.*" Such was capitalist interaction. He came back sweaty and stood in the kitchen drinking water directly from a jar his mother kept in the fridge. To assuage his guilt, he wiped the jar's rim with a tea towel and refilled it. In the middle of his bedroom floor, he knew, were his weights, because he had put them there earlier, when he felt ambitious and planned to work out.

He sat on the sofa, feeling the lace doilies under his arms and behind his neck. It was home, but also alien. Clearing space on the coffee table, he rolled ten cigarettes, turned on the TV, and smoked one after another, watching a fitness program led by a buff woman with a husky voice. Off-camera, she had to be a smoker too.

Marius came home from filling out unemployment forms to find his good buddy René, the Womanizing Anarchist, on the sofa, relaxed, handsome, and messy-haired as usual. His mother, Marie, sat in the easy chair, looking refreshed in a yellow dress, darning a sock. For a moment, he felt like a man returning from work to his wife and kid, a kid who was supposed to leave home.

"*Salut!*" he called out briskly. After leaving the papers on his bed, he took a seat on the couch. "Want to do a practice interview?"

René set down one of Marie's best plates, the ones with poppies on them. It still held bread crumbs and a smear of Brie. "*D'accord.*" He raised his head and looked into the distance, giving the topic deep attention, then said, "What are your plans for the future?"

"To work hard and stay out of prison," Marie offered, looking up from her needle and sock. "It shows an honorable character."

René crossed his legs. One foot was bare. So it was Rene's sock his mother was darning. Something in this scenario irritated him though he couldn't say exactly what.

"To *écraser l'infâme!*" René recommended, calling up the ghost of Voltaire. "It's literate and clever too."

"I'll do the answers," Marius said. He went into the kitchen and poured himself a bigger than usual glass of wine. Several new bottles were pushed into the corner of the cupboard. Marius's irritation softened. Even with the wages of an assistant carpenter, Rene's generosity was inexhaustible.

René called out from the living room, "I have a couple more."

Marius re-entered. "*Allons-y, camarade.* Let's go."

René sat up stiffly and said through his nose, "Discuss your qualifications."

With aplomb, Marius replied, "My degree in history is a perfect match for your archives, which, if I'm not mistaken, are filled with historical materials waiting for the right eye to assess and organize them. That eye, *monsieur,* is mine." He pointed sagely to his right eye.

"*Eh, bien*," René continued. "Now tell me, young man, what makes you want to work here—in this reactionary backwater?"

Both he and Marius cracked up and Marie stopped darning and joined in with her light laugh. Marius held his glass out so it would spill on the stained rug, not the couch. He stood and proclaimed with raised fist, "I plan to overthrow this fascist stronghold from within! So hire me, damn you!"

"That is not an appealing response, young man," René said severely.

"*Pardonnez-moi, monsieur.*" Marius sank to his knees. "The truth is I want a job that's out of the rain and comes with low wages and possibly a computer but only so I can better serve my God, who is French, and this great French nation!"

"*Bienvenue, mon enfant.*" René made the sign of the cross over him. "Welcome. You are hired!"

Few trains travelled between Côte de Mer and Saint-Luc, none of them high speed. Marius felt like an undercover agent, sitting in the second car dressed in his re-tailored secondhand suit (courtesy of *Maman*'s sewing skills,) head carefully shaved and rubbed with oil. He opened a free newspaper, saving *l'Humanité* for the ride home. But he was too agitated to read. The train passed through dry chalky hills speckled with goats, little mountain towns. At the end of an hour, it pulled into Saint-Luc, more a stop than a station, and Marius stepped down into an obviously "nice" neighborhood. Not a dry leaf sullied the lawns, not a doorstep was left unscoured. Not a drop of oil dirtied a driveway. In a few blocks, he caught sight of the archives surrounded by a bland lawn and severely-pruned shrubbery.

Up the marble stairs he stepped, heart beating. Was this where he'd end up? He opened the big door. Immediately to his right was a wall of portraits. Some faces were fatter, some had beards, but they went on forever. *Merde.* The rich formed such a tiny minority, and yet you couldn't get away from them.

After making inquiries at the front desk, Marius was directed to the subterranean office of Hélène LaFrance, assistant chief archivist. He knocked, and a woman's voice said, "*Entrez, s'il vous plaît.*"

Marius opened the door—seemingly made of cardboard—and entered a room whose concrete floor was covered by a Persian rug. On the walls were framed prints of classic, not quite pornographic Indian erotica featuring ultra-athletic participants with excellent posture. A lean, stylish woman, wearing a red suit, stood up from behind a desk.

"Marius? *Enchantée.*" She shook his hand, then waved him into a worn easy chair. Static electricity tickled his legs as the back of his pants legs slid against the Chinese silk.

"Have a seat. I brought it from home. At my own expense. Naturally." She rolled her desk chair toward the squat bamboo table beside Marius's chair and stretched out her long muscled legs in high heels. Marius glanced away.

On Hélène's desk were two mugs, a carafe, and an art moderne cream and sugar set. She reached over. "Coffee?"

Steam rose from the carafe with a rich roasted scent as Hélène poured them each a cup. Marius helped himself generously to cream and sugar. If he didn't get the job, he could almost make up the cost of the train ticket in coffee. But already he was thinking that an hour or two with Hélène was not as bad as many things he could name.

"I see your specialization was history," she said, looking over a file on her lap. "Which areas did you cover?"

"Seventeenth to twentieth century Europe."

Hélène uncrossed and recrossed her legs. "That's a large span. Any particular focus?"

Marius paused. Job or truth. He settled for a half-truth. "I focused on working-class movements."

"So you're a Romantic?" She gave him a quick look.

"I consider myself a realist." Marius held his ground.

Hélène considered this. "I suppose we all do. Personally, I never met a reality I liked." She continued briskly, "Well, let me tell you about the collections."

She listed titles such as le Baron de Frenedy, and other names that Marius associated with industrial products. He noticed a little red pipe on her desk. In the air was a hint of pipe tobacco.

"Let me give you a brief tour."

They took the elevator upstairs to the ground floor. Marius followed Hélène until she paused in front of a massive glass case. "On permanent display is a collection of seventy-nine porcelain kittens given to us by the daughter of Paul Louis the first, a shipping entrepreneur and major donor," she said.

"You're joking!" Marius burst out, forgetting himself.

"Sadly, no. It is of zero artistic and historical importance," she pronounced, "but endowments are endowments." The second floor held dioramas, short men of the past in noble poses with dogs and horses. The third floor held one minor gallery of local watercolors with the rest devoted to offices including Photocopying and the Mail room. In a hallway on the fourth floor, a woman wearing a necklace with a gold cross and gold-cross earrings looked fiercely at Marius's shaved head.

"Corinne," Hélène said, "Allow me to introduce Marius who's interviewing for the clerk job."

Corinne gave him a limp hand.

"And up we go to the Electronic Media room. There's one more floor but that's for the Director and his many activities requiring a penthouse view."

They descended on the slow elevator to Hélène's office, and she brought her chair back behind her desk. "Now you have an inkling of our collection," she said, her eyes crinkling at the edges. "Any thoughts on augmenting or maximizing the use of it?"

The pen ready in her hand made Marius's nervous, but he seized the moment. "Actually, yes. Several trade unions have headquarters in Côte de Mer."

"Do they?"

"Yes. They might lend us documents, photos, banners, things like that from years past."

"Interesting. Go on."

"We could set up an exhibit on labor history that could open May 1st. You know, Jean Jaurès was involved in labor movements not too far from here." *Nothing too radical in that,* Marius thought. A broken fluorescent light buzzed.

Hélène folded her arms and stretched her legs out to the side. "This is not exactly Paris."

Marius gave her a questioning look.

"Who in Saint-Luc would be interested?"

Marius flushed. "Well, union members, for one."

Hélène looked down at an imaginary list. "Let's see. How many union members do we have on our board of directors and major donor list?" She looked up brightly. "Zero."

"But this *is* a state archive," Marius protested.

It was Hélène's turn to look blank.

"Isn't the state supposed to represent the people?" Marius asked.

Hélène's stylishly-coiffed head bent forward as she laughed. "In theory, my friend. Unfortunately we live in reality." With great good humor, she poured herself another half-cup, gesturing to invite Marius. "Any other ideas?"

"Not at the moment," Marius said shortly. He poured coffee, the rest of the cream, and a heaping spoonful of sugar into his cup.

"Actually, unions might have materials of interest," Hélène continued cordially. "I wonder if they have any photos of old buildings. We have an architecture nut on the board." The heating system came on, surrounding them with a humming roar without warming the room. She glanced at her red pipe. "We operate here on the principle that hearing the heat is just as good as feeling it," and continued, "What do you do in your free time?"

René's likely answer came to mind: "Drink. Go to strip clubs and protest marches. Actively work for the overthrow of this stinking government." Marius said he followed national affairs to some extent, walked a lot, listened to music, and was active in an organization that aided the poor.

"Have you by chance held any leadership positions?"

"I was chair of my college commu—dorm," Marius said, replacing the word halfway through. He did not add that it was a rotating position, the opposite of coveted.

"Have you ever been responsible for organizing and assessing large amounts of material?"

Marius and René had together organized all the communal rent payments into Valid, Overdue, Partial, and Bounced. Marius had created and posted on each floor a much-ignored list of people and their respective weekly chores. "I kept track of some of our activities, income, and expenses at the dorm."

"Very good."

"And I am secretary and chair of the outreach committee of this organization I mentioned."

"Oh yes? What's it called?" Hélène's bright hard eyes regarded him.

Marius said in as natural a tone as he could, "CIASSG."

"CIASSG? Is it an acronym?"

Three thoughts whizzed through Marius's brain: One: it was going acceptably well up to this point, but that could end with the words *Anarcho-Syndicalist*. Two: people can read a lie in your eyes, and Three: maybe they can't.

"I'm not sure what it stands for," he said, "but it's basically charitable."

"Perhaps in the same sense that this archive is," Hélène said, arching her eyebrows. "More coffee?"

Just as Marius had always suspected, you succeed in this capitalist world by lying and cheating. Friday morning, he answered his cell phone, and when he came out to the living room where his mother was talking, again, with René, he said, "*Maman*. I got the job at the Saint-Luc Archives."

Marius's marvelous position at the Saint-Luc Archives came with a desk wedged into a basement hallway and archive boxes stacked five high, filled with dusty mementos of Saint-Luc's lusterless nobility and single-minded moneymakers. Some items Marius had to photocopy, some he had to scan, and some label and file. Then it all had to be entered into a database.

The first week he was hired, Marius felt lucky to have a job at all, but as day after day he pulled out rusty staples with a staple remover and carefully flattened newspaper clippings that had been folded for decades to scan or Xerox them, his sense of good fortune melted away.

Marie, however, remained ecstatic. Usually modest, shunning the evil eye of envy, she made an exception in this case and crowed about Marius's work in the "archives (a magical insider word she never tired of using) at Saint-Luc!" Swiftly chopping onions, cutting oysters from the shell, and de-veining shrimp on a cutting board, she turned a smug face to her son. The bangs of her new youthful haircut were streaked with scarlet. "And they said your education wouldn't pay off!"

"How wrong they were, *Maman*." Marius kissed the top of her shiny hair, keeping his complaints silent. "Thanks to you."

Now he could pay back her generosity, buying fine chocolates instead of stealing them, providing all the ingredients for bouillabaisse and the company to consume it: himself and, *naturellement,* René.

Marie and Marius's collective of two saved money on rent, heating, and TV. Who needed further proof of the superiority of collective action? Was it embarrassing to live with his mother, he quizzed himself, sitting at his gray desk sneezing over another box? *Pas du tout!* Theirs was a skirmish in the war on bourgeois individualism. And of course René too was part of that fight.

To keep himself awake, Marius mentally edited the curator's notes. *Gross Excesses of Capitalism* was the label he bestowed on one exhibit. He helpfully typed those words into the computer index for those few visitors who might be interested in the truth.

Hélène gave him the go-ahead to contact unions in Côte de Mer, and he did—with the result that union banners went on display in an exhibit entitled *Textiles of Bygone Years,* and photos of striking workers were cropped to maximize the stonework in the buildings and the wrought-iron factory gates (locked against them.) Although no union members apparently had time to visit the exhibit, Marius placed an anonymous note in the suggestion box on their behalf: *Shouldn't the focus be on these historic events and not the raw materials?* If anyone read his protest, he never heard of it.

But these frustrating projects were delightful in comparison to other duties. Each afternoon, for several hours Marius photocopied, preserving on long-lasting archival paper, the crumbling marriage proposals, yellowed deeds, and cracked telegrams of the locally important. First, he had to flatten the wrinkled or crumpled paper onto the glass, then slide his hand out carefully as he brought the lid down to hold it in place. And then he waited. The photocopier harrumphed as if about to begin an enormous meal; its green light flashed, the machine digested, and slowly, slowly, slowly the copy emerged at the other end. During that endless minute, Marius gazed at the wall, the institutional clock, the calendar of amateur landscapes, desperate for stimulus. After a half hour, he felt his blood pressure double. If only he could read a book! But Xeroxing was the perfect torture: long enough to seem interminable, but too short to allow any other activity. In the last hour he was a zombie, moving automatically. Near the end of two hours, he operated with the mental acuity of a mollusk.

Halfway through the afternoon's quota, Marius had to go to the supply cupboard for more paper. As he returned, arms stacked high, two board members walked past, tanned, in exquisite suits, talking of "Tahiti" and "amortization." One cut through his path, making him rock back on his feet. Without begging pardon, the man continued, as if he'd cut off a stray dog.

Marius burned. Staring at the man's back, he telepathically sent an array of sharp knives whizzing into it. Back at the Xerox machine, he turned the ink intensity to ultra-black. He should Xerox the whole file that way and waste a toner cartridge. To ease his tension, he rotated his shoulders. For now, he reminded himself, he had income, CIASSG, and comrades, and one day, by god, the revolution would come.

Back at Marius's desk, the phone rang, making him jump.

"I've got an urgent project for you, Marius," Hélène said. She sounded none too happy. "Could you come to my office, please?"

Happy to meet with his attractive boss, Marius dusted his clothes off and made for the staircase.

He could barely get inside Hélène's office for the boxes piled up. She waved at him over the top of a six-box stack. "Another stupid Paul Louis project," she grumbled. "All his family junk, which he considers worthy of preservation. Would you take these down to your desk and divide it into three groups: *merde absolute*, *merde probable*, and *possibly useful*. *Croyez-moi,* the third pile will be small. Be brutal!"

Energized by the prospect of a task more demanding than Xeroxing and filing, Marius went to find a cart and brought the boxes down the elevator. The physical work revived him. Back at his desk, he opened the first box: an 8 x 10 of a baron in front of an antique black Rolls grinned at him. "Don't tempt me," he told it. A second later, he said, "You tempted me," and ripped it right down the middle. That first tear was delightful, the next, less so. Now that it was too late, he wondered if the photo might be valuable. It *did* look old. Hurriedly, he tore the rest into microscopic bits and hid them in the bottommost drawer of his desk.

Though the revolution took its time, afternoon break did arrive. Pulling his cigarettes out of his jacket pocket, Marius hurried down the marble steps of the archive and into the "park" outside, a span of grass so perfect it could have been computer-generated. At regular intervals, rows of yew trees were pruned to exact squares and circles. What a street. He was surprised the clouds above weren't uniformly shaped. He sat down on a clean hard bench and pulled out a cigarette.

The days of unalienated labor at Jacques' bar were over. Now, first, again, and always, there was the archives. It amused Hélène to watch for projects that might interest Marius— easy enough since no one else wanted them.

"Here you go, my red friend. *Vive la révolution*," she said, dumping a dusty archive box on his desk. Inside were clippings of factory fires and bread lines, group photos of maids, dock workers, and miners.

Labeling the backs of pictures, Marius's resentment coagulated. Official archives policy was to name only the notable. "The Baron de Frenedy" for example, might be the title of a photo featuring the baron and twenty anonymous men with picks, shovels, and worn boots. Beneath bushy eyebrows, intelligence, character, and, at times, menace shone forth. Baggy clothes couldn't hide stupendous muscles. Who had they been? What was their story? He carefully typed on the label, "The Baron de Frenedy and those who made him rich" or "Regrettably anonymous but important members of the proletariat with the capitalist R. Franc".

One afternoon Hélène came to his desk, the side of her mouth scrunched with disappointment, and handed Marius a folder.

"Marius," she said, "Look at this. The date is cut off. And this one's smudged. I'm afraid you'll have to do them over. Archival bond is expensive." She stood beside him for a moment in her Chanel-ish suit and stiletto pumps.

Marius shifted a paper to cover the semicircles of dried coffee on his desk which only drew attention to them. "Okay." he said. "Sorry about that."

She was right, and he was embarrassed. But frustrated too. How was it humanly possible to pay attention to such insignificant details? He devised a plan. After inspecting each piece with exaggerated care, as if adjudicating fine wines, he adjusted his glasses and raised his chin. If the quality warranted, he placed the copy in a folder covered with gold stars labeled "Bravissimo!" If marred or sloppy, he let his head loll forward in exaggerated shame and slid the offending paper into the recycling bin making the sign of the cross over it.

Corinne, the director's secretary, came up behind him as he did this. "What on earth are you doing?"

"Xeroxing obviously," he replied, praying his face was not turning red. She was a lumpenproletarian if ever there was one. When the board members arrived, she turned her heavily made-up face to them like a sunflower to the sun, simpering, "Can I bring you anything, M.Louis? M. Barry?"

He had overheard her saying, "Marius takes forever on the Xerox machine!"

Well, you couldn't have it both ways. Either speed or quality.

Today she said, "How much longer are you going to take? I have important materials for the board meeting to do."

Marius wanted to say, "In that case, the rest of the day." Instead he said, not hiding his annoyance, "I'll be finished in a half hour, Corinne." However, before ten more minutes had passed, the copier emitted a burning odor, five or six red lights flashed, and it stopped working. Jubilantly, Marius placed a call to the service person. Corinne's work for the board was *completement foutu*, screwed and it wasn't his fault.

The voice on the other end asked in a condescending way whether the machine was plugged in, and Marius struggled not to lose patience with a fellow member of the working class. "Yes. My guess is it overheated"

"Ah. You may need a total replacement."

"How long will that take?"

"Up to two weeks, depending."

Marius felt the joy of the alienated worker released from routine by forces beyond his control. Suppressing the bounce in his step, he knocked on Hélène's door and told her the news.

She raised her fists in frustration, the fluorescent light glinting off her orange nails. "Two weeks? Those lazy bums! We'll have to take it down the street. Marius, would you mind terribly?" Her phone rang and she picked it up. "Oh yes? Well, Marius's going to a copy shop. No problem." To Marius she said, "Could you drop by Corinne's and pick up some urgent materials for the board meeting?"

Ten minutes later, Marius grabbed his files and that *conne*, Corinne's work, an umbrella, and a handful of CIASSG flyers he had copied at work. Up he rose on the freight elevator to freedom. In spite of the sky full of bruised clouds and his thankless mission, it was wonderful to see trees instead of walls, to breathe air that moved, to hear birds instead of the ventilation system. It was wonderful to stop and smoke one.

Out on the street, he passed a laundromat, popped in and left flyers on the folding tables. He also left several at a hairdresser's, dropping them into the rack with the fashion magazines. In his experience it was best not to ask permission. And though it was a couple blocks out of his way, he left a stack at the public library.

His hand was on the door of a photocopy place, when he saw a flyer for LePen taped to it! He let go the door as if it were ablaze and, with no alternative in mind, walked swiftly on.

Rain began to fall in fat, angry drops. He opened his umbrella and clamped the files tightly under his arm. Twenty blocks further, after going up hill, passing gas stations, houses, and fearing he was leaving the business district forever, he found a photocopying place that didn't advertise its fascism.

On the way back with twice the load, his arm ached and he had to duck under an awning and clamp the heavy package under the other armpit. It was now pouring. The street beside the sidewalk was a swift-moving brook that turned into a lake where driveways met the street. The thrill of being outdoors had lessened considerably. Mistaking a deep puddle for a shallow one, Marius stepped in, filling his shoe with freezing water. Blocks later, passing a trashcan near the hairdressers, he caught sight of something yellow. His flyers. Not only discarded but torn in half. The rain fell harder and colder.

Tired and soaked after his forty-block walk, Marius left the copies in Hélène's inbox and returned to his desk. An hour of work remained. The warmth from his walk gave way to a sodden chill worsened by a vent directly above his desk that blasted down cold air. Waving his arms briskly, he walked the dim aisles, one foot wetter and colder than the other. He passed long shelves of archive boxes and heard the stultifying hum of a heating system bringing heat to everyone but him. He thought of Mao's Long March, the Siege of Leningrad, the revolutionary volunteers marching on foot from Marseilles to Paris.

When the clock struck five, Marius, in spite of rain and cold, had already forged his way to the train station for the commute home.

A Real Tear

Anne Shewring

It started as a joke.
No, that's not right. It started as a regular piece of work, the kind of project we discussed every week at our Monday status meeting.
At that time, and I'm talking about the early 'nineties now, there were three of us in the Donor Development Department of *Save the Kids*, or *S the K*, as it was written on our pink and blue headed paper. Jed Norris was our boss. If you're in the business, you might know his name. He was real direct marketeer, worked for Sloss, McNally, Rice, who did all the big catalogues and insurance companies. Then he spent time with, of all people, the Conservative Party, which the top brass at *S the K* considered enough of a charitable experience to give him full reign over our direct marketing work. Personally, I thought it made him deeply suspect but, over drinks in the pub one night, he claimed his time at Smith Square wasn't a political decision, just a career move. Bollocks, I'd said. They're a bunch of money grabbing has-beens and you worked for them. Shame on you. He didn't care though. Jed was part of a trend, a migration of people from the corporate sector to the charitable one, nobly bringing their finely honed business skills to the not-for-profit world. Apparently, so these guys argued, charities needed to operate more like companies. They needed to be more professional. The fact that most charities were picking up the shit created by the failure of the free market to—what was the phrase?—trickle down—was by the by.
I digress...The *S the K* Board loved him, maybe because he wore a suit and played golf, or more likely, because half the Board were donors to the Tory Party and just got over-excited when they saw his CV.
After Jed, there came Martin and myself. We did all the real work. Martin in particular was a star. To be honest, I was a little in love with him. Just a little. He looked like a young Martin Sheen only taller. When we'd been in Birmingham the year before at the National Convention, we'd almost slept together. Well, there was sod all else to do in that stinking Metropolitan Hotel, stuck out in the middle of God knows where, drinks priced through the roof and only a thousand other fundraisers for company. I was certainly game, and so was Martin until, mid snog, he

suddenly had an attack of conscience. It wouldn't be fair on either of us, he'd said, being that he already had a girlfriend. I could have argued the point but I was too drunk and so the moment had passed. A shame really.

Martin and I were a pretty good team though. We'd been together for a couple of years when all this happened, and it would be reasonable to say that we shared something special, professionally speaking. I only needed to glance at him in a meeting and I could tell what was going through his mind, what he made of the work being presented or the state of our donor profile. And we both shared a healthy contempt for Jed and his corporate ideas, even if much of what he said actually made sense. It was our job to obstruct, like Old Labour or the Unions.

Before the era of Jed, we'd had a pretty standard approach to our donors, mailing them four times a year, plus the Christmas catalogue. Everyone got the same thing, no matter how much they gave. Jed put a stop to all that. He said that we should be segmenting our lists and mailing donors at least ten times a year. That's too much, we'd argued. Our donors will protest. They'll think it's a waste of our—their—money. No, Jed had countered. They'll think they don't like it and some will even complain but, you see, it will bring in more money. And, fair play to him, it did.

The only problem with all this (assuming that we never considered pissing off a large percentage of our donors to be a problem, and apparently we didn't) was that we needed to keep coming up with new and urgent subjects for our increasing output of appeals. That was a challenge, and why we needed the help of Janice and Carla from *Rolf & Mayer*.

"I've brought in a few samples of mail-shots we've been working on for other charities," Janice had said at that Monday meeting, spreading many branded, window envelopes over the table. "Obviously, they are not competing organizations to *S the K*, but they may give us a few jumping off points."

"How about another case study?" I said. "We still haven't used *Emma*, and I think she's pretty good."

Emma wasn't a real person. She was what P.R. called, 'a composite.' Her story was cobbled together from the real life tales our project workers heard on a daily basis: sexual abuse, poverty, a life on the streets. The photograph that accompanied the case study wasn't genuine either. The soft-eyed teenager in the picture, her face long with sorrow, she was a model made up to look like a victim. We had no choice. It would not have been appropriate to show any of the real children we helped. Plus, many of them, particularly the teenagers, were far too unappealing, wearing the marks of deprivation on their faces, bad skin, poor teeth or, worse, defiance.

"We've done case histories, over and over," said Jed. "We need something new."

Carla reached for a pack with her long, sharply manicured hands and briskly spread its contents over the meeting room table. "We did this recently for Dignity in Age Overseas," she said, tapping an envelop with a plum colored finger nail. "It contains this piece of plastic, which, when you look through it, gives you an idea of what it's like to have cataracts. Simple, but effective and the ask was for five pounds to fund a cataract operation, five pounds for the gift of sight."

We all took turns to hold the plastic square to our eyes and marvel at how little we could see.

"That's really excellent," said Jed, peering like a pirate. "D'you have the response rate for this?" he asked, removing the plastic from his eye.

Janice pushed a sheet of figures around the table. "And here's the same data when we used it with cold donors." Cold donors are people who have never supported the charity in question before. Usually, we'd acquire their names by swapping with other, similar charities, our donors' details for theirs. This was before all the data protection stuff we have today, before the prevalence of the little, 'no I don't want to receive information from other organizations' tick box which, I might add, has almost brought the noble industry of direct marketing to its knees.

Jed studied the figures, rubbing his chin as he took in the data. "This is good stuff," he said. "Really, impressive." He looked around the table, at each one of us individually. "So, come on team, what do we have that could work in the same way?"

Janice and Carla glanced at each other. They'd come armed with an idea. Janice produced a new envelope and unpacked it, placing a mailing piece and a yellow wax crayon on the table.

"Crayons," she said. "We thought about crayons."

Martin shifted in his chair. "I'm not sure I get it," he said.

Janice grinned. "We'd put a crayon in each pack, together with a drawing from a child, a picture illustrating their plight. You know, the kind of thing a psychologist might get a child to do. 'Can you draw how you see your disreputable family?' or 'Can you draw how it feels when you are left on your own?' The picture we'll actually include will be bleak, dark and angry, very disturbing. Then the recipient will find the crayon, which will be nice and bright, yellow or orange, and the message will be, 'Change the color of a child's life by making a donation.'" Janice sat back in her chair and folded her arms. She was deeply satisfied.

"It sounds a bit elaborate," I said. "I'm just not sure the donors will get it."

Jed nodded. "I agree. It's ok, but it's not, 'This is how it looks when you can't see.'"

Carla protested. "We think..."

"No," said Jed. "We need something sharper. Come on, people. What symbolizes suffering children? What says 'abuse' to our donors?"

Martin and I exchanged a look.

"Did you have a particular kind of abuse in mind?" I asked.

"Something that works," he said.

We sat in silence for a moment. "It's not easy to package 'neglect'," said Martin eventually.

"No, ok," said Jed. "But what about physical..."

"Or sexual?" I added. "The mind boggles."

Janice and Carla exchanged an unhappy glance. They were still sore about their crayon proposal.

"No, but you have something," said Jed.

"Oh, come on," said Martin, sitting forward in his chair. "You want us to put semen samples in tiny plastic bags, the wank of abusers, 'This is what it looks like.' That kind of thing?"

I started to laugh.

"Just not sure how we'll package it," said Martin.

"Or get enough," I added. "We'd have to go to a sperm bank, maybe. Would that work?"

"Because, of course, it doesn't need to be genuine abusers semen."

"Just composite semen, semen that represents the experiences of a number of abused children."

"Stop it," said Janice. "This is horrible."

"Yes, people," said Jed. "Obviously, we can't do that."

Martin and I laughed again, knowing that Jed's objections were more practical than moral. He just didn't see it as a money raiser.

I cleared my throat. "Well, what about tears," I said.

And right there, that was the joke that started it.

"Tears?" Janice didn't look any happier.

"The tears of a child," I went on, still smiling.

Martin started to laugh again.

Jed held up his hand. "No, wait. I think you have something."

Carla and Janice shot each other a look.

"Jed..." Martin began, but our boss shook his head.

"What could be more moving? Who could not put their hand in their pocket when faced with the tears of a child? It's brilliant." There was an eerie look in Jed's eyes. I think it unnerved the girls from *Rolf & Mayer*. The whole tear idea had made their crayon plan look hopelessly innocent.

Martin cleared his throat. "Let's just run with this for a minute. How would we collect these 'tears'?"

"We could poke children until they cry," I said. "I'm sure if we offered enough money, parents would be volunteering kids left, right and centre. I can name you half dozen members of staff right in this building who'd go for it."

Carla looked concerned. "But wouldn't that be abuse in itself? I'm really not sure donors would like that."

Jed rolled his eyes, although it wasn't clear whether this was in exasperation at Carla's failure to get the joke, or in frustration at the prospect of donors and their pesky objections to children being repeatedly poked.

"Obviously, we can't hurt real children. That would be totally unacceptable," he said, eventually.

"We are still joking, aren't we?" asked Janice. She looked at each of us, a degree of panic in her expression. "Tell me, no one is seriously considering this idea."

"I've said already," said Jed. "Collecting real tears is not possible."

"No, I mean…"

"But," went on Jed, railroading through Janice's objections, "Why couldn't we use salt water, a couple of drops of salt water in a small plastic bag?"

"No," I said, "a plastic bag wouldn't work. But what about one of those little plastic vials, the kind of thing used for perfume samples?"

"Excellent," said Jed.

Martin sucked in his breath as if weighing up the pros and cons.

"What would the unit cost be on something like that?" he asked, turning to the agency ladies. They looked nervously one to the other.

"I've really no idea," said Janice.

"Well, more or less than the plastic cataract thing?"

"Emm, well, I suppose the vial would be the expensive item. It would need to be airtight to stop the tears, oh, sorry, the salt water, leaking out. And then there'd be the usual art work, copywriting costs."

"It would be light though," I added, thinking of mailing prices.

"We might need some new photography," said Martin. "A picture of a super, ultra-sad child. Followed by shots of the same child now super, ultra-happy as result of *S the K's* wonderful and unique help."

"Never use the word 'unique'," I said. "Donors don't like it. They know perfectly well that very little is truly 'unique'."

"I think this bloody well might be," said Jed, a note of triumph in his voice. "Can you imagine what kind of coverage this will get, not just in the charity press but all over?" He must have sensed hesitancy from *Rolf & Mayer*. "Oh come on. Janice, Carla, you're professionals. You know that what we're about is innovation, eh?" He picked up the piece of cataract plastic, gave it a contemptuous look and threw it across the table. "You guys want to make your name? You'll need to be a whole lot more daring than fuzzy bits of plastic. Let's face it, blind old people just don't kick ass in the same way as sad kids."

Thinking back, we should have all walked out then and there. But you have to understand that those were different times, governed by a different set of rules. Or so it seems now.

To my credit, I did say, "And, of course, this appeal will raise some serious and much needed funds for neglected and abused children," and everyone in the room nodded gravely, although I suspect we were all really thinking about next year's Direct Marketing Awards and the coveted silver envelop for best charity-agency partnership.

"Will you get this past the Senior Management Team?" Martin asked.

Jed waved this away. "You leave them to me. Anyway, it's an operational decision, and I'm Head of this particular operation." He didn't need to say anymore. If we guessed that he wouldn't apprise them of the plan until it was a *fait accompli*, no one said anything.

There was a moment of conspiratorial silence. I suspect we shared something of the same sick thrill experienced by governments on the eve of war. If just one of us in that room had said no then, we would never have gone ahead. I mean, yes, we were all Direct Marketeers, but we were still people, and, let's face it, three of us were professionally charitable.

But we didn't. Instead, we doled out jobs, worked out a mailing schedule and a donor breakdown and even did an initial income forecast. When we left the meeting, it was with thoughts of sourcing tiny plastic vials and drafting appropriate copy.

The funny thing is that when the packs went out I was genuinely proud of them, and, to begin with, there were hardly any complaints. The day the mailing went out, Martin and I went for a drink to celebrate; three bottles of Californian Chardonnay later we ended up back at my flat and hey ho, it was Birmingham all over again, but this time Martin didn't mention his girlfriend. Maybe that was symbolic of how far we'd fallen. I don't know. At the time, it just seemed like we were having fun.

That didn't last and by the following Monday, the press had got hold of a pack. Donors were apparently outraged, as were our celebrity patrons, who resigned in droves, and, more embarrassingly, so were our front line project workers, who popped up all over the show to decry modern fundraising techniques. That made me cross. They never complained when the money was rolling in, but the minute there was a whiff of reporter and a brouhaha, a chance to get their picture in paper, they were all up on their moral high-horses.

Jed had to resign, of course, although he found a new job pretty quickly. While people appeared to disapprove, those in the business admired his balls. He went to work for some finance company. *S the K* sacked *Rolf & Meyer*, while Martin and I kept our heads down and hoped for the best, although, in the end, we both moved on too. I heard that Martin married his girlfriend and moved to Birmingham.

I'm no longer in direct marketing, but not because I regret the *Real Tear* pack; on the contrary, I think it was a landmark piece of work, and not just because of the government legislation it prompted. To be honest, everything I worked on after that seemed horribly dull in comparison. The new agency did something with free pens in the next mailing but really, who wants a stupid cheap biro? That doesn't get the message across. Maybe people need to be more honest. At the end of the day, it is about children's tears, and if you can't face that truth then you've no business working for a charity.

Pushing the Knives

Dustin Hoffman

He's supposed to be pushing the knives. Thrusting them up to the humming tube lighting of the supermarket so the polished steel sparkles, so you can almost hear the reflected twinkle slide across the blade. But gazing into vast ceilings, pure white girders grazed by boxed and shrink-wrapped bulk products towering in twenty-foot-tall aisles, makes him dizzy. He'd prefer to keep his head down. He should be showing off the sexy curves of the fillet knife, flaunting the no-nonsense power of the bulk cleaver. Instead, he runs his fingers over the name tag pinned to his white chef's uniform complete with the white hat that poofs at the top like an atomic mushroom cloud, his thinning hairline tightly concealed underneath the explosion. His name tag is bright gold. The grooves of his name are sharp and cut skillfully, deeply. It reads "Wyatt." But how can he live up to "Wyatt" engraved in gold, sparkling in tube lights like the knives should be?

A woman with short brown hair barely stretched into a ponytail and wearing gray sweatpants pushes a cart toward his stand. One of the wheels squeaks shrilly. It reminds Wyatt of the tenor in his trainer's voice, the guy with the sharp triangle of black facial hair below his lower lip who wore the managerial navy blue chef uniform. His two weeks of training just ended yesterday, but he can still hear his trainer shrieking, *This is your target audience! Mid-thirties, slightly overweight, listless eyes that wander over shrink-wrapped ground chuck looking like red brains. Reel her in, Wyatt. Make the sale!*

But he can't bring himself to do it. He is a pathetic salesman. Shy, terrible at talking. He feels lost in a forest of aisles the height of redwoods. He's glad to be standing near the meat, near squat refrigerated troughs less daunting. Still, in front of him, colorful displays and barcodes stack to the ceiling, obscuring his vision, and he wonders if there are actually more people somewhere in this store. Is this lady in her sweatpants his lone audience member, his only shot? If he had any courage he might scale an aisle, scout from pinnacle heights perched atop two hundred-unit diaper boxes, and proclaim his sales pitch.

Dustin Hoffman —

The woman is close now. Almost to the steaks, near where his promotional stand sits, painted blue with a big, yellow lightning bolt and a sign that reads THUNDER BLADES: STRIKE CULINARY PERFECTION. He wishes he had the wit and intensity his sign promises. She inches toward him, squeaking closer. This is his big moment, his first potential sale. He thinks back to his training manual, how he should approach this customer.

Ma'am, a moment of your precious time?
(Don't wait for her. Take it!)

Has your cutlery gone dull, uninspired, pointlessly pathetic? This is a common tragedy that befalls nearly nine of every ten households in America. A fact!
(Keep it up. Don't relent now. You've got the facts down, now show her the blades.)

Ha! Your troubles are solved!
(Brandish the Electroshocker Chef's Knife. But don't brandish too much; you don't want her to think you're a serial killer.)

On this planet, you won't find a sharper, more-balanced knife. As if forged in the fires of Olympus, it slices with incomparable power and accuracy. But I could talk all day. The proof is in the results. Observe as the Electroshocker slices with perfection. There! Impossible? No. Amazing! And so easy a child could do it.
(Note: don't sell knives to children under the age of ten. These things are sharp!)

A finer edge and I'd be splitting atoms. But there's more. So much more...
(Atta boy! That's how we do it!)

But he can't begin the pitch, can't dredge the words from his quivering abdomen. Standing so close to the steak troughs is freezing him. The frigid temperatures that keep grade A meat fresh stop him cold. This seems like a valid excuse. He must remember to not be so hard on himself, but he always is.

And now she's front and center, her eyes looking him up and down. Him, not the knives, up and down. He straightens his posture, pushes out his flat pectorals, tries to smile with his yellowed teeth. It makes him worry. In training, they explained how important appearances are, how you're not just selling products, but yourselves. He remembers how desperately he needs tooth whiteners and Chuck Norris' ab machine. She looks away. He can't blame her. Her cart squeaks onward toward the ice cream and frozen key-lime pies. She is gone. No sale. No commission. No money for whiter teeth and abs of steel. It's okay; he'll get the next one. He's still learning.

"Why didn't you get *that* one?" His supervisor, Lee, bursts from his hiding spot at the endcap of the cereal aisle, scattering cardboard toucans across the tile floor. He is a good hider; Wyatt didn't even know he was there. It's an impressive skill. Lee is a fat man, but short. He must have rolled up like a hedgehog to stow himself in the bottom shelf behind all those cereal boxes.

"You didn't say a damn word." Lee is breathing hard. Droplets of sweat form on his round, bald, baby-faced red head. Wyatt doesn't mean or want to disappoint him. He wants Lee to like him. But Lee will never be his friend until he starts making sales.

"Are you at least sawing the sledgehammer?"

Wyatt completely forgot about the sledgehammer. He fidgets with his name tag.

"Well, dammit." Lee pushes Wyatt out from the knife stand. He reaches under for the sledgehammer and thunks it down on the stand's massive oak cutting board. "You should be. You should have worked up a nice pile of shavings at this point. Start sawing for chrissake."

Wyatt unsheathes the serrated knife, the Thundertooth. Why didn't he remember the sledgehammer? It's sure to draw in customers. How could he be so absent-minded? He draws the blade across the head of the sledge a few times, a few more. Metal sledge shavings sprinkle the cutting board, his fingers, his hands.

"That's the ticket! Show them what the knives can do. How they'll never go dull, even when it's steel against steel."

Lee squeezes himself back into the bottom shelf of the end cap. He indeed does look like a balled-up hedgehog—tucking in his knees, clutching them tight with his short, hairy arms. His face is less red now, but he still looks nervous. He has two teenage girls and a baby boy on the way. His kids' welfare depends on the sheer selling prowess of his regional salesmen, and thinking about this makes Wyatt more nervous. Many people depend on him. Lee's daughters will not wear designer clothes, hence never find lovers. The baby will not utter genius giggles at educational mobiles and will grow up dull-eyed, uninspired, and stupid. Wyatt hates the pressure piling up like the metal shavings. A light gray line forms across the sledge head, where metal meets metal. A layer of shavings covers the stand top.

"Good. Great. Go get em, Wyatt. We're all behind you, rooting for you," Lee says, balled-up in his hiding spot. "Now, before you get too far, cover me up with the cereal boxes again."

Wyatt picks the toucans off the floor and stacks them around Lee in a colorful, tropical igloo. He leaves a slot for Lee to peep through, even though he doesn't want to. He'd rather not have Lee watching him so closely. His presence is pressure, a reminder of all the lives at stake. He focuses on sawing.

He wonders if he's really cut out for this vocation. Before Thunder Blades, he worked in a nursing home called The Best is Yet to Come. The residents thrived off his listening skills, stringing their stories along for hours. So many stories. But too many of the residents died in a freak outbreak of heart attacks and strokes and aneurysms. Everyone's coronary systems just stopped working one week, twenty-three all on one Wednesday. Clogged up or burst until the nursing home staff needed to be cut in half. These things happen. Hearts explode or just stop. There was no one to blame, Wyatt convinced himself, but secretly didn't believe. There must have been more he could have done, more stories he could have listened to, kept record of in his mind like a Venus fly trap of dead men's tales, which might have lessened the loads on their strained hearts.

One resident in particular, Mr. Henderson, never told him a story deep enough. He didn't want to share his family tree with Wyatt, or talk about children, or even reveal his first name. Instead, he told him about cars: his bright yellow Belair with the sexy tail fins, the Crown Vic lined with red upholstery, so sleek no ass deserved such classy cushioning. He told him about California roads, the smooth slinking blacktop, windows down at sunset next to the ocean, not a bump in the road. Then, the roads in Michigan for the second half of his life—cracked spine concrete, potholed, blowing out his alignment, windows shut tight in winter. This was all that Wyatt learned before Mr. Henderson's heart swelled to two times its original size and eventually stopped. A massive, useless organ. Wyatt wished he could have dug deeper past the cars to whatever made a heart swell so big.

After The Best is Yet to Come, Thunder Blades hired him over the phone. They didn't want experience. They didn't want skill. Blank slates preferred. Lumpy masses of clay to be sculpted into an army of unstoppable salesmen. Wyatt came to know a world of products, each one more amazing than the next. Products his training stressed that no one could live without. Products he realized he'd been living without. Was this why he lived alone, why he had no girlfriend or best friend or a close relationship with mom and dad? He had dead men's stories, but he needed stuff. Stuff and money. Everything was about money, commission, sale, paycheck, purchase.

By the time the next customer rounds the corner, swinging a shopping basket merrily, Wyatt has made a nice groove into the head of the sledge. The knives really are amazing. He likes the sound of the knife sawing back and forth, like the sound of old men's labored breathing as they near sleep on a comfortable mattress. He can feel Lee's eyes behind the boxes urging him. *Saw like the wind, Wyatt. Make an impression.* And he does. He saws more vigorously, sledge shavings accumulating like a metal blizzard, drifts of dust rising around the head of the sledge.

The customer reaches the cheese display, just before the meat troughs where Wyatt saws. He has messy brown hair and freckles, a dusty face with a thick shadow of stubble. He wears an orange reflective vest over a black T-shirt with asphalt-splotched jeans. A road paver, maybe a city worker. The guys that blur past his car windows at the side of the road on his way to work. The customer picks out a small curd quart of cottage cheese and plunks it into his basket. Then he's on his way, Thunder Blades directly in his path.

Wyatt is lactose intolerant, and watching the man at the cheese display puts him all in knots. It starts in his stomach and creeps into his arms fast at work, now cramping. How long can he last? How long until his arms melt into butter or cream cheese or small curds? How long until the blade goes dull?

Thunder Blades never go dull! Put your trust in the product. A master salesman is filled with faith.

Remembering his training slightly rejuvenates his confidence, gives him a burst of sawing speed. The customer stops, stares, rubs his sandpaper cheeks. Wyatt has captured his attention, is finally doing something right.

We got our hooks in him now. Don't stop. Saw that son of a bitch sledgehammer right in half! If he's impressed now, wait until he sees the rest. Break out the tomatoes!

From the deep pockets of his apron, Wyatt produces a bright red tomato. He holds it up for the customer, rotates it left and right. It might be the biggest, reddest tomato the man in the orange vest has ever seen. The man scratches his head. He should be explaining what he's about to do, how the blade will still slice with Excalibur sharpness. But his tongue is tar. The words catch like stones in his throat.

Pushing back his nerves, Wyatt slides the serrated blade over the tomato, and it sinks through like non-dairy butter. He breathes a sigh of relief. The customer widens his eyes with recognition, nods. Yeah, it all makes sense now. The pieces are coming together. These are the best damn knives you'll ever see or want or need.

Back to the Sledge. Wyatt is going for a world record with astronomically fast thrusts and pulls of his wrist. Einstein said nothing could move faster than the speed of light, but he was wrong. The passion and pressure fueling Wyatt's thrusts shatter the conventional theories of speed and physics. The shavings shoot out the deepening divot, spilling off the table top and onto the floor, like planets being born from astral dust.

From the opposite direction of the cheese—the seafood side with the giant tank of fat, mottled brown lobsters—a high-pitched and pleasant hum approaches. It almost sounds like a song, as if a mermaid might have been mistakenly plunked into the tank and is trying to sing her way out. It's really quite fantastic, and this distraction causes Wyatt to slip a bit and graze his knuckle—just a scratch, not much blood, but it seeps as bright and ripe as the tomato. He wipes his bloody knuckle on his uniform, under his apron where he hopes no one will see he's bleeding, that these products can be dangerous. Appearances are important. The customer doesn't notice because he looks toward the sound, too.

A woman with a bright yellow blouse and black pants hums past his stand with a small vacuum on a slim pole, sucking up the spilled shavings of Wyatt's salesmanship. After one pass, not a speck remains. She pushes her small vacuum in a full circle around the customer and stops in front of him, propping her elbow on the slim pole with a confident smile. She's small and skinny with short blond hair combed over like a school boy. With that tiny body, she could almost be invisible. But she assumes the presence of a greater-sized woman. Every movement—the curve of her wrist, her seductive twists of the tiny vacuum, the slight but unmistakable jut of her hip when she leans—are all executed with graceful showmanship.

"Sir, do you wish you had an easier life?" She winks at the customer. "I'm here to make that dream possible. Well, not just me. Our product was envisioned and designed by expert NASA engineers to bring you an out-of-this-world sweeping experience from Warp-Speed Vacuums."

She swoops her hand into her tight pockets and releases a handful of varied size gems and gold nuggets. It's amazing so many could fit into such a tight pocket. They sprinkle and bounce across the tile floor. "But Warp-Speed doesn't just handle small messes, it can tackle the heavy-duty work as well."

And then she's at it again, making quick graceful circles with the tiny vacuum, sucking up each precious stone with a flick of the wrist and a side-step here and there. It's like a dance. Wyatt is mesmerized. He's forgotten all about the sledge, wondering to himself what heavenly training program blessed her with such a persona, and why his hasn't kicked in yet. Perhaps some people are just born with salesmanship talent. She is certainly perfect. He begins to seriously consider upgrading to a new vacuum. But he'd need to sell more knives.

Stay focused on the knives! Get your head out of your ass, Wyatt. Don't be taken in by flashy false prophets. There's only room for one miracle product today.

He's back to sawing, stealing a glance as she swoops up the last gem. So perfect. The customer is in awe too. Blood wells up in the cracks of Wyatt's fingers, forming into tiny, red tributaries. Maybe the cut is a bit worse than he first thought. He wipes behind his apron again, hopes nothing shows through, hopes she might keep the customer's attention until his blood coagulates. Damn blood.

"And just like that, your floors are spotless," she says. "You'll never need to toil away again. Just think of all the time you'll save in cleaning the very biggest of messes to the very smallest, insignificant specks of dust."

The customer sets his basket down in order to clap.

Wyatt thinks about the last thing she said: smallest, insignificant. She very likely refers to him and his metal shavings. This is not just competition. This is an attack. His stomach burns now. Oh God, an ulcer! And no health insurance. He feels sweat build on the crest of his thinning hairline hidden under the poofy chef's hat. His finger bleeds on, wiped carefully on the inside of his pocket. He's glad his sweat and blood are hidden. Customers want effortlessness. For Wyatt to have a chance here, everything with his product must appear easy.

"But that's not all. Warp-Speed never needs to be emptied. All messes are broken down into their molecular states and exhaust in a refreshing scent of coconut or pine tree fragrance."

It can't possibly be true. The Thunder Blades suddenly feel much less miraculous. Her product has molecular innovations by NASA. Their knives are merely designed by some national culinary institute.

A colorful array of fruity Os spread across the floor—a box of toucans spilled, and Wyatt knows the culprit. Lee is trying to give him a fighting chance by keeping her busy. Or, possibly, is just as amazed by her miraculous product and wants to see more. Either way, it's a chance for Wyatt to swing the balance of salesmanship back in his power.

He really digs in now, breathing heavily, clattering the knife against the sledgehammer. The customer looks just in time to see an edge of the sledge head disconnect and thud on the floor. Just a slice, but the smallness makes it no less impressive, Wyatt hopes.

The customer lifts his eyebrows and awkwardly slaps his palms together a few times.

Toucan cereal boxes erupt from the end cap. "See if you can sweep that up, bitch!" Lee says, revealing his secret location.

The woman leans, shifts her weight, rolls her eyes. She walks over to the broken edge of the sledge and slips it into her pocket. Her pants are so tight, yet somehow she manages to make it disappear just as easily as she produced the gems and nuggets. She's quite amazing. Wyatt is dumbstruck. All his work gone in a flash, but he doesn't mind so much. He may very well be in love with the small vacuum woman in the yellow blouse. If only they could combine forces. He imagines an immaculately swept apartment fully stocked with blades that never go dull. Maybe a few toddlers pushing pop-ball vacuums and slicing plastic tomatoes with plastic knives. They'd all go for a drive down smooth California roads, their hearts nearly bursting at the seams. A beautiful thought.

But not to Lee, who is tearing open boxes of Toucans and flinging the contents in furious handfuls. His face is red. His leg juts from his cramped ball posture into the aisle. Wyatt's guilt overcomes him, seeing Lee flailing from his hiding spot. Lee already has a family, already has teenagers who've grown out of their plastic utensils. Soon they'll be leaving for college and will need real tiny vacuums and perfectly balanced blades. These things require money, which comes from sales, which come from Lee's salesmen, which Wyatt is one of. Maybe Lee hasn't been managing so great. Why would he be here adding so much pressure to Wyatt's first day? Why is his face so red, the silky hairs above his ears fraying violently in all directions?

From behind Wyatt's stand, he hears a rustling of cellophane and Styrofoam. He turns to see a ripple of packaged steaks in the refrigerated trough, and then the steaks erupt and a large woman in an even yellower blouse pops up. "Fuck you, Lee!" She hurls a T-bone at Lee who can't move from his cramped hiding spot and takes the meat right across the face. "He's our sale now. Get over it."

"You vulture!" Lee squirms, makes some progress and slides onto the floor like a walrus. "Candy Walton, I should have known you were behind this. When will you stop scavenging our sales?"

Wyatt wonders about their history, whether Lee was once in his position, enchanted by the beauty and grace of the competition, enticed into an affair. He imagines Lee and Candy in a dark motel room kissing passionately, but this is unpleasant so he skips to the morning after, when their large sweaty bodies touch again in the morning light and recognition of their huge mistake sets in.

Why take chances with your satisfaction? Only Thunder Blades offers a risk free trial.

The customer looks nervous now, caught in the middle of fiery competition. He sways to the left, but the small woman in yellow pushes the vacuum in front of him, leaving all in her path sparkling and smelling of coconut. He sways to the right, and she's there again. Spotless floors block his escape.

"Give em hell, Wyatt." Lee hurls a box of Toucans at Candy but misses, just before she tackles him. "Use the shearing scissors!" he cries, writhing on the tile floor.

Of course, Lee is right; the shearing scissors would be best for this situation—in making a mess and in impressing the customer with their ergonomical handle and dead-eye accuracy. But releasing this astounding product so early in the sales pitch is not only radical to his traditional training, it would also be cruel to the saleswoman, who probably needs the money as much as him, who's just trying to vacuum out a place in this cold world.

"What are you waiting for? Don't hold back now." Lee tosses him the steak that had hit him in the face.

Loyalty comes first. Wyatt tears away the cellophane and Styrofoam. He holds the flank of what was once a cow, and it bleeds in his grip, staining his white sleeve. In a way, it's a relief he doesn't have to hide his bleeding finger anymore—this cow's blood looks close enough to his own. He imagines this cow mawing lazily on its cud in an open pasture beside a Michigan freeway, cars zooming past with the windows up. The cow never had to worry about sales pitches or jarred alignment or the products it needed to sell itself. Cows sell good as is, except for a few organs, which can be processed into a marketable mush of flesh.

He raises the scissors. The small woman looks at him, jutting that hip slightly, waiting. He looks back at her, tries to express with his eyes that he's sorry it has come to this. He cuts into the meat, marveling at the control of the twin blades. If only the man in the orange vest could feel how perfectly molded the ergo grips are to the shape of his callused skin, the hours of shoveling asphalt would melt away. Wyatt wishes the customer stood in his place thinking road worker thoughts. Wyatt thinks nursing home thoughts. The road worker would've liked to have heard about roads. He might have cared to listen, might have been able to help.

He slices, snips. Chunks of meat plop in all directions. The tiny vacuum darts after each bloody piece. Sweat builds in tiny dots along the woman's blond hairline. The customer flicks a piece of meat off his boot, hops back to dodge another.

The results are undeniable now.

Candy lifts herself from the tile floor, kicking away Lee's grabs at her ankles. She pulls two retractable tiny vacuums from black holsters around her hips. "No job too messy for NASA design!" She pushes one in each hand, aiding her saleswoman.

Lee trots to Wyatt's side. "Can you believe this?" he huffs, spouting testimonial, wringing his hands at the customer. "I never thought meat preparation could be *so* easy. With Thor's Mighty Shearing Scissors, you'll never have to worry about dangerous fats again."

Wyatt tries to stay focused on the flesh in his hands. He whittles from the mass of flesh with the scissors. The meat in his hands, in the blades of the scissors, starts to form with two fat arcs on the top funneling to a point—a heart. But not a heart exactly like the one in Henderson's weak ribs with ventricles and aortas and tangles of swelled junctions, something simpler, a heart like on a Valentine's card, voluptuous and vibrantly red.

You can't make a sale without putting your heart into it.

Lee leans in toward Wyatt's shoulder and speaks through the side of his mouth. "What are you doing? Stick to the protocol. You'll lose your ass trying to get so fancy."

But Wyatt can't stop at this point. Protocol has been obliterated. There's no turning back. He looks up and sees all eyes on him—the customer dangling his basket, Candy swooping two vacuums in his direction, and the small woman with the blond hair. She gazes at him with an inquisitive twist of her hips. They all look at him, not the knives. The knives he should be pushing. They might as well be plastic props.

When faith falters, trust thyself.

"You're pretty good with those scissors." The customer speaks for the first time. He steps across the polished floors, his boots leaving ghostly prints behind. "How did you do that?"

How could he explain? Looking in the road worker's eyes, Wyatt sees an appreciation, as if the skilled cuts with his scissors led somewhere real, or maybe helped smooth the way like the constant filling and refilling of potholes.

Lee steps in between the man and Wyatt. "Anyone could accomplish such a feat with the power of Thunder Blades."

"But I really don't want to. I don't need new knives or a vacuum, but, damn, you all sure put on quite a show for some guy like me."

Candy and Lee crowd in on the man, telling him about four easy payments, free shipping and handling, then three payments, doubling his order, tripling his order. They pile boxes of amazing products next to his asphalt-scabbed boots. He slides his hands into his pockets and listens, smiling politely. Wyatt doesn't think he'll really buy a thing. He wonders about this man's home. His dull steak knives, fast food wrappers, a push broom with a broken handle. He goes to work, fixes roads, comes home, and is satisfied with less than miraculous. His roads do what they need to do, despite their pot-holed flaws; they get people places.

While Candy and Lee urge hopelessly, the small woman nears the Thunder Blades stand and plants her delicate fingers on the cutting board. Wyatt still holds the heart sculpted from cow. It almost feels like it pumps and thumps now.

"That *is* something I've never seen before," she says, shifting her hip. "Must be some training program you guys have."

"I'm learning still," Wyatt says.

She seems impressed. Maybe he's not such a terrible salesman after all.

"Can I hold it?"

Wyatt places his heart into the woman's hands, her soft-looking palms. Droplets of cow blood run down her thin fingers. She drops the heart to the floor and zooms the vacuum over it. The vacuum struggles at first, clogging, but sucks it through, and a large plume of coconut scent exhales. She wipes the blood on her hand across the outside of Wyatt's white apron that has been covering the pocks and slashes he's hidden all day.

Evie and the Arfids

Tania Hershman

Radio-frequency identification (RFID) tags are spreading, and they could soon be keeping tabs on every one of us. This has privacy advocates worried, and they are campaigning for safeguards to be built into the still-to-be-finalized standards for RFID.
                                       —*NewScientist 28 August 2004*

I got the job because I said I could keep a secret.
They said, "Excellent, excellent, that's precisely what we need."
I didn't know that what they really needed was someone to push buttons all day. I thought I'd be using my brain, that's what they'd said in the interview. They said,
"Mrs. Applegate, you're a bright woman, no one has given you a chance. We see your potential." They sat there, three of them in grey suits, one leg crossed over the other, smiling, every now and then all looking at each other and then looking at me and nodding. They were like one person with three heads and six legs, all nodding at me at once. "We need a woman like you," they said to me. It was all the same to them that I'd been doing nothing for the last thirty years, just raising kids, making breakfasts, lunches and dinners, cleaning, sorting, sweating, eating, losing my figure, losing my husband, watching my kids go off one by one, losing my mind. I'd seen the SanFirst International ad in the local paper, took one look at the No Qualifications Necessary, and thought, well, I've got the No Qualifications they're looking for, why not give it a try.
I started on the Monday morning, and here's what I did all day: sat on my backside behind the machine, and watched stuff come out of the hole in the floor and along the belt towards me. The first week it was jumpers, with some logo on them, a fancy thing, Tommy Hilfinger, like the one I'd seen my Jimmy wearing once and he got all snippy when I asked where the money came from. When one made it into the tray in front of me, I'd press Pause, then push the green button and this arm'd come out and grab the collar of the jumper and put one of them little ar-

fid things into the label so it sort of melts in there so no-one can see. It's bloody clever, I don't know how it disappears like that. It's a bit creepy, someone's going to buy that jumper and not know it's there, aren't they? But for the first few weeks I didn't think about that stuff; I was just thinking about my paycheck, not giving much of my brain over to wondering about bigger questions.

So then I press Start, the jumper moves on and down the belt and through a hole in the wall and that's the last I see of it. To be honest, a half-blind monkey could've done it.

"It's secret work," the three-heads said. "Classified. You understand. National security. You're doing important work, Mrs. Applegate. Your country thanks you." My country! Thanks, country, for the nice payslip, really nice, if you ask me. Way too much for just pushing a button and watching and not saying nothing to nobody.

The first day, I ate lunch by myself. At 12 o'clock, I left the machine on standby like they told me, like my video recorder when it's not really On or Off, and walked down the corridor. There were lots of doors but no noise. Maybe there are hundreds of other Evie Applegates pushing buttons just like me, I thought, loads of us women who ain't got nothing better to do, who don't gossip, who ain't got no one at home to tell it to anyway. What makes me think I'm so special, I said to myself, and grinned to no one. I came around a corner and there was the canteen.

I got shepherd's pie and a bowl of fruit 'cause it was healthy, even though it had bananas, which make me queasy. I looked to see if I could sit with somebody. I can keep secrets but that don't mean I don't like polite chitter-chatter with someone while I eat. I'm not one of them who never speaks, like my Jack's friend Ronnie, sitting in our armchair and saying nothing for hours and hours. I never understood why Jack bothered with him, Dumb Ronnie I'd call him and Jack'd get angry.

"He's a good man, don't call him names, Evie," he said one night while he tried to pull his trousers off standing up by the side of our bed. "He don't say anything 'less he thinks it's worthwhile…"

"He must think I'm not worthwhile then," I said, watching Jack struggle and holding myself in from saying, "For goodness' sake, just sit down and take them off, it's so much easier."

"Don't start," said Jack. "With your 'I'm just rubbish, no one listens to me'." And he got his trousers off and went to the loo. That was a month before he left. I should have known.

There were only three people in the canteen. It was quiet in a spooky way. No one gave me a you're-new-here-sit-with-me look, so I didn't. I sat by myself, ate the pie, which was OK, and the fruit salad. I left the bananas on the plate. It took me all of five minutes. What about my half hour, I thought, what do I do with the rest?

Nothing. I went back to work and pushed buttons until 5pm, then I put the machine back on standby, got my coat on and left. I didn't see no one then either. Strange, I thought, aren't they all going home? I hope SanFirst International don't want me to work overtime. I can't push buttons for more time than that.

My second day, I met Gina. I went to the canteen and got stew and a chocolate cake, which I shouldn't have, but I was feeling sorry for myself, thinking if I was eating alone then I was going to have cake and it didn't matter about my fat thighs, no one wanted to look at me with no clothes on anyway. I was heading for the same spot as the day before, but out of the corner of my eye I saw someone waving. She was a tiny thing with hair that was orange like a lollipop. I turned right around and headed in her direction. No way I was eating alone if I didn't have to.

"Gina Workley," she said, "Hi, you're new, aren't you?"

"Evie Applegate, nice to meet you," I said, and tried to hold my tray in one hand and shake her hand with the other. It didn't work, and she laughed.

"Here," she said, and took my tray.

"Thanks," I said, and sat down. Gina was eating sandwiches. "Oh," I said, "I didn't see any of them, do they make them for you specially?"

"Oh no, I bring them from home, there's so much I can't eat," she said, and laughed again like a little girl, but even though she was tiny, she was definitely not young, she might even have been coming up on my age, she just did it better.

We started chatting, and it was really comfortable. She was so easy to talk to. I told her about the kids, said quickly about Jack and me not being together. I wanted to ask how long she'd been working here, what she did, but I was supposed to be keeping secrets and she was probably too, so I didn't. If she asks me, I'll say, I thought, but only if she asks. *Don't screw up this job, Evie*, I told myself.

At half past twelve she stood up and so did I.

"Really lovely meeting you, Evie," she said, and giggled. I giggled too—you couldn't not.

"I thought I was going to eat by my lonesome every day," I said as we carried the trays back.

"It is rather quiet," said Gina, and bent down to slot her tray into the rack. "Most people don't come to the canteen, they're too busy. But I'm in here every day, I like the change of scene."

"Glad to hear it," I said, but then while I was putting my tray in she said, "Bye, Evie," and walked off really fast. Bit rude, I thought. I guess she didn't want me to know which room she was in. I didn't know then that she wasn't being rude, that she was just scared. I just walked slowly to my room, and got back to the button-pushing.

The second week, it was trousers, Armani and some others. A nice young man, Steve, came and did some adjustments, so the arfid went in the right place.

"We've got templates for most different kinds of clothes" he said. "And other...." He stopped, went pink, and then turned back to the machine and didn't say another word.

"Thanks," I said.

"OK," he said. "Just do...whatever you did before." Then he went. On the Monday of the third week, he came back.

"Shirts," he said.

"Fine," I said. When they started coming down the belt, I had a good look, but I'd never heard of the name on these. I'm sure they were expensive too.

Lunch was the only thing I looked forward to.

Gina and me, we'd got to talking about her life.

"I don't believe it, you with two grown-up kids, and twins at that!" I said to her. She was eating her sandwich. She doesn't eat meat, fish, milk, raw veggies, pretty much most things, for her health. Nuts she can eat, and weird stuff, seeds and seaweed.

"I got married young," Gina said, putting down her sandwich. "Young and foolish they say, and I certainly was." She laughed a not-so-happy laugh and I knew what that meant right away. "The children came along and it seemed like five minutes between them being in nappies and then off to university. It was a bit like a dream."

"A dream with no sleep and lots of screaming," I said. "Not the kind of dream I thought it would be."

"Actually," said Gina, pushing her hair back so it didn't get in her special smelly tea, "the twins were very quiet. They were different from other people's children. I wondered why they didn't make much noise. I kept thinking, well, they're just getting used to being in this world, and when they're accustomed to it, they'll start expressing themselves. But they stayed quiet, and that is just the way they are." She didn't laugh, she looked pretty sad. She stared at me for a moment and then looked down into her tea. I put my hand on her arm.

"You can never tell how they're going to turn out, love," I said. "They're like little puppies that someone drops round your house one day, and you do what you can, you feed them and all, but in the end they're not you, they're someone else. You ain't never going to understand them, and they ain't never going to understand you. That's how it's meant to be."

Gina smiled.

"Thank you, Evie," she said, quietly. "You're very easy....you're a good...listener."

"Big ears, that's me!" I said, trying to lighten it all up a little. "Just 'cause we're keeping secrets, don't mean we can't talk about stuff."

Gina's face went funny when I said the s-word. She looked like the tea'd gone down the wrong way. She looked at her tray, looked back at me, and then stood up.

"Oops," she said, in a trying-to-be-funny way, "I'm late. Better run. Bye, see you." And off she went.

Damn, I thought, shouldn't have said that.

Then this week was when things started going loopy. On Tuesday, Gina came into my room. I didn't know how she knew it was my room, there wasn't any hole in the door and all the doors looked the same. She gave me quite a shock.

"Gina, what....?" I said, standing up from my machine, forgetting that there were more shirts coming down.

"Sit down," she hissed, "and just carry on, or they'll pile up." She looked really frightened. I sat down and hurried to do the next arfid. Out of the corner of my eye I could see Gina pacing up and down.

"What is it, love?" I said, wishing I could turn around.

She didn't say a thing for about two-shirts'-worth of time.

Then she said, "I stole something."

"Oh god, Gina, what did you take?"

She crouched down next to me.

"They're probably bugging us," she said, like she was going to cry, "But they probably know anyway, so it doesn't matter. I don't want to get you into trouble, but I had to tell someone. I don't know what to do." It went through my head that I could lose my job over this, but then my mind said it didn't matter, that wasn't the most important thing.

"Tell me," I said. "What did you take?"

"I took a watch," whispered Gina. "With a tracking device in it. I needed it...so I just took it, and now I don't know what's going to happen."

I wanted to put the stupid machine on Pause and give her a big hug and tell her it'll be alright. She told me the whole story, while I kept pushing buttons: a few weeks before I started, she'd come into this room and taken a fancy watch. Seems they put arfids in all sorts of things. The person who worked here before me got fired when the three heads found something didn't add up. Gina didn't say anything because she really needed it. With the arfid in it.

"I work in tracking," she whispered to me, crouched down by my side. "If you have one of those in something you're wearing, they can follow you everywhere. That's why I took one. I needed the money."

"Money?" I said. "Who were you going to sell it to?" I stopped. This wasn't going to be something I should know about. But I didn't say anything when Gina carried on:

"Someone approached me a year ago and offered me ten thousand pounds. They just wanted one. I didn't ask what for. But I refused. I didn't want to compromise my job," Gina made a choking noise. "Then Brian got into trouble, he lost a load of money, a friend of his, he'd lent it to for his new business, and the friend left the country, ran away with all of it and....and he called me, and he was crying and saying, 'Mum, you've got to....'"

Right then, a voice came over the tannoy.

"Will all employees return to their stations please."

Until that minute, I didn't even know there was a tannoy. The place was always silent as a grave. It scared the wits out of me. I jumped. I looked at Gina, she was white as a bleached sheet.

"Shit," she whispered, and the word sounded all wrong in her mouth. "They know I'm in here. Evie, I have to go. Meet me at the bus stop when you finish." I didn't know what to say. I just nodded and she slipped out.

I don't know how I got through the afternoon, all these things whizzing round my little head: Gina stealing, her boy in trouble, she's just trying to help, ten thousand pounds, wouldn't I have done it for Jimmy, what's she going to do now, what can I do? Gina, she's the first real friend I'd had since...since a long time, someone who treated me like, well, like I'm just as good as her. Someone who trusted me with something big. I wiped away a tear just before it fell off my face. Didn't want to get the precious machine wet now, did I?

Staying calm till five o'clock wasn't easy, but I did all the things I was supposed to do, and then walked out a tiny bit faster than normal, and rushed up the street to the bus stop.

Gina was there, pale but smiling. She put her arm through mine.

"Let's go get a cup of tea," she said, as the 147 pulled up. We got on the bus, and sat quietly next at the front. I listened to the schoolkids chattering behind us and tried to keep the scary excitement in me from bursting out.

Gina didn't say anything until we had our teas in front of us and the waitress had gone off. Then she shuffled her chair around so we were both in the corner with a wall behind us and no one nearby.

"I gave them the watch," she said, "and they paid me. Cash. I have never held so much money in my hands. I took it straight to Brian and gave it all to him. I told him that I had got a bonus and his grandmother had lent me the rest. He didn't ask. He was in such a state, the bank were going to take his flat...." She stopped and looked at me, her eyes watery. "I felt like this was the one time I could really be there for him. I had to do it. I had no choice. Do you see, Evie?"

"Of course, love," I said, and I put my arm around her shoulders. She felt tiny, like a little kid. "You're a great mum, like a mother lion, doing whatever it takes for her kids. But what are you worried about? They fired someone, didn't they?"

"Something's not right," she said slowly, "I've been feeling it for a few days. I feel like they're watching what I do, and when I come in in the morning it looks the same but something's wrong. I can't tell you what exactly, but it makes my skin crawl."

I felt something running up and down my spine.

"What are you going to do?" I said.

"I already did it," she said, looking proud and scared together. "I put a tracker into me."

"Oh my good god!" I said. "What do you mean? Those things, they're not for that...they're for clothes and things, not. How did you...?"

"I put my finger in the machine, modified it slightly, quick sting, and there it is." She turned her hand over, and I could see a little red square on the tip of the longest finger on her right hand. If you didn't know, you'd think it was hard skin. I was gobsmacked. If you can put them in people, well...I thought about what the three heads said about National Security. This was going too far.

"I need to ask you something, Evie," said Gina, and when she said that, I really had no idea what she wanted. Did she want me to put one in myself too? Or in someone else?

Before I could say, 'Hang on...' she said, "If I am not in to work, if something happens, I want you to track me." She looked at me very seriously.

"Track you?" I said. I felt dizzy, like I was losing hold on myself and might fall right off my chair.

"Yes," Gina said. "SanFirst have people...if they know what I've... I think that they might..." Gina couldn't finish. She put her face in her hands and started crying.

"Oh love," I said again. "Couldn't you go to the police?" But I already knew the answer. They'd take the money away from Brian, and Gina wouldn't have that, not for anything. "Ok," I said, "Tell me what I've gotta do—if something happens, but it isn't going to, don't you worry." Gina looked up and tried a smile.

"Thank you," she said. "Thank you, Evie. You don't know how much this means to me."

For the next few days, Gina and I met for lunch as normal and tried to talk about ordinary things, like my Jeanie and her creep of a boyfriend, and some new food Gina's discovered, some strange seed. I couldn't help sneaking a look at her finger every few minutes. I just couldn't believe she'd done that to herself. She was brave, if you ask me, very brave.

Then on Friday, she wasn't there.

We'd arranged that she'd call if she was ill or there was some other reason. If she didn't call and she wasn't at lunch, I had to assume the worst, Gina had said, and go with the plan. I sat with my tray in the canteen, my chicken drumsticks going cold, a sick feeling in my stomach, praying for Gina to walk in and stroll up to me, a big smile, with her sandwiches and bad-smelling tea. I waited until the last minute, then put the tray back with all the food on it, and walked slowly to my room.

There was someone standing by my door. One of the three heads. This is it, I thought.

"Mrs. Applegate," he said.

"Hi," I said, trying to sound innocent and cheery. "Am I late? I was just getting back to...."

"Could you come with me for a moment?" He didn't seem to be asking, so I didn't answer. We went down the corridor in the opposite direction from the canteen. We got to one of the doors that looked like all the others, and he held it open for me. The other two were sitting at a desk.

"Mrs. Applegate," said one. "I am afraid we seem to have a situation here."

My tummy was doing flip-flops.

"I believe you and Ms. Workley have struck up an acquaintance," said the middle head. They know, I thought, should I deny it? I didn't know what to do, what would be best for Gina. I felt a bit dizzy, then I realized that I should just keep calm, play it down. So we were friends, me and Gina, I thought, that's not a crime.

"Oh yes," I said, in a jolly voice. "She's my lunch companion. Nice to have someone to talk to, you know." I laughed a little but these guys were making me nervous. They didn't smile or nod. They just looked at me really seriously.

"Ms. Workley has been suspended."

Suspended ain't the word, I thought. Been disappeared is more like it. Be strong, I said to myself. Throwing a wobbly won't help Gina.

"I'm sorry about that," I said, keeping my voice all non-involved. "She seemed like a nice person."

"You understand that when something happens here, it doesn't just affect this company, Mrs Applegate," they said. "This has ripples that go much farther than us. National security, you know." I nodded. National bloody security. "You're a clever woman, Mrs. Applegate, I am sure you appreciate the need for full candor in this matter. We are asking you to tell us what you know." They all stared at me hard.

What I know, eh? I thought. Clever woman, am I? So why weren't I doing something cleverer than pushing buttons? Why was I stuck in that room with a machine, doing the dirty work? I'm not clever, I'm stupid, I said to myself. I'm stupid to think that they would want me for anything important, for anything more than a little kid could do with just five minutes' practice. I've never done anything clever in my life. I let Jack leave me, when really I should have left him years before, should have taken the kids and gone. I would have been better on my own, without his sour face and his moaning and groaning. I could have done that, if I'd known which way was up, if I'd had an ounce of sense.

I looked at the three heads, who were waiting for my answer.

"I'm sorry, but I don't know anything," I said. "Apart from what she eats for lunch, if that helps. She brings sandwiches. She's very sensitive to loads of food, did you know that?" I sat back in my chair and stared. Keeping secrets is what they took me on for; well, that's what they're going to get. I smiled my sweetest smile and waited to see what they did next.

They didn't do anything, of course. What could they do, since I wasn't giving Gina up? They showed me out and I walked back my room. The plan was in full swing now, and I was going to do what I had to do. I felt a surge of bravery, like I was Popeye and I'd just had a can of spinach. I could do this.

At five o' clock exactly I left the building. I was worried sick about Gina. She'd given me a mobile telephone and I kept taking it out of my pocket and praying she'd call. But it never rang.

So I was supposed to do what we agreed. I had it all going round and round in my head, everything Gina had told me. Now was the Moment of Truth and I felt like I was in one of those dreams I had when I was a kid the night before a big test: I'm sitting in the classroom with everyone else writing and my mind all blank, and the panic just coming up inside me and everything spinning, and the teacher shouting at me, 'Eve Simpson! You are the stupidest girl we have ever had! Stand up! Everyone look at Eve Simpson!' and in my dream I stand up and they all laugh at me and point and throw paper airplanes. I felt exactly like that, with Gina's phone in my pocket, knowing that it was all down to me.

You've got to do it, I told myself, and shook my head to try and get all those thoughts out and away into the wind. "This isn't about you," I whispered to myself, "This is for Gina, and you don't have no choice but to do it."

I walked to the bus stop, pretended like I was waiting for a bus, and then, when everyone got on, I hid behind the bus stop and then crossed the road to the side with all the trees on and walked back to SanFirst International. I walked around the side of the building and there was the gate, like Gina told me, hidden among the bushes. There was a big plant pot, and I reached underneath and found the key Gina said she'd leave there. She'd worked it all out.

The key was big and cold in my hand, which was shaking from all of this like I had Parkinson's or something. It took me a couple of goes to get it in the lock, but finally I did it, and looked around quickly before squeezing through the doorway. I was in a yard behind the building, with high walls on either side. There was a door straight ahead. I told my body to stops its wobbling and marched to the door, where I typed in the number Gina gave me on the little number pad. I'd written it down because I've never had a head for remembering numbers, but when it came to it, I didn't need that paper, I'd read it so many times.

Inside the building, it was quiet as a graveyard. I went down a little corridor with only a small flickering light, and then turned left and right, and then I was there, the door to the Tracking room. Of course, it didn't say Tracking or anything like that, just another white door, like all the others. There was another number pad, and this time I fished the paper out of my bra, best place for keeping these things, pressed 62735 and the *, and there was a little click. I pushed the door, it opened, and my tummy suddenly went all queer. It was all going like we planned, and I thought I was going to be sick. I held onto the doorpost and let all the dizziness have a hold for a minute, then stood up straight and said to myself, *Evie, she's counting on you, just do it, like the adverts say.* I still felt a little queasy but I was firm with myself, and I went inside and closed the door.

Gina had told me that the room was always pretty dark; they didn't have any windows in case anyone was spying, just light from the computers. Blimey, were there a lot of them, just rows and rows of them, like they were all watching without anyone to watch them. Gina's computer was the fourth one along on the second row on the left. I walked over, feeling like any minute all the computers were going to scream or something, and the lights would go on and people would run in and grab me. But nothing happened. It was as silent as my house on a Saturday night.

I sat down in front of Gina's computer and put my handbag down on the floor. I put the mobile phone on the left side of the keyboard. Then, like Gina told me, I wiggled the mouse thing backwards and forwards on the table. Even though she'd told me what would happen, I jumped when the screen was suddenly all bright. Calm yourself, I said to myself, putting a hand on my heart which was banging like a train.

On the screen were lots of little pictures, but in the top right corner was a little picture of a green tree. That was the one I wanted. I took hold of the mouse again. I'd used one of them things a few times, in the library, but it never felt natural. It took me a few goes to get it to move the arrow on the screen in the right direction, and my hand got all sweaty. Finally I got there, and the arrow was on the tree, and I click the button and the whole screen changed. A line at the top said TrackID and I knew I was in the right place.

I got the piece of paper out of my bra again, and found the box on the screen to type in the number which meant Gina's arfid. It was very long, with letters and other symbols in it, like question marks, and I got it wrong the first time and had to press the back button. I was sweating so much I thought I might flood the keyboard. I couldn't believe no one had heard me yet. It felt like I was making loads of noise. But I had to get on with it. I got the right number down and pressed the Enter button, and there was a big whirring. I got a fright and I grabbed the phone and my handbag and stood up. But then no one came in and the whirring stopped, so I sat down again. *Bloody hell,* I said to myself, *You're on the way to a heart attack if you keep this up.*

The screen was showing a map, just like Gina said it would. At the top it said Roehampton Industrial Estate. I thought Roehampton was somewhere near Birmingham, I'd never been there. Anyway, that didn't matter. There was a little red dot on the map. Gina. The dot wasn't moving. It was just keeping really still, and I touched it with my finger.

"It's ok, love," I said to the dot. "Someone's coming, we know where you are." Around the map were letters and numbers, and I followed the dot down with my finger to the bottom, and wrote the number on my piece of paper. Then I followed the dot to the side and wrote down the letter.

I got the mobile phone, like she'd told me, and followed the instructions on the paper. I went into Messages, and then Write Message, and then I was supposed to write, but all the little buttons had three letters on them. I started writing 'Gina' but it came out all funny, like 'ggma'. I felt like crying. What did I do wrong? Then by mistake I press the 'g' twice and it turned into an 'h' and suddenly I got it. Then I was off. I wrote "Gina your mum in danger in Roehampton Industrial Estate 35D on map tell police from friend Evie." It felt like it took me hours, and my thumb was getting sore but I finished it. I pressed on the Send button and started putting in Brian's number. Gina said it would go straight to his mobile phone, which seemed like some kind of magic to me.

Just as I was putting in the last 354 there was a noise outside the door. It sounded like two people whispering. I panicked, I stood up, holding the phone and my handbag, and looked around for somewhere to go. There wasn't anywhere, just tables with computers on them and no windows. My head was spinning round and round and I thought I was going to faint. The door opened and a voice said,

"Mrs. Applegate, put down the phone and put your hands up."

Ohmigod, I thought, *Gina, what do I do!* But Gina was just a red dot somewhere, a red dot in big trouble and I was it. I was the only one. They came into the room and they had guns pointing at me and I was breathing a thousand times a minute and all I could do was look at the phone and press the Send button and they ran towards me, but before they grabbed it I saw that it said Message Sent and I knew I'd done it, and I sank down into the chair and put my hands up.

"Mrs. Applegate, you are in big trouble," said the man holding the phone. The other man came around and pulled me up out of the chair. He held my hands behind my back and put me in handcuffs, like you see on the telly, but I didn't care. I did it, I thought, I sent the message!

As the man pushed me roughly by my shoulders towards the door, I suddenly felt very calm. *Gina, love,* I said to her in my head, hoping she could hear me, *It's all going to be alright.*

The man who had the mobile phone was talking into his phone, saying, "We've got her but she made contact, I'm bringing her in."

Bring me in, I thought, *and do your worst. You ain't getting nothing out of me.* I smiled a little smile to myself and let them drag me down the corridor.

Monkey-Men in Office Suite 209

Nick Kocz

Jones and I are sitting in the office one night, discussing changes we'd like to see in our company's management practices, when a man wearing a monkey suit wanders in eating powdered donuts from a box of Krispy Kremes that he's holding. We know it's a man because he says "Hello." He tosses a donut at Jones, who's been working hard trying to reach a settlement on the Tri-Narrows project. The donut whacks Jones on the ear and, when it falls onto the carpet, the Monkey-Man leaps upon it. Powdered sugar smudges the black fur of his costume. He's rolling around the floor, wrestling with the donut. It's the most ridiculous thing we've ever seen, this costumed fool carrying on, when suddenly the monkey-man gasps. He clutches his heart. Through the eyeholes in the costume, we see a look of panic pass over his eyes. He lets out another gasp, anguished. His right leg kicks feebly at a desk chair, then falls limply on the carpet. Jones jumps to the floor and tries to administer some kind of first aid, though I can tell by the way he smacks the monkey-man's chest with his balled fists that, technique-wise, he hasn't the slightest idea what to do.

"Maybe you ought to call 911," Jones says. And then he stares at the monkey-man's face a full minute before walloping him again. "This isn't looking good."

I call 911 and explain that we've got a monkey-man down in our office, that he's had a heart attack or something, but the dispatcher insists on giving me the phone number for Animal Control. Then, because it's after hours, the dispatcher makes a point of telling us that we'll have to call that office tomorrow during standard business hours. Washington, it appears, has not had enough reports of erratic animal behavior to justify round-the-clock staffing at Animal Control. And then 911 hangs up on me.

Things with the monkey-man aren't looking good. For one, he's not breathing. His eyes are closed and, because the zipper has jammed, the suit is impossible to remove. Jones's hands are sore and he's given up trying to beat the creature back to hale health. "So what do we do now?"

I shrug. Our firm's Rules of Employment do not specify the course of action to take for the removal of monkey-men, dead or otherwise, and I am not about to put myself at risk of early termination just for making up company policy on the fly. Having dispensed with the civic duty to alert 911, I tell Jones that our obligations in the matter have been fulfilled, that we can just walk away, or at least back away to our cubicles so we can work on official company business and crank out the billable hours.

Jones kicks the body. "But he isn't moving."

"So how bad can it get? It's not like he's in any position to demand that we cart him off to an emergency room. And just think of how long that might take: there's no way we can recover those billable hours."

And billable hours, of course, are the prime measuring stick in any standard of efficiency. So we go back to our respective cubicles and type onto our keyboards, preparing memos that perhaps no one, not even the parties that are paying our billable hours, will ever read. Washington is a city of paper. If you stripped away the marble buildings that house our immense paper holdings, one good rain would wash the whole city into the Potomac. That's all it would take: one good rain. Or at least that was my conclusion last year when the Department of Unspeakably Bad Things contracted our firm to study the situation. I'm now engaged in a follow-up study: what might the environmental effects be of having so much paper wash into the Potomac? I'm tempted to say that those environmental consequences shall be great, very great, but until I max out the allowable hours specified in the contract, I am contractually bound to refrain from drawing conclusions.

Leaving the office at ten o'clock, I'm misted by the light rain that's in the air, nothing heavy, which is just as well seeing that I've forgot my umbrella again. The lampposts along Connecticut Avenue are posted with flyers advertising yet another weekend rally protesting the current Administration's global warming policies. Bums accost me for spare change. Might some of them be secret monkey-men? Riding the Metro home, I wonder if any of my fellow passengers—the group of Capitals fans returning from a hockey game at the Verizon Center, the drunk Georgetown students wobbling the aisles, and the ladies with their noses buried in romance novels—are capable of donning a monkey costume.

When I get home, the children are already asleep. Clarisse is reading a bodice-ripper in the den, chewing on a strand of her auburn hair. Reading is a new pursuit for her; until recently, she'd be watching whatever was on the room's wall-to-wall plasma television. She's wrapped up in a terrycloth bathrobe, her bare feet plopped upon the ottoman. There's a neon pink band-aid, the type we buy to placate our youngest daughter, on one of her toes and I wonder how she might have cut it. She turns a page slowly. In years past, staying up late in her bathrobe would have been my clue that she was in the mood. Instead, she pokes her head from the book when she finally senses my presence. "You forgot your umbrella today."

"Are the children asleep?"

"What do you think?"

"I'm guessing that they are." I drop my briefcase on the floor. Why I carry the thing fro and back to the office every day is beyond me, since by the time I come home I'm too tired to crack it open and look at any of the materials that I've diligently crammed into it.

"What were you doing at the office?"

"Billable hours. I would have had a good bedtime story to tell the children tonight."

Clarisse picks her bodice-ripper off her lap and thumbs through the pages. The cover has an illustration of a bare-chested Tarzan-like figure with shoulder-length brown hair, a dimpled chin, and the icy blue eyes that one never encounters in real life. The man's pectorals gleam as if they've been rubbed with olive oil and the fair-haired young lass that he's holding, she of the French-braided blonde hair and diaphanous red chiffon peasant dress that (with its black satin corselet that fastened with leather cords) could double as a kinky nightgown, stands defiantly as if in possession of some bold and previously unexplored truth. Clarisse shifts on the sofa, tucking her feet beneath herself. Outside, a Sikorsky MH-60K gunship flies over the neighborhood, the *swoopa-swoopa-swoopa* of its helicopter blades making it impossible to hear each other; in the security-crazed aftermath of 9/11, these nighttime chopper sorties have become routine in metropolitan Washington. Through the living room window, I can see the helicopter's search light briefly sweep over our lawn before turning its beacon to the neighbor's property. Clarisse flips through a couple more pages and pouts. "You made me lose my page."

"Your toe. How did you hurt it?"

"Huh?"

"Your toe?"

She unfolds her legs from under herself. Flexibility has always been one of her greatest attributes, the way she can bend and stretch. She folds herself into a lotus position and touches the neon pink band-aid with the tip of her fingernail that has been coated with nail polish of the identical pink shade. "I can't remember."

The next morning, everyone's stepping over the monkey-man as they make their way across the office. The Federal Express man, overweight and with a tangled mess of brown hair, stiff, as if each unkempt strand has been gelled into place, trips over the critter's rope-like tail. Standing up, his hair not moving at all as he shakes himself off, he collects the Fedexelopes that spilled from his basket, then kneels down to examine what tripped him up. His eyes narrow and he flashes me a look like, *What the fuck?*

"Our new mascot. Pretty swank, eh?"

No one else so much as mentions the monkey-man, so intent are they in the quest for billable hours as they march across the office to take important conference calls and cuss out the support staff for screwing up the strength of the office coffee. And really, just how hard can it be to brew a pot of consistently über-caffeinated coffee?

That night, Jones and I are talking. Again it's late and we're the only people in the office, both of us on some unspoken quest to become the kings of billable hours, but Jones is upset. He's beside himself. He's picking at a pea-sized growth at the corner of his eye, squeezing and pulling it. Over the years, the pigmentation of this growth has darkened; now it is as dark as the screen of a computer monitor that has been turned off. What Jones is upset about is his Tri-Narrows project.

The Tri-Narrows Dam, located on Idaho's Spago River, was once the nation's largest concrete structure before the Grand Coulee Dam was completed during the Roosevelt Administration. For decades though, its electrical generators sat idle because a consortium of hydro-electric power concerns, environmental groups, and a plethora of state and local governments disputed the costs and parameters of its refurbishment. Because of its proximity to the Canadian border, the provincial government of British Columbia even weighed in with a brief, mainly to protect the rights of their citizens to make use of the dam's lake during wintertime for makeshift hockey games. Re-equipping the aging hydro-electric plant with the turbines and widgets (Jones' term, not mine) necessary to restore the facility to operating condition was not in the interest of any of these parties.

Jones's contract, in terms of billable hours, is open-ended. Legal loopholes allow him to bill out 72 hours for each day his work on the project continues, the federal Department of Wouldn't It Be Nice picking up the tab. For years he has been able to prevent even the terms of mediation from being discussed. But now his luck had changed: conciliation is in the air and, unless Jones can think of something quick, the parties will likely hammer out the differences in a matter of days, leaving him without a source of billable hours.

"I don't understand it," Jones says. He gives his growth another tug and lets it snap back into place. "I'm such an asshole, yet everyone's sending me emails, thanking me for the wonderful job I'm doing. The premier of British Columbia invited me up, all expenses paid, to watch a hockey tournament. I'm not even sure where British Columbia is."

"It's in Canada, isn't it?"

Jones arches his eyebrow. "You're asking me to draw a conclusion, aren't you?"

The office's front door opens suddenly. In walks another monkey-man, again with a box of Krispy Kremes. He goes, *Ooo-Ooo, Ahh-Ahh* and beats his chest. Unlike the previous monkey-man, this one's acrobatic. He races through the office, vaulting off chairs and swinging from the tops of the orange prefab partitions that divide our cubicles. He latches onto an overhead fluorescent light fixture and lobs chocolate-iced crullers at us. From this vantage, his accuracy is uncanny. A Krispy Kreme thumps against the side of my head, smearing me with a chocolate icing that, to be honest, is a bit rancid. Every time the monkey-man scores a direct hit, he goes *Ooo-Ooo, Ahh-Ahh* and gives us the finger. Jones is howling back at the monkey-man. He's been hit three times and his face resembles a hockey puck, so dark is the chocolate icing that covers his face.

"What do we do?" I ask, dodging for cover behind one of the oversized waste baskets.

"Wait him out. He's bound to run out of doughnuts."

My first thought is, in a world where something as fantastical as a monkey-man appears in your office, who's to say that said monkey-man is not blessed with an inexhaustible supply of chocolate crullers? I mean, if a monkey-man appeared in one of Clarisse's bodice-rippers, she'd fling the book down and chastise it as a flawed work of fiction. But here, crouched behind a waste paper basket late at night in a near-empty office with chocolate crullers raining down upon me, things seem to happen in ways I've never been paid to study.

...Did I tell you that I have children? Scads of them. That much I can conclude, though no study has yet been commissioned to ascertain my findings. Clarisse leaves the bills on the propped-up pillow of my bed—department store charges for their glow-in-the-dark sneakers, an invoice from the Soccerplex for their summer league registration fees. One of the girls logged onto my Amazon account and bought Hello Kitty paraphernalia that set me back three hundred dollars. Though I rarely see the children, the bills are irrefutable proof of their existence. The oldest boy must have had his braces tightened recently; so great was the bill from Smart Teeth, Inc., the orthodontia practice that he frequents, that I began to cry when I saw it...

Monkey-man's still dangling from the light fixture and hurling doughnuts at us when he slips. It happens so suddenly that he doesn't even *Ooo-Ooo Ahh-Ahh* one last time. He falls head-first and lands upon the back of the previous monkey-man. From the angle his neck snaps, my guess is that mouth-to-mouth resuscitation, thankfully, is not going to help matters.

Jones opens the monkey-man's box of Krispy Kremes, which landed upside-down on the seat of an office chair. Though generous portions of chocolate icing are stuck to the sides of the box, no doughnuts remain. Jones shakes his head. "Just my luck. No more doughnuts."

I arrive home just before midnight. Clarisse is in the living room. Again, she's in her bathrobe, her feet resting on the Ottoman. The band-aid is nowhere in evidence. When I ask if the kids are still awake, Clarisse shushes me. She's watching television. Or, more precisely, she's ogling a shirtless Tarzan-like man; the same glistening savage featured on the cover of yesterday's bodice-ripper is now on our television screen. On High Definition, a notoriously unforgiving medium, he looks fantastic:

muscles ripple as he flexes his arms, a healthy sheen in his brown hair, his eyes icy radiant. The young lass, also from the bodice-ripper, leans her head on his muscular shoulder. The shoulder of her peasant dress is torn, exposing a provocative glimpse of her bosom, again so appallingly and tantalizingly realistic on HD. The savage turns to me and grunts. The picture is so life-like, it's like he's looking at me. He grunts again, tilting his head as if he's asking a question.

"Billable hours," Clarisse says.

The savage nods. For some reason, the lass on his shoulder has begun weeping, sobbing actually, a minor rivulet of tears streaking her cheeks. He wraps his arm around her.

Clarisse shifts on the sofa, pulling her legs up and wrapping her arms over her knees. The sash on her bathrobe has become undone but, in the room's darkened light, her exposed skin lacks the vividness of what is on the screen. She bites the corner of her lip, a signal to me that she is uncomfortable about something. She clears her throat. "Honey, can you give us a little privacy maybe? There's cold cuts in the fridge."

And indeed, amid the bottles and bottles of baby formula, cold cuts are in the refrigerator—not just any cold cuts but slices of prosciutto, dry-cured Genoa salami and an herb-encrusted pastrami that is not to be believed, the fine fruits of billable hours. I slather honey-Dijon on two slices of a coarse-grain bread and make a sandwich. I pour a glass of red wine and set it on the table next the sandwich. From the next room, I hear groans of pleasure. The Savage howls. Because of the sub-woofers in the 5.1 surrround sound theater system, the house rumbles pleasantly with each groan.

The day's billable hours have taken their toll and though I am barely able to remain awake, I conjure images that surely must be flickering over the plasma screen. Clarisse begins to groan and it reminds me of something and….Did I tell you I have children? Children who require constant care and loving attention. Children who require billable hours. Children whom I am told run constantly throughout the house in the daylight hours, children who are constantly breaking their toy trains and Hello Kitty merchandise, requiring additional purchases (authorized or not) of said merchandise. The children, Clarisse says, run her ragged and she has so little time to wear the dresses that she buys.

Monkey-men have been accumulating in our office. Because our Rules of Employment have yet to be amended to address their removal, no one dares to push them out of the aisle between our cubicles. Currently they're stacked five-high. This morning, our office ergonomics freak finally stuck an orange pylon atop the pile to prevent the Fedex guy from falling over them again, but it was no use; like clockwork, the Fedex guy wags his butt into the office and, as he's sorting through the Fedexelopes, he trips over a dead monkey-man's leg. Picking himself off the monkey-man pile, his cheeks burning red with embarrassment, he shoots me this

It's a job glance. Clumps of monkey-man fur stick to his blue Fedex jacket but, amazingly, his mass of hair is unaffected by the fall.

"Those things would make cute pets," he says.

"Yeah. If they were alive."

"Even still." He pushes a Fedexelope into my hand and makes me sign his manifest delivery log, certifying that he has indeed delivered the Fedexelope to me. "They're easy to care for, aren't they?"

The Fedexelope does not bring good news. It's from the Department of Unspeakably Bad Things, and it's about my study on office papers that might someday wash into the Potomac. The current Administration is no longer supporting environmental research. Not that they ever were. In the Administration's waning days, they wish to focus on what the Administration feels it does best: terrorism. Or anti-terrorism. Or weapons of mass destruction. Or the military occupation of foreign lands that were believed to hold caches of weapons of mass destruction. From the letter, it is hard to tell exactly what the Administration hopes to do in its waning days because, as the letter says, "there is so many things we do well, no?" But one thing is clear: it is pulling the billable hours plug on all environmental projects.

When I show this letter to Jones that night, he can barely speak. The office is rank with the smell of scorched coffee that we brew throughout the day to keep us awake. Too much caffeine is not good; ever since the Fedexelope arrived, I've been suffering from that jittery sensation that makes sustained thought impossible. Jones seems to have aged decades over the past few days: his brown hair has thinned, making legible a fork-shaped birthmark at the back of his head. The growth at his eye is larger. Liver spots have appeared on the back of his hands. He has taken to wearing bifocals

"I've got gray hair on my chest," he says.

"I don't need to know that," I respond.

Jones has aged because the Tri-Narrows dispute is officially resolved. His billable hours gravy train is over. Kaput. Each day, the premier of British Columbia sends him another letter inviting him to a sporting event: curling, a salmon derby, spelunking festivals held in funky-smelling caves. Jones stuffs the invitations into the hands of the dead monkey-men, into their mouths and up the cracks of their... well, I can't print that. But Jones is despondent. He's got nothing to do. He doesn't know what to do with his time. He slams his liver-spotted hand on his empty desk. He had been hoping to bum some billable hours off me. "Give me some."

"Me?"

"Yes, you. Why should you have all those billable hours and me have none?" This, from a man who only last week, was billing out four times as many hours as I. He gazes into my eyes. "I'm talking economic justice here."

And then the glass office door swings open. In steps another monkey-man. He wanders through the office, past the humming photocopier and the bank of fax machines that are so rarely used now that the world is connected through electronic mail. The monkey-man scratches his head, unaware that he is being observed. He has the posture of a gorilla, crouched, swinging his arms as he walks and letting his knuckles graze the carpet. He picks up a stapler, the industrial kind that is used to bind thick pamphlets, and squeezes it. A silver staple zings out of the stapler, causing the monkey man to jump back and grunt. Slowly, he re-approaches the stapler, which he has dropped on the floor. He clucks his tongue loudly. He nudges the stapler with his toe. Then he nudges it again until the stapler is up against the wall, cutting off the stapler's avenues of escape, should the stapler suddenly wish to take flight.

"What are you doing?" Jones asks.

The monkey-man throws himself on the stapler, gripping it with both hands as if to strangle it, his eyes wide open, the stapler offering no resistance.

"You have no idea how to operate that thing, do you?" Jones asks. There's something scathing in the way he asks this question. He tugs at the growth at his eye. The thing is as thin as a gnarled rubber band but maybe an inch long. He wraps it around his finger, stretching it further than it ought to go, causing him to grimace. "There's no need to pretend to know what you're doing."

The monkey-man, who's still sprawled out on the carpet and clasping the stapler, looks up at Jones. He's got the reddish-brown fur of an orangutan. He lowers his coal-black eyes. He lets go of the stapler. "*Ooo-Ooo.*"

"That's more like it," Jones says. "*Ooo-Ooo, Ahh-Ahh* indeed."

I had thought monkey-men were hygienic creatures with well-developed self-grooming skills but the cigarette butts and doughnut crumbs lodged in his matted fur makes me reconsider this notion.

"*Ooo-Ooo, Ooo-Ooo Ahh-Ahh,*" Jones says. Gone is the scathing tone from his voice. He reaches down and extends a hand to the monkey-man, lifting him to his feet. When he pats the monkey-man's back, dead fleas fall off.

The monkey-man chitters in response to Jones, who nods thoughtfully.

"So what do you really want to do with your life?" Jones asks.

The monkey-man reaches into the thick nap of his orangutan fur and retrieves a box of Krispy Kremes. I am astounded still by the variety of doughnuts God grants to monkey-men, for there is no telling the flavors that might pop out of a Krispy Kreme box: Boston Creams, cinnamon twists, caramel-filled doughnuts that have been rolled in granulated sugar, to say nothing of the special blueberry-iced cream puffs that have been so heavily advertised on television.

A jelly doughnut falls from the paperboard box and the monkey-man watches it roll a few yards into the sprawled-out pile of his dead simian brethren. He picks it up but stares down at the most recent monkey-man casualty, a gorilla-like figure with the slate-gray hair of a silverback. This is the first time that any of the monkey-men have displayed a consciousness to those who preceded them. He lifts one of the dead monkey-men's arms and lets its fingers brush his wrist.

"It's what happens to all of us," Jones says.

"*Ooo-Ooo?*"

Jones nods. "*Ooo-Ooo, Ahh, Ooo-Ooo.*"

The monkey-man lets go of the arm, which flops to the floor. For a moment, he looks lost. He looks at Jones. Then he gazes at me with vacant eyes, giving the impression that his thoughts are elsewhere. I want to ask why monkey-men eat doughnuts when, after all, it would make more sense for them to run around with bunches of bananas but when I consider the consequences, how the monkey-men would probably litter the office with the slippery skins of their yellow jungle fruit, then where would we be: a bunch of comically inept government consultants falling all over each other? He starts gorging himself with doughnuts, stuffing them one after another in his mouth, coughing, swallowing them whole, coughing again.

This is where the story should end, but monkey-men are not blessed with the common sense that has allowed the likes of Jones and me to prosper for so long. He jams yet more doughnuts into his mouth, his elastic cheeks expanding. This is not going to end well. He doesn't even want a glass of water to help wash them down. His cheeks bulge from the strain of so many doughnuts. I lose count of how many doughnuts he has gone through. Powdered sugar dusts the paper-thin translucent skin of his shriveled chin.

"Easy does it," Jones says. "Think about all those unnecessary carbs."

The monkey-man shoves another cruller into his mouth. He starts to gag. His eyes pop open in urgent attention. He's got his hands to his throat. He's choking. His cheeks are still puffed full of doughnuts. A rapid series of gurgled rasps issue from his mouth. I knew this was going to happen.

Jones, ever the Good Samaritan, jumps behind the monkey-man. He wraps his arms around the monkey-man's torso and presses his hands into the creature's abdominal cavity. The Heimlich maneuver. With the first thrust, doughnut chunks spew from the monkey-man's mouth but he still can't breathe. Jones tries again and again but the monkey-man shakes his head. Something is still lodged in his windpipe. Each thrust is swifter, more violent. And then something happens: there's a crunching sound, the sound of the monkey-man's sternum shattering. The monkey-man slumps from Jones's arms and Jones tries again to dislodge whatever is preventing him from breathing. The monkey-man's face turns purple, and I'm wondering if an adherence to a banana diet could have prevented this tragedy. Someone ought to study the relative choking hazards associated with different foods. Surely the idea has billable hours potential, whether it be during this Administration or the next and I'm feeling suddenly good about myself even though there are mouths to feed at home and, for the moment at least, I'm "between hours," as the euphemism goes. And then the monkey falls down.

I look up to see that Jones has given up Heimliching. He slaps his hands together, just as one might to clear them free of dirt when gardening.

"What is it about monkey-men and doughnuts?" Jones asks. He picks up the paperboard Krispy Kreme box, which is empty. "And the worst part of it is, there never are doughnuts left in the end."

There is an unexpected situation at home. Clarisse has dyed her hair blonde and is wearing a simple peasant dress cut from coarse fabric, the type of dress which a heroine wears on the cover of a bodice-ripper. A Tarzan-like man is directly atop her. They're lying on the sofa, he thrusting his groin and she making the soft cooing sounds a dove might make. The skirt of her dress is pulled up over her hips and it has been a long time since I last witnessed the creaminess of her skin. He is not wearing a loincloth. Her legs are stretched out, her feet arched and her toes pointing toward the plasma screen. The backs of his legs gleam from the apparent application of olive oil. He's grunting, louder and louder with each thrust. I'm tempted to say that things are not going to end well. If only someone will toss billable hours my way to study the situation. Upstairs, the baby begins to cry. Did I tell you I have children?

No-See-Um

Michael Zadoorian

Quite suddenly, one day at the office, there are tiny insects in the air. Everywhere: copy room, lunchroom, conference room, shipping department, personnel. We see them when we fax a letter or go to the bathroom. Wherever we look up, there suspended against a nimbus of humming fluorescent white, is a shadowy funnel of tiny flies, bobbing in the air.

No-See-Ums. This is what one employee calls them. This is true. Although we often cannot see them, we feel them, floating around our ears, flitting through our regulation-length hair, pelting the skin on our throats with their invisible bodies, as if trying to collapse bones and meat with their infinitesimal insect blows.

Soon it is all we employees talk about. The bugs. *Where did they come from? Why are there so many? Is that one in your Latte?* It is strange to see us so preoccupied because we are usually such a happy bunch. We always celebrate each other's birthdays with pudding cake and little pointy hats. Once a week, we all chip in a dollar for *Donut Day,* which is Wednesday. (Nothing like a choco-custard breakfast stick to get you over the hump.) We are all astonished that something like this has been allowed to happen. Our company is usually so efficient in most matters. But in this case, it is days before they even acknowledge the problem. By that time, the No-See-Ums have multiplied exponentially.

Corporate action is in the form of an email. This is a surprise since, in our office, we still generally get paper memos. Ostensibly, the equivalent of eight Yellowstone National Parks are leveled annually for our memos alone. These are issued by our boss, who rarely emails, and is, in fact, still reserving judgment on whether or not this whole Internet thing is going to catch on. His memos are always reminding us of something, the more trivial the matter, the better. *Re: the issue of mens shoes with big tassals; Offically, no mens shoes with big tassals are permitable by the company within the confines of the office.*

The No-See-Um email is not like this. The spelling is correct and there are uncharacteristic phrases such as *sudden proliferation, the health factor,* and *descending like locusts.* The fact that this missive is articulate is some cause for concern.

The No-See-Um email further states that work stations must now be kept clean: no more half-eaten sandwiches left out, no more half-drunk cups of *Sanka* or *Dr. Pepper* left sitting on conference room tables for days at a time. According to the email, it is in these places, especially the liquids, that the insects lay their eggs. Since their gestation period is about 24 hours (the email is also suspiciously rich in factual detail), this accounts for the extraordinarily high number of insects in our humble office.

Knowledge is power, so thinks our company. *Right.* Soon, employees begin to cover all things comestible—coasters atop shaky cups of coffee, Kleenex wrapped round a nutty donut, white bond over Snickers bar. After a single sip of Cherry Vanilla Coke, a piece of foil is clamped over the top of the can. Anything to keep the insects from spilling their terrible seed.

Before long, covering our food and drink is not enough. After reading the email, one secretary (the boss' paramour) starts holding a tissue over her face wherever she goes. When one of the other employees asks her if she has a cold, she says *What if they fly in my mouth and lay their eggs there?*

The other employee does not laugh. In fact, he says nothing. You can see the wheels turning. It had not occurred to him that the insects might lay their eggs in such places. We all start to wonder what grotesque maladies these teeny arthropods might introduce into our bodies via the old cakehole or mucus membranes. *Rocky Mountain Fever? Legionnaire's Disease? Elephantiasis?* Or will we just rot like a melon left too long on top of the refrigerator, starting at the bunghole and spreading rapidly from there?

The next day, there are a few surgical masks being worn around the office. Soon, our dress code (*All employees must wear suits of dark blue or dark gray, black or brown shoes, white shirts/blouses and subdued blue or maroon ties with designs that do not exceed one half-inch in diameter*) is completely disregarded. When the secretaries start showing up in goggles and netted pith helmets, no one even questions it. Among the employees, there is talk of how to seal other orifices. It seems likely that the local hardware store is experiencing a run on caulking guns.

It is as if everyone in the office has suddenly become aware of some indiscernible otherworld, where the air is not simply something that we breathe, pure lung fodder, but a place where things happen. We employees are like the drunkard comedian who believes water is unhealthy to drink because fish go to the bathroom in it.

Donut day is cancelled indefinitely.

So many insects now that when we walk into a room, we see pieces of darkness in the air, ragged shapes that hang like rents in the spatial fabric. The bugs are no longer "No-See-Ums." We can indeed *see-um*. One employee, caught up in work, inadvertently walks into one of these dark spaces and immediately begins slapping himself. While jabbering, crazy-like, he starts slapping the air around him, including the person next to him, which happens to be our boss. This continues for quite some time.

After what the spectators deem a sufficient interval, the slapping man is restrained and taken away. Our swollen boss hastily retreats to his office while the snickering dies down. The slapping man is currently under observation. The company continues to pay his salary for the duration of his stay at the hospital.

We notice the days slowing. This is something that never happens in office life. Of course, there are many bad, *boring* days, but in an office, there is always a sense of the blur—weeks, months, the company anniversaries that pass and pass. Employees are always talking about how time flies, yet now we are living on Fly Time. We are conscious of the *days.* They crumble slowly behind us, as if we are sleepwalking in front of an ever-widening ravine.

The company continues to do nothing about the insects. We begin to wonder if they think the email was enough, when something happens in the coffee room. One employee, hungry enough to risk disease, tries to find some well-sealed item in the honor system snack box. The No-See-Ums light on his head as if it were roadkill. In a fit of pique and panic, he knocks the whole box of snacks onto the floor.

Word quickly gets back to another employee, whose brother-in-law works for the snack supplier. He rushes into the coffee room and accuses the hungry employee of stealing, of breaking the sacred code of honor of the snack box. A scuffle ensues. People start to leave their desks and mill around the coffee room to watch the action. Two men under a halo of flies, rolling around on a floor strewn with Zagnuts, Cheez-its, Mallo Cups and Bar-B-Q Fritos. Then one of them falls backward onto a stale Charleston Chew and lets out a horrible animal shriek.

The boss comes in and a group of employees, feeling a collective vicarious blood rush, ask him, in ways that one would not normally speak to their boss, *when is the company going to do something about the bugs? What is wrong with you people?* A few employees start working out an impromptu chant when one of the female reps walks in ashen-faced. She announces that the secretary who has been holding a tissue over her face for the past three days is dead in the ladies' room. The two men stop beating each other. The boss faints.

Upon investigation, a spray can of Off! is discovered near the woman's body. We surmise that she has been surreptitiously inhaling it so to keep her nose and mouth from becoming a breeding ground for larvae. Ironically, it is not long before there is a higher concentration of flies in the bathroom. Swarms of them.

After the police arrive, one employee stands outside the ladies' room ranting to all of us. *Spray can nothing, it's what I've suspected all along.*

— NO-SEE-UM

Killer insects! Rare poisonous FLESH-EATING No-See-Ums sent here by the company to downsize our staff so they save money on unemployment insurance. Much easier and cheaper than lay-offs. It makes sense, doesn't it?

Others of us know the truth. She is dead and they are flies. Nature.

A paper memo is issued. It is addressed directly to the bugs. *It is to be understood that all insects will discontinue mating and leave the office at once. Or security will be notified.*

The memo is circulated throughout the entire department before it is noticed by someone and quietly gathered up. Soon, our boss has a visitor from Corporate. The man behind the email, we suspect. The door is closed for a long time. No one sees our boss after he leaves work that day.

On Friday morning, we receive another email. *Fumigation is to take place on the premises over the weekend.* We are told to cover objects in our offices, those with which we have everyday contact—computers, telephones, calculators, fax machines—everything not already sheathed.

Doing it, we are reminded of all the things we touch each day with our hands and ears and mouths—keyboards ingrained with communal grime, greasy ear-pieces of telephones, the teaspoon with a dull patina of artificial coffee whitener that carries the thumbprint of the last person who stirred. We are reminded of everything that the flies touch.

That evening, we look back at our office before getting on the elevator. It is as if we are exiting a quarantine room. There is a baffled, bandaged silence. One of us sneezes on the way down and everybody jumps. Then we move away.

Our habits from work carry over into our weekend lives. We are afraid to make contact with our loved ones for fear we are somehow infested, afraid to leave beverages out (cringe as we watch our children do it, but dare not say anything so not to look foolish or crazy), we look toward a light and check the air before entering a room. We are seeing much more these days.

Our families ask us what's wrong. We give them hollow smiles and say *Nothing.*

On Monday, when we return to work, the flies are once again invisible. There are many dead ones fallen on blotters, on the memos piled on our desks, but those in the air are difficult to see. They weave around, flying the logy half-flight of the toxemic. When you spot them against the light, they are easy to trap in your palm, but no one does so, at least at first. After a short while, rage catches up with us and we do start killing them manually, snatching them out of the air when we can see them, and crushing them between the heels of our hands. Once we see that victory is ours, we realize the ludicrousness of our fears. *They're only tiny insects—We are humans! How could we have been so scared?*

By Wednesday, things are normal. A few employees have become sick from the insecticide, but they are the weak ones. Friday arrives quickly—a blur. By then, sandwiches are left out unprotected, half-filled mugs of coffee sit on desk tops for an hour then are topped off with more warm liquid and consumed. *Donut Day* will be resumed next week.

    The company seems pleased with itself. Our boss comes back after a few weeks as if from vacation. He holds no grudges toward anyone. A new secretary has been assigned to him and she is quite attractive, a redhead. We are getting memos again most every day.

LIGHTS OUT

Steve Himmer

Some days the only advantage the top floor had over the mailroom was its view of the sky. In his years at Horizon Illumination, Clark's view had improved a floor or two with each promotion and now he was at the top. As he'd climbed his offices had grown larger—as Clark himself had—even as the number of people around him had shrunk until now he knew there were people at work behind walls and closed doors near his own, he heard photocopiers churning and telephones ringing, but he seldom saw anyone else on his floor. There were internal email addresses he wrote to every day with no idea who the recipients were, what they looked like or where their desks were. He made phone calls and sent emails and occasionally someone came into his office to drop off his mail or pick up a package for shipping, but mostly he was alone. Since he had so few visitors, he'd given up on decorations and personal touches apart from a couple of pictures taken of the Grand Canyon and Hollywood sign and other landmarks he'd visited on team-building excursions from conferences over the years.

Colleagues had called his rise graceful, being in the right place at the right time while doing the right work the right way. He'd climbed quietly without leaving problems behind, and now there was only an access and utilities floor over his office, then the roof, where a pair of peregrine falcons nested. Clark spent whole mornings as he'd spent this one so far, with his chair swiveled toward unopenable windows to watch his avian neighbors swoop and wheel outside. They usually circled a floor or two down, and he watched from above as their graphite bodies slid through pale sky like a pencil point across paper, writing their story on air. Only the tiniest tremors in the tips of their wings and the slightest lateral roll gave away any motion and showed any sign of the winds they had mastered. They hovered, as he did, over a landscape of opportunities, awaiting the right time to move and hoping that moment would not be missed.

In the months he'd been in this office, Clark had tried to get onto the roof to look for the nest. Despite his senior position and long tenure, building management had refused him access, or had refused by default since they never replied to his emailed requests. Every morning he looked at the keyhole beneath the elevator's buttons, the route to the roof, and was reminded that the building still held a higher story than his. Since he wasn't allowed up in person, he'd emailed building management a second time to ask about having a webcam installed the way other buildings had done with their birds. That request brought no reply, either. He wrote again two weeks later, anticipating their objection for security reasons and preemptively asking what harm it could do—what threat were birds to a company as large as Horizon? They sold lightbulbs, not birdseed. Lightbulbs and everything else that a century of lightbulbs had spawned. Again building management had nothing to say.

Clark's computer weather widget said the temperature outside was just over fifty degrees, but he wondered how much colder it was up as high as the falcons were flying. As high as he was, too, but he couldn't feel it. Most days, between his parking garages at home and at work and the elevators that rose from within them, Clark never set foot outside. Even on the coldest days of winter he left his coat in the closet. He watched the birds rolling on what must have been updrafts along the side of the building, and he thought of the fast-flowing paper and email and data rising up through the inside of the tower, through other departments and offices, up elevator shafts and staircases and ethernet cables, flooding his inbox and voicemail and spilling into his briefcase to be carried home. The falcons swung lower, almost out of sight, and he leaned forward with his forehead pressed to the glass as they reeled in long ovals below.

He hadn't meant to stay with the company as long as he had, so long now that it wouldn't make sense to leave before he retired. It was meant to be a job in a mailroom right after college, while he figured out what he would really do, who he would become, but before he'd decided Horizon and its lightbulbs had done so on his behalf. With each year and every promotion—from the mailroom to filing and records, from filing and records to public relations, and now vice president of community outreach—it had become harder to justify leaving. His salary kept on increasing, not that he spent it on much without a family or time for vacations. A senior position had looked attractive from the distance of other departments, drawing him closer to the top floor, and by the time he realized those promotions may not be what he wanted, he was moving too fast to stop. He'd been rising on updrafts of commerce for years, rising simply by being in the way of the current, circling and waiting for the right moment to swoop down from his office and do something else, but he'd risen too high now to see what other chances might be down below. He didn't have the eyes of the falcons, as much as he liked to see himself in them.

And *BLAM!*, something slammed into the window. The impact rocked Clark's head hard against the glass. Stunned from the blow and pulled out of his dour daydream, he looked up at the gruesome sight of red blood and gold feathers pasted onto the window. He'd seen the falcons chase smaller birds into the glass a few times before, unwilling prey frantic to make an escape, and he felt sad for the birds that died in a crash more than for those killed by the raptors. Breaking your neck against an invisible wall seemed so clumsy and wasted, nothing gained for hunter or hunted. At least there was something romantic in one bird surviving by besting another.

There was nothing romantic about the grim smear on the glass, dead center of his lofty view, and he turned his chair back to his desk and to work. But his head hurt too much to get anything done so he spent a while looking at websites he couldn't remember a few minutes later. He heard the murmur of conversation out in the hallway, almost inaudible through his thick door, and it only lasted a minute before all was quiet again. He decided to go down to the convenience store in the lobby to buy some pills for his head.

The elevator was mirrored inside, like windows all looking nowhere, and Clark half expected a bird to fly into them. From where, he wondered—from behind the glass, or somehow from inside the elevator—and he wondered if he'd hurt his head more seriously than it seemed. He had the car to himself all the way down, but between all those mirrors he was surrounded.

Downstairs, a few steps from the convenience store entrance, Clark decided to walk the two blocks to another store, less conveniently located in the lobby of another building that housed the offices of other firms. The walk might do his head good. So he revolved through the climate-equalizing door for the first time in weeks, and found the air colder than he'd expected but the sun was much brighter than it had appeared through his office's UV-safe glass. Outside, near the doors, were a few concrete slabs suggestive of benches but not so suggestive that anyone sat there for long or ever lay down for a nap. Clark sat and took a deep breath. There were some smokers clustered around one of the slabs, puffing and laughing together, and Clark thought they might be onto something— an excuse to get outside a few minutes each day, looked down on for smoking instead of for wasting time in the sun, one transgression concealed by the other. He thought he might take up smoking himself or pretend that he had, standing around by the building with an unlit cigarette in his hand. Or a pipe, because a pipe seemed so insistently restful.

The benches backed up against deep concrete planters, and he noticed for the first time the pale green and white and bright purple of decorative cabbage, and the miniature evergreens already planted for winter. The planters, he knew, rotated crops every season, fully-grown bushes and trees hauled in from somewhere and the last season's dug out and dumped. He knew all that from building management's memos and from approvals he'd signed—"beautification" fell under community outreach—but he went seasons without stepping outside the building and when he did there was no time for plants.

He leaned back, palms supporting his weight against the cold concrete, and he scanned the sky alongside the glass walls. He couldn't tell if this was his side of the building because all four sides of the top looked the same from the bottom just like the bottom looked the same from the top. His headache seemed to be fading, but he'd still buy the pills just in case. He was about to get up and move on toward the store when his eye caught a red flash beneath a white cabbage. A dead bird, grayish brown with a red hood and breast, lay crumpled and broken under the plant. One leg was cocked close to the fist-sized body and the other stuck out too far to one side. Clark didn't recognize the species; he knew very few birds, pretty much pigeons and seagulls and peregrine falcons, and he only knew what the peregrines were after some time with an online bird guide. He knew this couldn't be the same bird that had struck his window, but its red patches were too much like blood. His headache came back but he didn't feel like a walk any longer and decided to just buy his painkillers inside, in the lobby, where he should have gone in the first place—better yet, he should have sent someone else down to get them and stayed in his office to wait.

He rose from the bench and moved toward the doors, but had only taken a couple of steps when he saw another bird, just as dead but yellow this time. And, like a joke, like an insult, a third lay crushed in a pile of dirt at the base of the building like someone had swept it aside with a broom. All those birds, all at once. He circled the base of the building with a sick stomach, and he found thirteen more bodies, different colors and sizes and broken shapes. Some were already picked over by rats or by bugs, and some looked so perfect they might have been sleeping or stuffed. His building was some kind of deathtrap for birds, and with his head pounding he went inside and purchased his pills.

He shared the elevator with a man he thought was named Chapman, the Chapman in international sales who was rumored to be joining the top floor very soon. But Clark wasn't sure so he didn't say anything and Chapman or not the man stepped out of the car one floor from the top.

Back in his office, once his pills had taken effect, Clark emailed building management to report the dead birds. He'd learned by now not to expect a reply, but he hoped someone might look into it, anyway, even if they never told him.

With all the events of the morning, Clark fell behind on his work and was still at his desk after dark. There were a few other people at work on his floor, and every so often he heard a cough or the scrape of a chair, but he didn't see anyone except the janitor pushing a green trash bin with a wobbly, rattling wheel. He rolled up to Clark's door, saw that he was still inside, then rolled on to return when the office was empty.

At night, the lights of the city spread away from his building and the other towers downtown like sparks from the tail of a rocket. At night his office felt like a capsule halfway into space and Clark himself was one of those cosmonauts stuck in orbit when the Soviet Union collapsed. At night, he wondered if air became thinner because his thoughts always seemed to turn strange if he was still up high in the building.

He typed with half his attention, going through the motions of memos and critiques of marketing plans, more concerned with completion than content. Then *Bang! Bang! Bang!* on the window in popcorn succession. Clark jumped in his chair so the pneumatic risers first relaxed then compressed when he landed, hissing out a quick gasp and long sigh. He spun toward the window, but he was too late to see anything but three smudges dotting the glass like a ghostly ellipsis. There were no feathered bodies hung up on the thin concrete sill of his window, but he knew what the noises had been and he knew there were three more birds on the ground far below him or on their way to it, still falling, perhaps half-alive and still fighting to fly or relying on glider-built bodies to coast them more slowly than his own awkward building-bound body would fall.

He looked down at the lights of all colors and imagined them feathers instead—red, green, and yellow; pink, purple, white; concentric rings and rich patterns like a Tibetan sand painting made from the corpses of birds. Birds all killed by his building. He felt his headache returning and he felt sick from not eating; he'd worked through lunch then forgotten about dinner while trying to finish, and it was all enough for one day. He would just come in early to finish, while the sky was still dark enough for the building and its lights to stand out like a candle as he drove toward it through the city. He came in that early most mornings, and he always got his work done.

Before leaving, he sent another email to building management, updating them on the bird situation and informing them of these latest strikes. He considered getting off on the ground floor to check outside for bodies, but he had no coat and the night could be cold or it might be too dark on the sides of the building, so he rode down to the garage like he did everyday.

The next morning he came up from the parking garage through the street exit instead of straight into the elevator and to his office. The sky was still dark but two maintenance workers with brooms and long-handled dustpans were already sweeping the concrete desert outside the building. When he walked closer, Clark realized they were gathering birds and loose feathers.

He asked one of the sweepers how many birds he'd found that morning, but the man stared back with no indication he knew what

Clark had said. His dustpan was overstuffed, and beaks and tails pushed their way out of its mouth. Maybe, Clark thought, building management had noticed his emails and was doing something.

But only a little while later, when the sun had risen on one side of the building but his was still in the dark, two more birds struck the glass. They must have been small, whatever they were, because the collisions were quiet and almost like rain, but they left the same oily smudge as the ones last night had. He'd already emailed to request window washing, but right away he began a new email, an ultimatum demanding a stop to these deaths. But as he typed he realized that if he proposed a solution instead of just asking for one, it might actually be implemented. So he went online and searched for "birds hitting windows" and "bird collisions skyscrapers" and other combinations like that. He learned that cities squatted on migration routes, and that while some birds—like the falcons above him—had become urban fixtures, others still traveled each year. Millions died as they followed the routes they had followed forever, and most of the impacts came in the dark to birds disoriented and drawn to bright windows in buildings like his.

Other cities, he read, had convinced building managers to turn out their lights, to darken the sky and to let the birds pass. In other buildings that darkening had worked, and he copied three articles all saying so and forwarded them to building management in his email, insisting they adopt the same plan. Then he waited for a reply.

He waited that day and the next, and though he got some of his work done it wasn't much because every minute he was listening with one ear and holding his breath for the sound of a body behind him. It happened a couple of times, and each morning he saw the sweepers at work.

Building management still hadn't answered by the end of day three, and Clark couldn't wait any longer. Late at night his floor became quiet, photocopiers no longer churning out pages and shredders no longer chewing them up, no more eruptions of laughter followed by rushed, self-conscious silence. He waited until he heard only himself and the water cooler bubbling like a stream in a bottle. Then he rode the elevator all the way down to the parking garage and took a black bag from his trunk. He walked to the end of the basement, to the unmarked grey door behind which all the electrical systems connected. He had no key, but between the drill and the saw and the hammer and files he'd packed in his bag, he was able to force the door open. Inside was a jungle of wires climbing into the ceiling, and grey boxes all over the walls, and none of it meant much to him. But inside the boxes were labels detailing which circuit breakers corresponded to where in the building, and it was easy enough—as easy as it had been to identify birds from a guide—to turn off all the lights in the upper reaches of Horizon Tower.

He could feel all that darkness above him, like the top of the tower had floated away and the sky could dip close to the ground. He drove out of the parking garage to the street, then stopped a few blocks away to stand on the sidewalk, looking back at what he had done. There was his building, the faintest outline against the black sky, all of its windows and mirrored walls reflecting the night back onto itself. His office was up there somewhere, he knew, but he couldn't find it, only a single dark square in all that dark sky. He wondered if the falcons would care that the building had vanished beneath them, or was it the same to them either way—their nest was still there and so was the wind, so concrete and steel could come and could go.

Building management would know who had done this, if they were reading their email at all. If not, if their inbox was meant for appearances only, to create the illusion of communication between the building's occupants and its owners, they might never find out it was him. But with his office gone for the moment, and the candle—the bulb—of Horizon Tower unlit, Clark didn't feel like going back the next day to find out. He thought he might go away for a couple of seasons, drive out of town and keep driving until he found some place he'd like to stay for a while, and maybe come back in the spring.

THE LAST FINAL COPY

Peter Anderson

The voice on the line sounded like so many others—young, excited, breathless while not trying to sound that way—from over the years, although unlike the old days this one came from a cell-phone inside a car instead of a phone booth on the street or in some drugstore.

"So is this it, Mr. Heitman? The last one?"

Heitman liked the kid, this Miguel Garza. Enthusiastic, energetic, fresh out of college and still revering the profession. And maintaining respect for his seniors—nobody called anyone Mister any more, not in anything but jest, not even in the formal hierarchies of the corporate world.

"Hard to say, *mi amigo*. It just might be."

Heitman didn't need to address Garza in his native language—the young police reporter spoke perfectly good English—but did so from familiarity, sensing a bond between them despite their obvious differences. Garza grew up in Little Village, in what Heitman used to call the *barrio*, graduated from Benito Juarez High School and spent two years at Malcolm X before applying to the bureau. Right away Heitman saw the reporter in Garza, that bulldog spirit, and quietly hired him without the standard bachelor's degree. Heitman didn't have a four-year degree either, but it hadn't hindered him at all during the past four decades. In fact, skipping college got him out on the streets four years earlier and gave him a head start on the newly-minted journalism grads, all of whom seemed more interested in moving up to the big league papers instead of doing any of the dirty work, the real reporting at the bureau.

In the old days Mullaney only hired English or political science majors, always saying that the former knew how to write a sentence and the latter knew what facts are, while journalism majors didn't seem to know much about anything. Years later, Heitman still agreed with him. Most of the college boys today knew even less about reporting than back then, as they now stayed in school longer, getting master's degrees at Medill or elsewhere and striving to move directly to the city or editorial desks at the dailies while avoiding beat work altogether.

Garza wasn't like those pretty boys—or pretty girls—and, despite their cultural differences, Heitman saw a lot of himself in the young reporter.

"Alright, I'm on my way," Garza replied. "But man, Englewood? I don't like going around there, know what I mean? The Village is tough, man, but Englewood is *scary*."

"There's plenty of worse places," Heitman said mildly. "Or a few, anyway. But it's senior citizen housing, so hopefully there won't be any gangbangers around to give you any trouble."

Garza didn't seem like that type to Heitman. He clearly knew the streets, and could speak the language—probably even the kind spoken in Englewood—without being a troublemaker. More than likely, Heitman imagined, Garza spent his teenage years in the library or honest part-time jobs instead of running with the gangs, the Kings or Padrinos or whomever. But he talked the talk, probably learning it from survival instinct, and maybe even knew a few Kings on a first-name basis to protect himself.

The call had come in earlier over the police scanner—an electrical fire at a seniors high-rise at 63rd and Halsted—and the dispatcher assigned it to Garza who, at that moment, was on his way back downtown, driving up the Dan Ryan after covering a bar brawl on the far South Side. Heitman had taken Garza's earlier report over the phone— the information raw, like that of most rookies—and eased the facts into final copy in his mind, crafting them into no-nonsense bureau language before they were even typed out.

"New Year's Eve festivities deteriorated into a brawl at McGladrey's Harp, 11614 S. Western, Saturday night as revelers..." Heitman's copy began before detailing the injuries, the arrests made, the comments of the bouncer and two patrons, the entire incident neatly summarized in six crisp paragraphs. Let the papers dig deeper if they wanted to, expound on a developing pattern of bar violence, editorialize on society's lamentable loss of decorum and respect. None of that was the bureau's job. Their job was to cover the story on the scene, compile the basic facts, and get the story out on the wires before quickly moving on to the next one.

There was always a *next one*, Heitman reflected, especially on this night. It was New Year's Eve, Amateur Night, an evening rivaled only by St. Patrick's Day and the city's rare championship celebration for incidents to be covered. But for the bureau there weren't many next ones left.

Harry Heitman had seen it all during his forty-three years at the bureau—apartment fires, head-on collisions, shootings—but this night, the last night, was one he never saw coming. Or saw it coming but instinctively looked away, avoiding the inevitable. His cold, unflinching reporter's stance wavered at the thought of it coming to an end.

But soon it would end. At that moment, as Heitman waited for Garza to phone in his report, the city news bureau would exist for only thirty more minutes. Another half hour and it would be just a memory.

After one hundred fifteen years of unparalleled civic service, it would become another victim of corporate cutbacks—killed off by bean counters chasing pennies like rats in a maze, Heitman grumbled more than once. He also wondered, as much as Garza did, if the Englewood story would be the very last one the bureau would cover. The dispatcher would shut down at 11:45, allowing just enough time to pass out styrofoam cups to the entire newsroom staff for the midnight sendoff. The dispatcher's last call would go out to the reporters in the field to return to the office for a goodbye drink if they were nearby; otherwise they were free to head home or wherever else they preferred.

No more stories would be assigned after 11:45, ones which couldn't possibly be filed by midnight. The post-midnight shift, long known as "last watch," would be no more, along with every other shift.

The scanner was fairly quiet, its staticky chatter limited to cops making after-work plans back and forth, arguing Willie's versus Lanegan's, a bar near the precinct versus some place closer to home. Between eleven and twelve, partygoers were already where they wanted to be and were still on their best behavior, not wanting to miss out on midnight, so for now there was little official police business and little for the reporters to report on.

Heitman figured Garza's transformer fire wouldn't be much of a story. Old people evacuated, maybe some hospitalized with smoke inhalation and kept overnight for observation. Most or all of them would be back in their rooms, nestled under the covers in their steel-railed beds, before sunrise. Although Heitman would never hope for a tragedy, he still wished, just a little, that the bureau could go out with more of a bang.

Though it would probably be a nothing story, one that might not even get picked up by the papers, Garza had gone after it eagerly. Heitman admired his commitment, his enthusiasm. All rookies were like this to some extent, but Garza took it much further. Here he was, on New Year's Eve, completely justified if he asked to knock off early to join his buddies for a party somewhere, getting there just in time to kiss every pretty girl in the place at midnight, and instead he was chasing down an electrical fire in Englewood.

Garza was covering the story partly for the glory, Heitman realized, to become a future trivia answer in Chicago newsrooms. ("Who covered the bureau's last story ever?" "Miguel Garza." "Garza, *right*.") But he was mostly doing so because he was a true reporter, and to him every story simply had to be covered. He certainly wasn't doing it for brownie points, some gold star on his employee evaluation. For there would be no more evaluations.

Heitman didn't have to be here tonight, either. As senior editor, he hadn't worked evening shift in years. But tonight's shift was one he couldn't miss, even though he tried to ignore its significance. Lillian would understand, he thought. She was out on the town with the Wilkersons and would just have to enjoy herself without him, her as a third wheel, this one time. Heitman offered the regular evening editor the night off, and the latter gratefully accepted.

Heitman looked across the newsroom through the plexiglass walls of his cubicle. The glass gave him privacy, barely, to take incoming calls from his reporters on the streets and type up their reports into bureauese, while also keeping watch on the comings and goings of the other editors and rewrite people. As he watched the staff move about, the old and familiar plaque caught his eye, its gold lettering gleaming under the fluorescent lights through layers of lacquer: "If your mother says she loves you, check it out." The plaque was a gift from Mullaney, passed along to Heitman on the old editor's last day before retirement. It was the credo of the bureau, and meant *Follow up on every fact, take nobody's word or anything, verify*. He reflected on the words in silence.

As the senior editor on staff, Heitman had unspoken authority over the other editors. His seniority gave him something of an aura, compelling the other editors to defer to him. But despite his authority over the newsroom, the staff formally reported to the executive editor, Lundgren, a man thirty years Heitman's junior in both age and tenure, and to whom the words of Mullaney's plaque probably meant little.

Lundgren had much less experience than Heitman, but more importantly to the suits in the executive suites he was a j-school grad, from Medill—the best school, according to people who cared about such things—and Wilmette, and mixed easily with his North Shore neighbors at the Tower, much more so than Heitman with his high school education and bungalow-belt upbringing.

It might have been said that Lundgren didn't mix well with the bureau staff, were it not for the fact that he didn't mix with them at all, badly or otherwise. Lundgren was never even seen around the bureau's offices. He had stopped in just once, a few weeks after being hired away from a Milwaukee daily, but only stayed long enough to show his obvious distaste for everything about the office: the lingering smoke from cigarettes and a few pipes, the plaid, polyester and otherwise fashionless sportcoats and soup-stained ties, the orange-vinyled and green-fabricked chairs, the formica-topped desks, the worn and dirty linoleum floor. After that single appalled viewing of the newsroom Lundgren conducted all of his business with the staff over the phone, delegating most of the messy everyday details to Heitman from an office two floors above which he claimed and promptly had renovated to his considerably higher standards. Standards lower than those of his colleagues and superiors at the Tower—with whom he spent the majority of his day on the phone, schmoozing and currying favor—but not vinyl, formica and linoleum either.

With Lundgren keeping his distance, Heitman ran the newsroom with a velvet fist, letting the other editors do as they pleased as long as he saw good work being done. He only raised his voice in anger when

Peter Anderson —

dealing with some of the younger reporters, particularly those whom he saw as sloppy or indifferent or only interested in goofing off out in the streets, far from the prying eyes of the editors.

He had worked the job long enough to know how long a story took to cover—an hour for a car accident, two for a holdup, three for a fire—and if a reporter went a half hour over Heitman would be on the phone, blistering the kid's ears, with a pay cut or being shipped back to Fort Wayne being the most common threats. He also could always tell, after hearing a phoned-in report, when a youngster hadn't asked enough questions. In those cases he had no qualms about sending the kid right back to the scene, no matter how embarrassing it might have been for the reporter.

"Cruel world, Jaworski," he would say, or Greenbaum or Morales or Jefferson. "Bosses want you to work hard. Get used to it, or get out."

The kid would learn standards, Heitman's tough standards, if he wanted to keep his job. There were enough young aspiring reporters out there enamored of the bureau's legend and distinguished alumni— Royko, Vonnegut, Seymour Hersh—that no hesitation was needed in firing underperformers. There would always be others to hire. The bureau's seminal stature in the city's newspaper history gave Heitman that luxury. The papers which sucked their lifeblood from the bureau's reports, sometimes even stealing them outright, enjoyed no such luxury. To the general public the bureau was all but unknown, but within the cloistered world of Chicago newspaper journalism the bureau was the big man on campus. Or would be the big man, Heitman saw from a glance at the clock, for another twenty-two minutes.

At 11:38 the newsroom was winding down. Lundgren had knocked off at five, as usual, without calling, without any mention of this being a landmark day in the bureau's storied history. Instead he left the office like it was any other workday. He had probably been at his New Year's party for six hours now, Heitman guessed, with a big steak already in his gut along with who knows how many scotches. He'd be at the Drake or the Ambassador East, weaving slightly in place, watching the champagne being ferried into position, quietly awaiting midnight with frequent glances at the mirrored ball suspended from the ceiling high above. At twelve the ball would finally descend from the rafters—lusty and drunken cheers roaring up, champagne uncorked with a flurry of pops, kisses and hugs all around—as Lundgren eased into another blessed year of employment. He was being kicked upstairs with the bureau's demise, the staff's lone survivor.

All of this was inevitable, Heitman surmised with sadness. Corporate altruism just wasn't what it once was. Dailies cutting loose a money-losing news bureau, airlines and car companies dumping their pension plans, manufacturers abandoning small towns and moving overseas just to boost their next few quarterly reports—it was all the same. The likes of Andrew Carnegie, supporting retirees well into their dotage and spending millions building libraries across the country, would never be seen again. Carnegie probably wasn't any less of a thief than today's Dennis Kozklowskis and Ken Lays, Heitman reasoned, but at least he gave some of it back to the community, lavishing some of his gains on the common good instead of jeweled collars for his poodle or solid gold shower curtains in the guest bathroom of one his vacation houses.

Those days of altruism were over for the bureau, never mind that Heitman ran an extremely lean operation, paying his people no more than they needed to get by and not bringing the newsroom's decor to within forty years of being up to date. Never mind that Heitman's bureau gathered the city's most basic news more efficiently than the dailies ever could on their own. Never mind that, all cost considerations aside, the papers couldn't cover the stories more effectively on their own. No one knew the streets better than the bureau's reporters—the quickest route to South Lawndale, which cops at the Austin Precinct were the most likely to blab indiscreetly, which shopkeepers in Portage Park had the best dirt on local gang activity—and no one could whip the raw information into tight copy better than the bureau's editors.

From now on, starting in January, those responsibilities would fall to the dailies themselves, to reporters and editors who shared Lundgren's indifferent mindset, to Medill grads who spent their formative years in North Shore classrooms instead of pounding the pavement chasing leads, to pampered kids who couldn't keep their eyes on the streets for all their daydreaming about the editorial desk or the Washington bureau. To well-bred reporters and editors who could never do half as good a job of covering the city as Heitman's mongrel staff was already doing.

Or would be doing for the next sixteen minutes.

At 11:44 the dispatcher rose from his desk, stretching languidly with hands clasped and arms raised overhead.

"About time to knock off," he called across to Heitman.

"Still a little early, Stan," the editor replied over the plexiglass barrier, his tone somewhat irritated. He wasn't bothered as much by the dispatcher's haste—Heitman knew there wasn't any sense in sending out any more assignments at this late hour—as by what it implied: that there wouldn't be any more stories covered. There were plenty more to cover, of course, with this being Amateur Night, but those would have to be covered by somebody else.

The dispatcher hesitated, sensing Heitman's disapproval, but the editor relented.

"Go ahead. Might as well get the cups handed out."

The dispatcher nodded in relief and hurried away toward the break room.

So this would be the last time, Heitman reflected, that the end of a shift would be marked by the opening of the bottom drawer of his filing cabinet and the solemn pouring of Jim Beam from a half-empty bottle into styrofoam coffee cups. The subtle tip of the cup toward one's colleagues and the one-gulp swallow of the biting amber liquid had always implied *Good work tonight... Until next time.*

The dispatcher returned with a tall stack of cups, distributing one to each desk in the newsroom. As he approached Heitman's desk, the editor's phone jangled. Heitman lifted the receiver with one hand while reaching for the proffered cup with the other, nodding to the dispatcher in acknowledgment.

"Heitman."

"Mr. Heitman, it's Miguel," the young reporter said, his voice full of anticipation.

"Hey there, Miguel. Got a story for me?"

"Yes, sir, I do."

Garza related the basics. Electrical fire, transformer short-circuit, no threat of injury or loss of life, forty-six seniors evacuated temporarily to St. Bernard Hospital to keep them warm, temperature twenty-two degrees, firemen said transformer not adequately maintained, high-rise run by a management company—a politically well-connected one, Heitman immediately recognized—which offered no comment for the record, Com Ed denied responsibility, fire quickly extinguished, residents being moved back in.

A routine story, Heitman thought with disappointment, the final copy of which was already composed in his head and would be out on the wires in a few short minutes.

"Is that all?" Heitman said, already aware of the answer. He turned to his keyboard and began to type, the receiver wedged between his ear and shoulder.

"Yeah, that's about it. Do you want me to come back in?"

Heitman typed up the story as they spoke, arranging the words in his mind without interrupting their conversation.

"No, Miguel. I mean, only if you really want to. We're going to have a quick drink here and then probably head over to the Merrimac, but if you've got something else going on you can just take off."

"I do have somewhere else to go," the reporter affirmed. "Party in Canaryville, at El Gato Negro. You don't mind?"

"No, of course not. Have yourself a good time. Oh, and good work tonight. Until—"

He paused, realizing there would be no next time. Yet even as he admitted this fact to himself, he dreaded the reporter's inevitable last question. They only danced around it earlier, during Garza's call before he headed to Englewood, alluding but never spelling it out. Heitman swallowed hard before continuing, with what he hoped was an air of finality.

"Miguel, it's been a pleasure working with you," he said as flatly as he could, hoping it would keep the question from being asked.

— The Last Final Copy

"Pleasure for me too, sir," the young reporter replied, hesitating, as if he still had something to say.

Heitman heard the reporter's phone click off, and returned his own to its base. He turned to the keyboard, giving his full attention to banging out the last few sentences. His eyes quickly scanned the three paragraphs—his years of experience having eliminated the need to edit any more formally—and seeing it to be perfect, hit the Save key, followed by Send. The story was finished: dispatched, reported, written, filed.

Heitman's phone rang a second time.

"Sir, I'm sorry, it's Miguel again," Garza said. "I meant to ask...was mine the last story?"

The editor glanced around the newsroom, where the other editors and rewrite people had left their desks and were milling around, waiting for their empty cups to be filled. Clearly, no more stories would be filed.

"Yeah, Miguel, that's the last one." He sighed. "Congratulations, I guess."

"Thanks, sir. I appreciate that."

"Take care."

Heitman hung up the phone again. Clearing his throat, he pivoted, the desk chair squeaking in under-oiled complaint as he reached down and grasped the handle of the bottom drawer of the filing cabinet.

At 11:59 the bottle was emptied, a quarter-inch into each cup, everyone looking at each other in silence, no one knowing what to say.

At midnight, the bourbon was tossed back, quiet handshakes exchanged, futures pondered.

Tonight, there would be no last watch. No more watches at all.

Contributor Note (Trench)

Michael Martone

    Michael Martone was born in Fort Wayne, Indiana, and grew up there, leaving, at seventeen, to work as a roustabout in the last traveling circus to winter in the state. He has held many jobs since then, including night auditor in a resort hotel, stenographer for the National Labor Relations Board, and clerk for a regional bookstore chain run by the associates of the Gambino crime family. For the last twenty years, Martone has been digging ditches. As a ditch digger, he has helped lay agricultural tiling, both the original fired-clay tile and the flexible pvc tubing, in the farm fields of northern Indiana, Ohio, and southern Michigan. He worked on the national project that buried thousands of miles of fiber optic cable along active and abandoned right-of-ways of North American railroads. He has often contracted to do the initial excavations at archaeological digs throughout the Midwest's extensive network of mounds, built by archaic pre-Columbian civilizations, where he would roughly remove the initial unremarkable strata for the scholars who followed at the site with hand trowels and dental instruments. Often when digging ditches, Martone would employ a poacher's spade made in the United Kingdom by the Bulldog Company and given to him by the Nobel Prize-winning Irish poet, Seamus Heaney, who ordered it from the Smith & Hawking catalogue and gave it to Martone as a going away present when Martone left Boston where he had been digging clams. Its ash, "Y" shaped handle still retains a remnant of the ribbon that decorated the gift. Martone has operated a backhoe, constructing drainage ditches, and he has used a DitchWitch when digging a trench for buried electrical conduit in housing developments around Las Vegas, Nevada. He has been certified to run a drag line as well as licensed to maintain boilers in obsolete steam shovels. He is proficient at foundation work, having been employed for four years in the area of poured form and precast concrete retaining walls and building footings. Briefly, he worked as a sand hog, tunneling a new PATH tube between Manhattan and New Jersey. Martone has mined coal and gypsum in Kentucky and repaired the sewers of Paris and Vienna. Honorably discharged from the SeaBees, he once helped fortify, through the entrenchment and the construction of sand berms and tank traps, the Saudi Arabian city of Qarr during the Gulf War. He has buried culvert in Nova Scotia and created leech fields and septic tanks in Stewartstown, Pennsylvania. Having installed irrigations systems on the Trent Jones designed golf courses of Alabama, Martone recently took a position as a grave digger at the Roman Catholic Cemetery in his home town in order to be closer to his family. Using the newly purchased Komatsu excavator, he dug the grave for his mother who died unexpectedly in her sleep. He observed the funeral from the cab of the machine, waiting until the mourners had departed to remove the Astroturf blanket covering the spoil and then back-filling the opening and replacing the squares of real turf on the dirt. Since that time, on his days off, Martone digs, with the poacher's spade given to him by the Nobel Prize-winning Irish poet Seamus Heaney, his own grave. Or, at least, attempts to dig his own grave as all of these efforts, so far, have been filled back in, as the resulting holes, to his professional eye, were never quite right.

Concentrate

Pete Fromm

I make orange juice everyday, earlier and earlier it seems, now that he's doing so much out of town work. But I'd never thought about it much before. Who does? You zip off the ring, slide the frozen stuff into the pitcher, add three cans of water, and presto—orange juice. Not much in that most people'd wonder about. Most people are hardly even awake during all that. But I get to thinking about things, usually while the kids are down for their naps and the whir of the air conditioner's all that's left in this trailer.

I can't think everyday though. Some days I'm so worn down by nap time all I can do is sit and listen to that air conditioner. Every time it cranks up it sounds like an old person trying to get going in the morning, wheezing and grumbling before settling down into the same old routine. It shakes the whole wall when it starts. Nobody ever said they made trailer homes to stand up to much. That's why you always see them blown wide open after tornadoes, when the big houses aren't touched at all.

Boy, but I'd like to see one of those big houses by the golf course break open. Just imagine all the wonderful things that'd get scattered around.

Days the kids've been good, or days Tom can sleep in a little before going off to work, I use nap time to think. Thinking's what's going to get us out of here. I know that. I make plans for things. I once thought how if I could design a trailer house that wouldn't get gutted so easy by tornadoes we'd be sitting pretty. But after a while I saw I didn't have the training for it. People go to schools to design buildings, even trailer houses I suppose. So I tried to scale down my ideas.

The next thing I tried was designing an air conditioner that wouldn't shake walls, or be so loud it'd wake you up if you happened to be lucky enough to doze some at nap time. I got so far as to getting out Tom's tools and taking apart that whole air conditioner, so I could see how it worked. But the kids got up then, before they were supposed to, and they started scrambling around in all the parts I'd taken out. I shouted at them, but Tommy got hold of the fan blade and tore all around the trailer with it, pretending he was a fighter plane. He kept shooting at me and for some reason I just couldn't stand that. I couldn't stand his little screwed up face or his spitting machine gun noises. Why did he have to keep shooting at me?

I went after him until I got him cornered in the back bedroom, but he went through the door there we never use, the fire escape door, and I had to chase him down the street through the middle of the trailer court. When I finally caught him he kept screaming, "Don't shoot me down, Mommy! Don't shoot me down!"

I wanted to paddle him so bad, but I was standing in the street then and there were a lot of women watching me, women putting out laundry—women just sitting on the steps in the heat, waiting for who knows what. Not a one of them would've thought twice about calling the police. Not that they didn't whack their own, but reporting me would've made something happen, which most everybody stuck here would've been happy for, just so they could crowd around the trailer singled out by the police car.

None of them could see Tommy was holding anything more than a toy propeller. They didn't know the first thing about air conditioning. They didn't know the first thing about any of my plans.

I dragged Tommy back to the trailer, him digging in his heels and hollering and crying the whole way. When I launched him up the steps I was ready to light into him, but there was Jenny, sitting in all the parts of the air conditioner, teething on a black fan belt she'd wound around herself. The belt had painted a big black frown down from the corners of her mouth.

I stood and stared at her, holding that dusty propeller in my hand, and I just told Tommy to go to his room. I told him to take his sister there too. He knew he was getting off light, and he jumped right to it. I stopped Jenny long enough to pry away the control knobs she'd balled into her fists. Then I went and sat down where Jenny'd been, and I tried to gather all the parts back together, but all of a sudden it seemed like more work than I could do, and I wound up just sitting there until Tom walked through the door, after another day of work. I knew he was doing shovel work then, and I knew he'd be tired. But he sat down next to me and asked me what had happened and I couldn't tell him one thing. Though I hated to, I just sat there and cried. I hated to let him see that. It'd worry him for days. He carried me back to our bed then and said he'd take the kids to McDonalds for dinner. It's no wonder they say they like him more than me.

When I got up the next morning to fix him breakfast, the air conditioner was back in the wall, rumbling away, shaking half my world, and Tom didn't say a word about it. I feel about him the same way the kids do.

He kissed me and asked if I'd be all right, and I said of course. Then he left like usual—before the kids got up. I watched his car disappear then peeked into the kids' room, just to see them while they were still asleep and quiet. They both had their sheets pulled clear over their heads. It gave me the shivers, and I wanted to pull the sheets down, just so they'd look a little more alive. But I didn't want to take the chance of waking them any earlier than I had to and I snuck away.

As I was closing the door I noticed a poster over Tommy's bed. It was a picture of Ricky Henderson, Tommy's absolute hero, diving into second base. I figured Tom must've bought it last night, after the kids had told him their version of the air conditioner.

I closed the door, but until the kids got up I kept seeing Ricky Henderson's face, so tight with concentration, like he had to reach that base or die. I wondered if my face ever looked like that, and when the kids got up and started fighting right off, I wondered what there might be that I could dive for.

Days the breeze'd go out toward the gulf, and it wasn't so sticky hot, I'd take the kids for walks; Jenny in the stroller and Tommy just barely staying in sight. We'd go up to the golf course mostly. It was like our park and I'd let Tommy tear around and do whatever he wanted there, and I'd look at the houses, wondering what was inside them. I thought if I could come up with something the people in those houses would want it wouldn't be too long before we'd have one of those places ourselves.

I was thinking on that, trying to come up with a plan, and I didn't notice when the greens on that golf course got to be too much for Tommy to resist. Four of the golf people caught him pretending he was Ricky Henderson, sliding head first into second. He was diving for the flag stuck in the hole, like it was a base, and when those men collared him and dragged him to me they were more than upset. They said I could be fined for what Tommy'd done. They said they paid men a lot of money to make that green just so, and that Tommy had ruined it.

I looked at them in their fine, colorful clothes and their funny shoes—men who paid other men just to grow grass—and instead of cussing them out, like I should've, I wound up laughing so hard and for so long that they all got looking uneasy, and finally turned Tommy over to me and told me not to let him loose on their course anymore. All the rest of that day I'd get the giggles, and if Tommy was in reach I'd rub the top of his head. I hadn't had a laugh like that in a long time, and I wanted to let him know he wasn't in trouble. The idea of those men thinking I could pay them anything they didn't already have was just too much for me.

But we kept going back up there, at first just when it was rainy and the golfers were all someplace else. I wondered about the houses, and when no one was around I'd go ahead and let Tommy free on the course. Sometimes I'd see him edging around a green and I'd yell out, "And Henderson's off with the pitch!" At first he used to look at me to make sure it was all right, but after he got used to it he was off as soon as I said Henderson, and he'd dive head first, skidding across that short, wet grass like it was plastic. Those were about the only grass stains I didn't mind working out of his jeans.

He slid right through the little flag pole once, snapping it off clean. He came running then, his face white, thinking he was in real trouble, but he saw me laughing and as we ran away, the stroller hopping like mad over the cracks in the sidewalks, he kept asking, "Did you see me, Mommy? Did you see me?"

All that day he was wound up that we'd been partners, and when his dad came home Tommy told him about it before I could stop him. Tom looked at me then, so hurt in his face that I knew I'd have to make Tommy stop sliding on the greens. Sometimes Tom would never say a thing, but all the same I'd suddenly see myself like he did, not the way I always saw myself—spending all day every day in a trailer house with these two kids. I'd see what I thought was fun, the way he would, and instead of being fun anymore it'd seem stupid, even scary.

Of course I couldn't explain all that to Tommy. I just made him stop, and when he kept on asking why, I wound up shouting at him. I'd get so mad at him sometimes, always getting me into trouble I wouldn't've even thought of myself.

The day before I got the orange juice idea it'd rained, and when we went to the golf course Tommy kept begging me to say, "And Henderson's off with the pitch!" But I couldn't do that anymore and we'd already been through it, more than once. But Tommy wouldn't let it go and he got so whiny and mopey I finally gave him a slap. That ruined everything and we wound up going home before I even had a chance to look at any of those big houses. When Tom came in from work he could see right off that something'd been brewing. He took one look around, and said, "How about a baseball game? I just happen to have some Astros tickets here."

Tommy went nuts, streaking straight out to the car, and Jenny toddled out after him, thinking if he thought it was so great she better not miss her turn. I sat still, looking at Tom, at the black dirt still caked onto the knees of his jeans and the thin lines of it wrinkled into the sweaty creases of his face. He didn't have any tickets, I knew that. If he did he'd be waving them around like a bouquet.

He pulled me out of my chair and gave me a hug and said we'd pick the tickets up at the Dome. He said it wasn't any good for us to be cramped inside all through a rainy day, and I went out to the car too. I didn't tell him that we went to the golf course everyday now, rain or shine. One by one I was going through the things that must be in those houses, knowing something was going to come to me if I just gave it a chance. And when I figured it out, I was going to surprise him with it. I could already practically see his face.

Pete Fromm —

Once we got in the Dome, first thing, Tommy complained about the seats, because he couldn't even see as much as he could on TV. When he found out Ricky Henderson wasn't playing I was ready to take him out to the parking lot and lock him in the car the rest of the night. Tom tried to explain that the A's were in another league, and that Henderson never played the Astros, but Tommy didn't calm down until Tom promised that we'd all ride up to Dallas some time, when the A's were taking on the Rangers.

I knew there wasn't much chance of that ever happening and looking at Tommy's sulky face the rest of the night I just wanted to shake him. Couldn't he see that his dad was just about killing himself, just to keep his snotty little face cleaned and fed? Couldn't he see how it ripped Tom up to have to lie about trips to Dallas that we couldn't've afforded for anything, let alone a stupid baseball game? I decided I was going to rip his poster to shreds as soon as we got home, right in front of his face, so he could see what he was doing to his dad every single day.

But on the drive home Tom went through every close play, marveling how some Puerto Rican kid could handle the ball. I saw we'd gone to that game for him too, and when we got home I put the kids to bed in a hurry, then climbed in with Tom, who was still all excited about the game.

The next morning we got up early because Tom was working clear on the other side of Houston, and when we finished breakfast he said again how much fun that game had been. I wanted to ask him if he hadn't noticed Tommy the whole night, but I let it go.

Then, out of the blue, Tom started talking about money, asking how we were making out on what we had, asking how our savings looked. I handled the money for us, and I said our savings didn't look like anything. I laughed and I said our savings were downright invisible. He had a way of even making things like that seem fun, and I wished again that he didn't have to work so hard—that he'd be able to be around more.

He kind of poked around with his feet under the table and he said it looked like he might be having some down time coming up, just until the hoe operator picked up his next job.

I gave a quick glance around the trailer when he said that, knowing already there wasn't a thing more we could cut back on. My eye settled on the sweating pitcher of orange juice, and I said that juice was high right now, and that we really didn't need it.

He laughed and said that things weren't that bad. He said he'd been having his fresh glass every morning since he was a kid, and he figured he'd keep on doing that. "The kids like it too," he added, patting my rear and stretching, getting ready to walk out the door. He said, "Don't worry. It's not as bad as all that." Then he kissed me and asked if I was going to be all right. Somehow that'd become part of our morning routine and I said, "Of course, I'll be fine," he drove away, and I slumped back down at the kitchen table.

I couldn't bring myself to tackle the dishes right then and I just prayed the kids would sleep late. If they started to fight this morning I didn't know what I'd do. I didn't know how we could face another layoff and I started blotting it out of my mind. I started trying to blot everything out. Without even knowing it I started running my finger back and forth across the pitcher, drawing lines in the beady drops of sweat.

That's when it hit.

Orange juice.

I sat up straight. The kids didn't like orange juice as much as Tom thought they did. I made them drink it. I made them drink the whole pitcher everyday. You know how juice gets if it's left around. It gets stale somehow, and it never has that same bright taste it does when you first mix it up. So I'd always made the kids finish the pitcher, so I could make it up fresh in the morning, so Tom'd at least have that before going out for another day.

It all fell together so pretty I couldn't believe it. I could see those golf people. I could see how their mornings went in their big, solid houses. They weren't like us. They didn't get up at the crack of dawn and have cold cereal. I couldn't even remember ever seeing any of them with kids. I figured they'd drink one, maybe two glasses of juice a day, tops. And they'd be in those dinky little glasses you see in stores, that aren't big enough to hold anything. A pitcher of orange juice would last forever in a house like that. Staler and staler every day.

Then, for a second, I thought, hell, those people'd just throw it away if it tasted less than perfect. But I knew people like that didn't get to live in those houses by throwing out good money. No, they'd see what I had.

You see, it'd been that obvious. How long's orange juice been around? Forever, right? So long that nobody thought about it anymore. Nobody but me.

I remembered the crates of oranges they'd had for sale at the store yesterday. Boxes and boxes, all marked down for quick sale. They were dirt cheap.

What I figured, just that quick, was that I could get a whole load of those oranges. Me and the kids could spend all day smashing them up, getting out the juice. It might even be fun for them, the way they love to smash things.

Then I'd set the juice to simmering on the stove, boiling off all the water, don't you see? Making concentrate myself! It was so easy I couldn't believe it.

Once I had it boiled down, I'd freeze it, but not in pitcher size cans. No. I'd freeze it in ice cube trays. Concentrated cubes! One bright, fresh glass of juice, perfect every single time. Nothing stale, no waste. It was a world record idea. Those golf people, the ones in the big houses, would pay for it too. They were the kind of people who'd pay big if they could see that someone had used their head and had really come up with something they needed. For Chrissakes, they paid people to grow them grass!

I jumped up from the table and ran to the kids' room. Jenny was awake and looking at me when I came through the door. "Come on, Hon'," I said, "We got to go to the store."

Tommy woke up as I was dressing his sister, and I told him to get his clothes on. Usually he's kind of cranky first thing, but he could see something was up and he moved pretty quick. He was sitting on the edge of his bed, trying to tie his shoes when I was ready, and I grabbed his hand and yanked him after me down the little hall way. He said a couple of times that he still had to tie his shoes, and I could feel him keep trying to bend over to tie them, even as I was pulling him out the door.

He was mad by the time we got to the car and he sat down on the ground to tie his shoes. I picked him up and sat him down in the front seat and he gave me one of his looks. I said, "You sit tight, buster. Things work out, we'll get you some of those shoes you don't have to tie."

"The ones with the velcro?" His face lit up that quick.

"You bet," I said. I was so excited I could hardly get Jenny buckled into the car seat. My key doesn't work on the driver's door, but when I ran around Tommy didn't even mess with me. He leaned right over and unlocked the door.

When I slid in and slammed the door behind me, Tommy asked, "Are we running away, Mommy?"

For some reason that stole my thunder. I stopped trying to ram the key into the ignition and I turned and looked at him. "You mean without Daddy?" I said.

He just shrugged and looked away from me.

"No. Of course not," I said. "We're going to the store."

"If we're running away I want to get my poster is all," he said, nearly into his morning pout, but not quite. He wasn't sure yet what was going on, if it'd be something he'd like or not like.

"Don't you worry about Ricky," I said, finding the key hole at last. A big blue cloud of smoke wrapped around us and I backed out. "We'll
He looked straight ahead into the dash, just like he was saying, *We'll see about that.* The tires screeched a little after I got it in drive and Jenny hooted.

On the way to the store I stopped at the Salvation Army. Months before I'd noticed they had a mound of plastic ice cube trays. I remembered thinking who in the world would go to the Army looking for ice cube trays? But now I bought all I thought would fit in my freezer. Nickel a piece. When I threw them in the back seat, Jenny picked one up and started gnawing at the corner.

At the grocery I told the guy in the white apron that I wanted oranges, boxes of them. He rounded up a couple of baggers and we filled the back of my little wagon. Cheap as they were, I was still about cleaned out at the cash register.

The man in the apron wanted to know what I was planning to do with all those oranges. "You can't freeze them," he told me.

"I know," I said.

"Do you can them?" he wanted to know. "Making marmalade?"

"No," I said, "that's all been done before."

"Well, what are you going to do then?"

I smiled at him, sweet, and said, "None of your beeswax." Tommy giggled.

Riding home, the three of us cramped in the front seat, the whole car filled with the smell of those oranges. It smelled like a vacation, like Florida or something, and the kids were excited and laughing the whole way.

I rumpled up Tommy's hair. "Running away!" I said. "Where'd you ever get an idea like that?" But he was embarrassed about that now and wouldn't say a word. He just pretended he didn't know what I was talking about. I never once thought of running away. But now the idea was there—foreign, but bright kind of, and shiny, like the smell of all those oranges, and I knew it wouldn't go away.

When we got back to the trailer I lugged the first couple of boxes inside, and when I went out for another I found Tommy'd pulled the top off a box. The boxes were too big for them, and he and Jenny were both carrying oranges into the house, three or four at a time. Right then I could've scooped both of them into my arms for great, giant hugs. What I did was said this'd be enough and that the fun was just starting.

I got them set up at the table and gave them each an orange. I told them to roll it around, mashing it up without breaking the peel. Pretty soon they were thumping them all over the place, but they were careful about breaking them. They wanted to see what I was up to.

I pulled out the big soup pot and set it in the middle of the table. I took Tommy's orange from him and it felt like a baggie full of water. I said, "At-a-boy. Just like that." Then I cut that orange in half, and the first squirts of juice splashed against the clean silver bottom of the pot. Then I rolled the halves between my palms, same way they made ropes out of Play-Dough, and the real juice slurped out.

Pretty soon Tommy got the hang of the rolling part, and we were elbow to elbow over the pot. Jenny couldn't do much but bang around the oranges, but that seemed to hold her all right.

By the time we got the whole pot full we'd burned up more than three boxes of oranges. I'd hoped they'd go farther than that. The way you always add three cans of water I figured I'd have to boil it down to about a quarter of a pot before I froze it. Didn't seem like a lot of return for all that work.

I put that first pot on the stove, setting it on medium-high just to get the ball rolling. I strainered out the seeds and stood and watched, stirring until I saw the first bubbles. I cut it right back to simmer then, and when

I saw it'd be all right I brought the next pot to the table and sang out, "Fill her up!"

My wrists were already tired from all the squeezing, and Jenny'd given up a long time ago, but Tommy grabbed another orange and started softening it up. I was surprised to see him hang on. I asked him where Jenny'd gone, and he just shrugged and kept rolling that orange around on the table.

I rounded Jenny up, her sticky hands and pudgy little arms all blue and hairy from the fuzz off the carpet, and I sat her back down at the table, telling her she didn't have to work, but that she had to stay here. I told her I didn't have the time to be tracking her all over the place. I half expected Tommy to squall about her not having to work, but he just held out an orange for me to cut in half for him. Then he started rolling the halves over the new pot, just like a pro. I would've rumpled up his hair right then, but my hands were all sticky too.

By noon we were almost done with the fourth pot and my own forearms were pretty near to being on fire—something about the rolling and squeezing that they just weren't used to. And I'd always figured I could work forever if I had to.

Tommy'd gotten awful quiet but every time I'd look over he was still rolling oranges. He started doing it all crippled up though, trying not to move his wrists at all. I bent my head down low, so I could see his face, and he was biting on his lip and he had tears just started in the corners of his eyes.

I pulled the orange away from his hands and said, "For heaven's sake, Tommy. Don't hurt yourself." I took his wrists in my hands and tried to massage them a little, but he flinched.

"Your hands are too sticky," he said. "They hurt my skin."

I looked down at my fingers and saw how our skin was stuck together, his smooth skin puckering behind my rough fingers, trying to stay with them and move the same way they did. I took my hands away and I said, "I'm sorry, Hon'. That must've felt like pulling off a band-aid."

"It's not that bad," he said, trying hard to be brave.

I set the last pot on the stove then, though it wasn't quite full. I turned the burner up to medium-high, like I'd done with all the others, just to get it going. I said, "Well, we've got all the burners filled up anyway. Nothing more for us to be doing for a while."

Tommy just sat at the table. I said, "I'll run you a tub. We'll soak those wrists of yours. That'll make them feel better."

"I'm all right," he mumbled.

"I know," I said. I was tired too, and I picked up Jenny and headed for the bathroom. I was proud of him for working as hard as he had, and I didn't want to watch him go into a sulk on me.

Jenny likes sitting in the tub while it fills, so I sat her down and turned on the water. She started splashing and giggling and I was able to yank her out and set her on the toilet as soon as she started to pee. That's one of her tricks—something about the water. Normally I let her go, but I thought Tommy might want this water, and I didn't think that'd be too fair after all his work.

Soon as I turned the water off and began working over Jenny with the wash cloth, Tommy stepped into the bathroom. He was naked al-ready, looking skinny and breakable. His arms were stained brown from the juice, halfway to the elbows. He climbed right into the tub, though recently he'd started saying he was too old to share with his sister anymore.

I gave Jenny a floating duck dressed like a sailor and started going over Tommy with the cloth. Somehow I knew that's what he wanted, to be cleaned up just like a baby, to have the nice scratchiness of the cloth rubbed over his body and to have my hands on him when they wouldn't hurt.

When I started to massage his wrists this time he didn't flinch. He asked, "What are we doing, Mommy?"

"We're making orange juice, Tommy," I said. "We're going to sell it to your friends up at the golf course."

He looked up at me then, to see if I was making fun of him, but I smiled and he smiled back a little unsurely. "Really?"

"You bet," I told him.

"Is Daddy coming home tonight?"

"Of course he is. What ever got in your head today?"

He shrugged then and looked at his hands. I was massaging his palm, pulling on each of his short, thin fingers. "Does that feel good?" I asked.

He hummed an answer and nodded his head. "Sometimes I'm so bad I think you'll both run away without me," he whispered.

"Nonsense," I said. "We never think like that. We aren't going to leave you anywhere."

"When I broke that flag that day, you laughed, but I thought Daddy was going to cry."

"Oh, Tommy," I said, switching to work on his other hand, "you're just tired. Daddy wasn't going to cry. He was surprised is all. If he was mad at anyone it was at me."

"But I was the one that did it."

"No, no. I shouldn't've let you play out there in the first place."

"But he wouldn't be mad at you if it wasn't for me."

"Hush now, Tommy. You're not making any sense. Daddy isn't mad at me."

I gave him a little hug then and stood him up. I pulled Jenny out of the tub and wrapped a towel around her. Then I pulled the other towel from the bar and started to rub Tommy dry. "I think you're both about ready for your naps," I said.

Tommy reached down and pulled the plug and I thought I heard something else. I stopped to listen. The towel was still draped over Tommy's head and his voice was muffled when he started to say he didn't want a nap, he wanted to help.

Then I heard the noise for real; splashing, hissing, burning, and I knew I hadn't turned that last burner down and even before I'd blurted, "Goddamn it," and started running to the kitchen the trailer was filled with a sweet, black smell that stung my eyes and made me want to throw up.

I yanked the pot from the stove and shut the burner off. The sides of the pan were scorched, and I knew that was going to be a scrubbing job for sure. I dumped the pot in the sink and ran cold water into it. The burnt juice poured over the side and swirled around like orange smoke, going down the drain.

"Damn it," I swore again. "Goddamn it to hell."

"I didn't do it," Tommy said, quietly.

He startled me and I spun around. "For Chrissake's, Tommy. Nobody said you did anything." I said that before I'd seen him—before I'd even thought. He was just standing there, at the edge of the counter, naked and tiny, that towel still hanging half off his head. When I saw that I squatted down to be at his height, and I held my arms out for him. His lip trembled some and he looked me right in the eyes and then turned and walked away.

I waited a minute, just trying to catch my breath. I stood up and ran the big spoon through the other three pots, to keep them from burning. Then I went to look for Tommy.

He was in his room and already in his bed. So was Jenny. I couldn't remember the last time that had happened without a fight. Jenny looked up at me and smiled, but Tommy had his back turned purposely to the door and even through the sheet I could see how stiff and hard he was holding his little body. I told them to have a good nap and I shut the door before going back to the kitchen.

The smell really was enough to make me sick, and I opened the door and the windows and that old air conditioner started going right away, like it could cool down the whole world. I stood and stared at it until it was over the wheezing and groaning, and I shivered.

I stayed over the stove all afternoon, and the kids stayed down much longer than usual. I wondered if the work'd really worn them out that much, or if maybe the smell was scaring them. I wondered if I was scaring them. I wondered if they'd learned to be afraid of me by now.

I went and checked on them once, and Jenny was sitting on her bed, playing with an old Barbie she'd found a while back. It was missing its arms, but she was holding it by the hair and didn't seem to mind. Tommy still had his face to the wall. I went and sat on his bed. "I'm going to freeze the first batch now, Tommy," I said. I was excited about that myself, and I thought he would be too. "Don't you want to see? After you did all that work?"

"I'm sick," he murmured. "I don't feel good."

"Are you going to be all right?"

"Yes."

"OK," I said. "I'll bring you the first glass though. That'll make you feel better."

He didn't say anything to that and when I stood up I saw him scrunch back to the far side of the bed, where he'd been before my weight had dragged him down.

Back in the kitchen I pulled the big pot off the stove and set it in the sink. I ran cold water around it, on the outside, to help it cool faster. The stuff in the pan was pretty gross looking, heavy and syrupy, but when I put my nose right down into the pot it still smelled like oranges. It was a nice smell after all afternoon with that burnt stuff in my nose.

When it was cool enough, I poured it into the cube trays and slid them into the freezer. I turned the freezer all the way to the coldest. I could hardly wait to try it.

As the rest of the pots boiled down to the same gooey mess, I poured them into trays and stuck them into the freezer, shifting the early ones to the top, so I could try them first. Then I sat down to start squeezing the next batch, but Jenny came down the hallway and wandered over and leaned up against my leg, grabbing a fistful of my jeans. The table was a mess; dust stuck all over it from when I'd opened the windows. I'd have to clean that before I did anything, and I decided I'd wait until I sampled the first batch. That'd get me going again.

So instead of going back to squeezing oranges, I picked Jenny up and sat down with her on the couch. She sat there, quiet as could be, with her head resting back against my chest. I could just see the top of her head and her eyelashes, sticking out longer than mine ever had. Every once in a while she'd blink and I'd know she was watching something. I looked out across the trailer; at the sticky table snatching at every bit of fluff, the piles of withered orange halves overflowing the waste basket, and at the stack of gluey pans next to the sink. I wondered what in the world she could be seeing.

What I started to see were the ladies who live in those big houses. I really never had seen one of them with children. I knew some of them must have kids, but I knew they didn't ever paddle them, and I knew none of their kids stayed in bed all day, saying they were sick, just to make them feel awful, right when they'd been so proud of them.

I knew most of those ladies worked downtown in Houston, in the skyscrapers, and I knew they worked because they liked to, not because they were trying to survive. They worked like a hobby, and they made more money than I could imagine, just so they could dress up so nice everyday and drive their foreign cars around and be seen going in and out of those buildings made of glass.

I looked around my trailer again and I thought of those women getting ready to come home. I could hear the clicking of their high heels snapping against cool tile floors, and smell the breaths of all their perfumes mixing in the noiseless elevators, like an everyday trip to a flower shop. What in the world had happened to me, I wondered. What in the world did they have that was so missing in me?

I petted the thin hair on Jenny's head and closed my eyes, waiting for my juice cubes to freeze.

Jenny fell asleep there on my lap, and just before I figured Tom would get home I set her down on the couch, careful not to wake her. I went to the freezer and took out the first tray. It was frozen hard and I scratched it with my nail. An orange curl came up and I sucked it into my mouth. My whole head filled with the burning smell again, and I got all loose feeling in the bottom of my insides. I figured it was maybe just from something that was on my finger, from messing with the burnt pot maybe.

I broke out some cubes and put one into a highball glass. I filled it up the rest of the way with water and I stirred it all around with a teaspoon. It was sort of fun, something ordinary, but so much smaller than I was used to. It seemed to mix all right, but my hands were shaking still, from that first taste.

When it was all mixed up, I took a sip and instead of spitting it out, like I should've, I made myself swallow it down. I took another drink. It was all burned up, even though I'd been so careful. It tasted like orange juice from a forest fire. Drinking it down, I could feel it filling me up with all the ashes of everything I'd planned.

I looked around the house which I'd meant to get cleaned before Tom came home, when I was going to give him his single serving glass of orange juice. I set my glass on the counter, but I missed and it crashed to the floor. If it'd been real glass it would've shattered all over the place.

That woke Jenny up and she started to whimper, and when I just walked away she got mad and began to cry for real. I went into the kids' room and I caught Tommy flipping over so his back was to me again. I walked over to his bed and got right in there with him, curling myself around his toasty, naked body.

Tommy didn't turn around or soften up one bit, and the last thing I saw before I closed my eyes was Ricky Henderson, so close to that base and safety, but frozen in mid air, his face forever twisted in concentration and effort.

I didn't cry. I was afraid of what would happen if I ever started that. But I wondered how I could've been so stupid to trick myself into thinking I could've concentrated anything down. I couldn't even concentrate my own life. I'd never once been able to boil away the bad parts, but had always left them there, clouding up the bright, flavorful core.

I held Tommy tighter and tighter, trying to melt him I suppose. And, just before I heard Tom pull up and walk through the door, Tommy finally started to relax. I told him I was sorry about everything I'd ever done to him. He didn't say anything but he started to play with my fingers, where they were wrapped around his chest. He twisted my wedding ring back and forth, like he used to when he was such a little boy.

My mouth was right against his ear, and I whispered again that I was sorry. Then I heard Tom come in and I heard his low whistle when he saw the kitchen. I could hear him pick up Jenny, who was still whimpering alone on the couch.

He said, "Where's Momma, Sugarbaby?"

I heard Jenny laugh and knew he was tickling her, but I could hear the nervousness in his voice. You can hear everything through these walls. I heard Jenny say I was in her room, sleeping with Tommy. Tom asked if we were sick and Jenny said, "No."

And when Tom said, "Well, let's go see if we can wake up the sleepyheads," I couldn't hold back the tears anymore, and I whispered into Tommy's ear that I loved him and that he should never be afraid that we'd run away.

When he squeezed my arms tighter to his chest, I opened my eyes and saw Ricky Henderson again, in mid-dive. But, for the first time, I noticed—blurred and in the background—the umpire in his black suit, legs spread wide and low, his arms already starting out to his sides, giving the safe sign.

Contributors

Peter Anderson left his first employer to go back to grad school, survived two downsizings at his second employer but then left the company prior to a looming third downsizing that would have inevitably cost him his job. He enjoyed a good five-year run at his third employer before a corporate takeover finally left him unemployed. Though he did land a stable but uninspiring position with his current employer (a small Chicago bank), he is now looking elsewhere. He lives and writes in Joliet, Illinois, and welcomes any and all career suggestions.

Rick Attig is a writer and editor for *The Oregonian* newspaper in Portland. He grew up working on a Willamette Valley grass-seed farm and building houses with his father, a longtime union carpenter in Corvallis, Oregon. Attig has worked as an Oregon journalist for more than 25 years and was part of a team at *The Oregonian* that won the 2001 Pulitzer Prize for Public Service for a series of articles and editorials about wrongdoing in the U.S. Immigration and Naturalization Service. In 2006, he and a colleague won the Pulitzer Prize for Editorial Writing for a series revealing abuses at the Oregon State Mental Hospital, which served as the backdrop for the movie *One Flew Over The Cuckoo's Nest*. Attig is now in his second year in the low-residency MFA program at Pacific University. This is his first piece of published fiction. His wife, Courtenay Thompson, is also a writer. He has two sons, Mitchell, and Will.

Matt Bell is the author of the short story collection *How They Were Found* (Keyhole Press, 2010), as well as three chapbooks: *Wolf Parts*, *The Collectors*, and *How the Broken Lead the Blind*. His fiction has been selected for inclusion in anthologies such as *Best American Mystery Stories 2010* and *Best American Fantasy 2*. He is also the editor of *The Collagist* and of Dzanc's *Best of the Web* series, and can be found online at www.mdbell.com. Over the past fifteen years, he's been (occasionally simultaneously) a bartender, a restaurant manager, a data analyst, a laboratory technician, a teacher, and an editor.

Bonnie Jo Campbell was a 2009 National Book Award finalist and National Book Critics Circle Award finalist for her collection of stories,

CONTRIBUTORS —

American Salvage. That collection won the Foreword Book of the Year award. Campbell is also author of the novel *Q Road* and the story collection *Women & Other Animals*. She's received the AWP Award for Short Fiction, a Pushcart Prize, and the Eudora Welty Prize. Her poetry collection, *Love Letters to Sons of Bitches,* won the 2009 CBA Letterpress Chapbook award. Campbell teaches at Pacific University Low Res MFA program. She has worked as a bicycle tour leader, a snow cone seller for the Ringling Brothers and Barnum & Bailey Circus, and a mathematics instructor. She lives with her husband in Kalamazoo, Michigan, where many of her stories could take place. She practices martial arts and tries to train her two donkeys, Jack and Don Quixote.

Jim Daniels' latest books include *Having a Little Talk with Capital P Poetry*, and *From Milltown to Malltown*, a collaborative book with photographer Charlee Brodsky and writer Jane McCafferty. He has published eleven other books of poetry, along with three collections of short stories. He has also written and produced three films, including, most recently, "Mr. Pleasant," based on his short story of the same name. His poems have been featured on Garrison Keillor's "Writer's Almanac," in Billy Collins' *Poetry 180* anthologies, and Ted Kooser's "American Life in Poetry" series. Other recognition includes the Brittingham Prize for Poetry, the Tillie Olsen Prize, two fellowships from the National Endowment for the Arts, and two from the Pennsylvania Council on the Arts. He is the Thomas Stockman Baker Professor of English at Carnegie Mellon University. He was born in Detroit, where much of his prior work experiences occurred. His jobs have included soda jerk, short-order cook, stock boy, liquor store clerk, bookkeeper, janitor, deliveryman, factory worker, among others. He currently lives in Pittsburgh with his wife, the writer, Kristin Kovacic, and their two children, near the boyhood homes of Andy Warhol and Dan Marino.

Pete Fromm won a fourth Pacific Northwest Booksellers Literary Award for his novel, *As Cool As I Am*, which will be filmed this summer. Earlier winners were his novel *How All This Started*, story collection *Dry Rain*, and memoir *Indian Creek Chronicles*. Before turning to writing full time, he worked as a river ranger in Grand Teton National Park and in Big Bend, Texas. Having spent a winter alone in the Bitterroot Wilderness tending 2.5 million salmon eggs for the Fish and Game, and two springs in the Bob Marshall wilderness with thousands of grayling eggs, he's the world's foremost fish egg babysitter. He's also done time as a carpenter, a lifeguard, and even a paperboy. He now works restoring his home in Montana, writing, and teaching in Pacific University's low-res MFA program.

Lolita Hernandez, born and raised in Detroit, is the author of *Autopsy of an Engine and Other Stories from the Cadillac Plant* (Coffee House

Press), winner of a 2005 PEN Beyond Margins Award. She is the author of two chapbook collections of poems: *Quiet Battles* (Wayne State University Writers Forum) and *snakecrossing* (Ridgeway Press). Her poetry and fiction have been published in numerous journals. She worked for over thirty-three years as a UAW member at General Motors—on the Cadillac motor line for five years and then in an engineering skilled trade at Cadillac and the Warren Tech Center. She holds a UAW journeyman's card in Experimental Product Engineering Layout and Assembly. She has worked for the UAW in a quality program for the last eight years of her time at GM. She now teaches in the Creative Writing Department of the University of Michigan Residential College and is currently at work on a novel.

Tania Hershman's first short story collection, *The White Road and Other Stories*, was published by Salt and commended by the judges of the 2009 Orange Award for New Writers. A former science journalist, many of her stories are inspired by science, and she is currently writer-in-residence in Bristol University's Science Faculty. Tania once did work experience on the women's page of the UK *Daily Mail* newspaper and at British Aerospace, and worked for 6 months for ICI Chemicals testing the stickiness of CDs. Tania blogs about writing at www.titaniawrites.blogspot.com, and her website is www.taniahershman.com.

Steve Himmer's stories have appeared in various journals and anthologies, and he edits the webjournal *Necessary Fiction*. He teaches at Emerson College in Boston, but before that he was (in no particular order) a conservation laborer, medical database troubleshooter, convenience store overnight clerk, line cook, program coordinator for psychoanalytic training, lobsterman (briefly), and boat builder's apprentice (badly).

Dustin M. Hoffman spent ten years as a house painter and drywaller before getting his MFA in fiction from Bowling Green State University. He also worked a bit as a movie theater usher and art gallery assistant, but in both jobs he ended up painting walls. He is currently pursuing his PhD in creative writing at Western Michigan University. His work has recently appeared or is forthcoming in *Takahe*, *Sugar House Review*, *Palooka*, *Conclave: A Journal of Character*, *Echo Ink Review*, *Marginalia*, *Black Warrior Review*, and *Gargoyle*.

Billie Louise Jones has worked as an insurance and credit clerk, typist, Welfare caseworker and supervisor, substitute teacher, bookstore cashier, telemarketer, mail prepper, and Third Key (corporate term for cashier.) She's been published in magazines, including *Struggle*, *Phoebe*, *The New Orleans Review*, *Palo Alto Review*, and *The Storyteller*. A short story, "Port Bon Temps," won honorable mention in the 2008 Lorian Hemingway Short Story Competition.

Nick Kocz's short stories have appeared or are forthcoming in *Black Warrior Review*, *The Florida Review*, *Mid-American Review*, and *The Normal School*. He has been awarded a MacDowell Fellowship and is currently a finalist for The Hudson Prize. Prior to pursuing his MFA degree from Virginia Tech, he worked for 19 years at a government consulting firm in Arlington, Virginia, where he worked long hours in the pursuit of billable hours.

Lita A. Kurth, a Wisconsin native, Jungian, and Anarcho-Syndicalist sympathizer, has worked selling popcorn and soda at a county fair; doing piecework packing greeting cards into plastic bags and plastic bags into boxes; filling in circles fully and darkly on Scantron forms; devising lists of experiences for a survey; photocopying, photocopying, photocopying; transcribing hard-to-hear workshops from a labor conference; entering bibliographic data into a computer; substitute teaching in pre-schools; writing abstracts of computer articles; writing grant proposals, teaching English Composition, and editing fiction and academic writing. With degrees from the University of Wisconsin, UC Berkeley, and San Francisco State, her most recent educational acquisition is an MFA from the Rainier Writers Workshop at Pacific Lutheran University. She has published poetry, essays, and short fiction in such venues as the *Santa Clara Review*, *The Exploratorium Quarterly*, the *Vermont Literary Review*, and *Tattoo Highway*, and contributes to *Tikkun* magazine's online version. She is at work on a novel, *The Rosa Luxemburg Exotic Dance Collective*.

Sean Lovelace teaches creative writing at Ball State University. *How Some People Like Their Eggs* is his award-winning flash fiction collection by Rose Metal Press. His works have appeared in *Crazyhorse*, *Diagram*, *Quick Fiction*, *Sonora Review*, and *Willow Springs*. He blogs at seanlovelace.com. He likes to run. His jobs have included dog groomer, produce store cashier, chemical company shipping and receiving, roofer, busboy, pizza delivery, construction worker, Mercedes plant worker, air conditioner cleaner, landscaper, registered nurse, columnist, and college professor.

Michael Martone was born in Fort Wayne, Indiana, and after taking his engineering degree from Purdue University in 1973, returned home to design tire tread patterns for the local B.F. Goodrich plant in the suburb of Woodburn, specializing in the cross-hatching located on the sidewalls of all-weather radial r-16 tires. Transferred to the Tuscaloosa installation in 1996, Martone refocused his effort on the evolving and increasing complex construction of active osmosis-acting induction in side-channel scoring on tubeless hard-rubber "donut" temporary tires or "spares" as these models replaced the full-sized tire that had been standard before the advent of the "compact" car. Martone has patented several designs that have garnered notice in the small but intensively competitive world of vulcanated hydrologic engineering, including the famous irrigation template of zig-zaggery based on the repeating pattern of his initials—MWMWMWMW—known in the field as the 1313stroke44 or more simply the "M&M."

Daniel Orozco's work has appeared in the *Best American Essays*, *Best American Short Stories*, *Best American Mystery Stories* and Pushcart Prize anthologies, and in *Harper's Magazine*, *McSweeney's*, *Zoetrope All-Story*, and others. He is the recipient of a National Endowment for the Arts fellowship. He teaches in the Creative Writing Program at the University of Idaho. A collection of short stories is forthcoming in March 2011. Prior to teaching and writing, he has toiled in offices in the Bay Area and in Seattle, providing—in job description parlance—administrative and technical support services: phones and reception, typing and transcription, filing, data entry, occasional project management (proof letters and stuff envelopes, burst and collate incoming apps, prep employment and benefits packets, process payments for the bank deposit), and—the catchall, the bucket at the end of the sentence— "other duties as assigned." Although he encountered many kind and good people over these eleven or so years, he is relieved that he never has to do this kind of work ever again.

Matthew Salesses is the author of *The Last Repatriate* (forthcoming from Flatmancrooked) and *We Will Take What We Can Get* (Publishing Genius.) His stories have or will appear in *Glimmer Train*, *Witness*, *American Short Fiction*, *Mid-American Review*, *The Literary Review*, and elsewhere. He has worked as a financial planning assistant, literary journal editor, EFL teacher, knife salesman, online auction manager, dishwasher, blog editor, and is currently a faculty assistant at Harvard and a contributing writer to *The Good Men Project*.

Anne Shewring, born in the Wirral, across the River Mersey from Liverpool, England, has since lived in Cambridge—where she was an unsuccessful student of literature—and in Portland, U.S.A.—where she was a much better student of history. She currently shares a small flat in Central London with a husband and a ten year old son. She has worked as a charity fundraiser for almost twenty years, helping to find the cash to pay others to save children, cure the sick and, nowadays, to help migrants and refugees who arrive in London with little but hope. She continues to be interested in writing about the kind of work most people do and, in particular, office-based work. Anne has recently completed an Mphil in Creative Writing at the University of Glamorgan for which she completed her first novel *Ordinary People are Peculiar Too,* as well as a study of office-based fiction, *The Ordinary Office.* She is currently working on a second novel set, of course, in an office.

Kennebrew Surant, the daughter of an autoworker, was raised in the Detroit area with her three brothers and younger sister. She credits her siblings for shaping her sense of humor, her mother for her ability to write and her father with teaching her how to dream. She worked eight years for the Chrysler Corporation, spending most of that time in several of their manufacturing facilities where she supervised fork truck drivers. "It was those long days on the shipping-and-receiving docks that inspired me to write about factory life. I'd tell non-automotive friends and family stories about my day or things that happened at work like how the coolest part of the stamping factory was usually somewhere around 100 degrees and the warmest area, somewhere around 120 or how routine it was for the skilled tradesmen to cause fires because of their inside-the-factory barbeques. But rarely did anyone believe me. It is such a different work environment. I knew I had to write about it, that the factory was an endless well of stories." Surant is the author of the murder mystery novel, *Life on the Line,* based on her experiences at the Sterling Stamping Plant.

M. **Kaat Toy** grew up in the oil fields of central California. She has worked (in chronological order) as a camp counselor, lifeguard, department store fashion office go-for, newspaper reporter, high school substitute teacher, teaching assistant, swimming instructor, professor of English and mass communication and faculty adviser to the student newspaper at a private military college and Presbyterian college, busperson, maid, and self-employed housecleaner. She has an MFA. in Creative Writing (fiction) from the University of Arizona and a Ph.D. in English (creative writing—fiction) from Florida State University and has lived in eleven states while teaching and writing. Taos, New Mexico, is her current home. "Any Failure to Obey Orders Will Be Considered an Act of Aggression" is from her short prose collection *Many Worlds: An American Odyssey.*

Michael Zadoorian is the author of two novels, *The Leisure Seeker* (Morrow, 2009), winner of Columbia University's Anahid Literary Award, and *Second Hand* (Norton, 2000), which was an ABA Booksense selection, a Barnes & Noble Discover finalist, and winner of the Great Lakes Colleges Association New Writers Award. His collection, *The Lost Tiki Palaces of Detroit* (Wayne State University Press, 2009) is a 2010 Michigan Notable Book. It features stories originally published in *The Literary Review, Beloit*

Fiction Journal, American Short Fiction, North American Review and *Detroit Noir*. He has worked as a lawn boy, shipping room clerk, Chrysler plant guard, UPS mail sorter, free-lance journalist and advertising copywriter. He lives with his wife in Ferndale, Michigan.

Editors

Josh Maday lives and works in Saginaw, Michigan. His writing has appeared in *New York Tyrant, elimae, Apostrophe Cast, Lamination Colony, Keyhole Magazine, Action Yes, Barrelhouse*, Dzanc's *Best of the Web 2010*, and elsewhere. His book reviews have appeared *The Collagist, The Quarterly Conversation*, and *NewPages*. He keeps a website at www.joshmaday.com. His first job was in a restaurant. Then he was a mason's laborer for four years. He has been working as a mason during the winter and an estimator in the summer for six years.

Jeff Vande Zande has worked as a fast food worker, furniture deliverer, usher, projectionist, telemarketer, hotel maintenance man, gas station attendant, painter, welder, stringer for the Associated Press (two assignments) and as a small university administrator. Currently, he teaches English at Delta College in Midland, MI. His books include *Emergency Stopping and Other Stories* (Bottom Dog Press), *Into the Desperate Country* (March Street Press), *Landscape with Fragmented Figures: A Novel* (Bottom Dog Press) and his most recent collection, *Threatened Species and Other Stories* (Whistling Shade Press). He can be found on the web at www.jeffvandezande.com.

RECENT BOOKS BY BOTTOM DOG PRESS
OUR 25TH YEAR

WORKING LIVES SERIES
Church of the Backyard Fire: Poems
By Vladimir Swirynsky
$15

Strangers in America: A Novel
by Erika Meyers
140 pgs. $168

Riders on the Storm: A Novel
by Susan Streeter Carpenter
404 pgs. $18

The Long River Home by Larry Smith
(cloth) $22; (paper) $16

Landscape with Fragmented Figures
by Jeff Vande Zande
232 pgs. $16

Reply to an Eviction Notice: Selected Poems
by Robert Flanagan
100 pgs. $15

An Unmistakable Shade of Red & The Obama Chronicles
by Mary E. Weems
80 pgs. $15

Cleveland Poetry Scenes: A Panorama and Anthology
eds. Nina Gibans, Mary Weems, Larry Smith
304 pgs. $20

d.a.levy & the mimeograph revolution
eds. Ingrid Swanberg & Larry Smith
276 pgs. & dvd $25

Our Way of Life: Poems by Ray McNiece
128 pgs. $14

HARMONY SERIES
Bottom Dog Press Poetry Anthology
edited by Laura Smith & Allen Frost
156 pgs. $16

Come Together: Imagine Peace
eds. Ann Smith, Larry Smith, Philip Metres
224 pgs. $18

BOTTOM DOG PRESS HTTP://SMITHDOCS.NET